Leila

In memory of Colin

Leila

Robin Jenkins

Polygon
EDINBURGH

© Robin Jenkins 1995

Published by
Polygon
22 George Square
Edinburgh
EH8 9LF

Set in Meridien by WestKey Ltd, Falmouth, Cornwall
and printed and bound in Great Britain by Page Bros Ltd,
Norwich, Norfolk

A CIP record is available for this title from the British Library

ISBN 0 7486 6204 9

The Publisher acknowledges subsidy from

THE SCOTTISH ARTS COUNCIL

towards the publication of this volume

Part One

1

On the eighth green, among the casuarina pines, with the South China Sea shining beyond, the Sultan, about to putt, asked, unexpectedly: 'What do you know of Dr Abad, Andrew?'

Taken aback, Sandilands had to be cautious as well as deferential. What did the all-powerful despot want him to say about the meek idealist? 'Not much, Your Highness. I've seen him about the town, that's all. I've never met him.'

The Sultan nodded and then concentrated on his putting. With utmost care he tapped the ball. It rolled timidly towards the hole and stopped well short of it. It hadn't helped that the head of his putter was solid gold. Like golfers everywhere he was very cross with himself.

It was then Sandilands' turn. When he had first been invited or rather summoned to play golf with the Sultan it had been hinted, though to be fair not by the great man himself, that it would be politic to let His Highness win more often than not, but Sandilands had never been able to bring himself to do it. It would have been insulting to the Sultan. No matter how he hates losing no golfer likes to be let win.

Sandilands' ball rolled smoothly into the hole.

The Sultan sighed. 'I'd give a million dollars to be able to putt like you, Andrew.'

Such things were said on golf courses all over the world, but only here was the claim not extravagant. A million dollars was a trifle to the Sultan.

Suppose, thought Sandilands, such an exchange was possible, would he agree to it? Would so large a sum, enabling him to travel throughout the Far East, staying in five-star hotels and entertaining fabulous beauties, compensate for the loss of a gift that had given him so much pleasure and satisfaction?

They were followed to the next and final tee by their caddies, two in the Sultan's case and one in Sandilands', and also, at a discreet distance, by His Highness's bodyguard, six soldiers in red and white uniforms carrying automatic guns at the ready. The nine-hole course in the palace grounds was strictly private. Trespassers were warned that they would be shot on sight. Not that the Sultan feared assassination. He was confident that his benevolence towards his subjects caused them to love him. Did not even Dr Abad, that earnest democrat, praise him in his speeches?

'And what was your impression of the good doctor?'

Again, Sandilands had to be careful. 'To tell the truth, Your Highness, I thought him an insignificant wee man.'

The Sultan laughed. As a young man he had spent some months in Edinburgh and liked Sandilands to use Scottish words.

'Harmless, would you say?'

'Very much so.'

The Sultan kept some peculiar pets: a cheetah, a cageful of snakes, hawks, and a couple of orang-utans. Dr Abad could be included among them. He had been given royal permission to form his People's Party and make speeches in favour of democracy, provided of course there was no criticism of the Sultan. It was believed that the British Resident had not approved.

Sandilands placed his ball on a tee and got ready to drive.

'Yet I am being persuaded to get rid of him, to scotch the snake before it grows too big.'

Sandilands wondered just what getting rid of someone meant nowadays. In the Sultan's father's time it could have meant a public hanging or a private garrotting. Thanks to the wealth from oil the country nowadays could afford to be more civilised. Sir Hugo, a suave Etonian, the present British Resident, would hardly connive at judicial murder, but he might well suggest having Abad packed off to practise medicine among the tribes in the interior where, if malaria or heartbreak did not dispose of him, recidivist head-hunters might.

The Sultan wiped sweat from his brow with a handkerchief handed him by a caddy but he was silent, as every golfer must be when his opponent is about to play.

As usual Sandilands' ball soared high and far and landed safely on the fairway.

'Good shot,' said His Highness, enviously.

His own, alas, was not good. In spite of his determination not to, he swung his club much too fast so that his ball shot sideways into a green swamp where snakes lurked whose bite could mean instant death.

He groaned with disappointment and self-disgust. His clubs were the best money could buy, he had been coached by famous professionals, he had studied books on the techniques of the game, and yet he still hit duff shots.

His caddies were aghast. Would they be ordered to wade in waist deep to make a token but futile search? Their eyes appealed to Sandilands. They knew he was only a teacher but they thought he must be a man of great importance to be allowed to play with His Highness. Also they had watched him outshine the Sultan at hole after hole and yet he hadn't been dragged off to have his arms broken.

'Not much chance of finding it in there, Your Highness,' said Sandilands.

'No.' The Sultan indicated that he needed a new ball.

Greatly relieved, his caddy placed one on a tee, as delicately as if it was an egg. The other caddy looked up at the sky, appealing to Allah to make His Highness's second attempt have better fortune. There were thickets with poisonous thorns as well as ponds with venomous snakes.

One of His Highness's weaknesses as a golfer was that he did not keep his mind on the game.

'I'm told his daughter's keener on politics than he is,' he said. 'Quite fanatical, they tell me. Have you seen her too about the town? The beautiful Leila?'

Impressive would have been Sandilands' word for Madam Azaharri. She had struck him as too stern, too austere, too dedicated to be called beautiful; but then her husband, a lawyer like herself, had died a year or so ago in Malaya. No doubt she was still grieving. Sandilands had once got a good look at her in the Gardenia Restaurant. Half Scottish, for her mother long since dead had been born in a village near Edinburgh, she was tall for an Asian woman and carried herself as straight as a peasant with a basketful of durians on her head. She had been wearing a blue and white kebaya-sarong and had made every other woman in the restaurant look dull and dowdy.

'Does the lady merit so much reflection?' asked the Sultan, laughing.

His Highness was in the market for beautiful women. He had a harem full of them. Madam Azaharri would make him a regal wife, but would the prospect of a palace with two thousand rooms, a yacht as big as the *Britannia*, and dozens of servants, entice her? Sandilands did not think so.

'How does she compare with the ladies of the Shamrock Hotel?' asked the Sultan, laughing again.

Sandilands grinned sheepishly. It had been dark when he had visited that haunt of the elegant whores from Hong Kong and Singapore. He had slunk in and out and yet he must have been seen and reported to the Sultan, whose spies were reputed, rightly it seemed, to be everywhere.

The Sultan was amused. Small and fat himself, he liked to make fun of Sandilands who was tall and spare. 'In my grandfather's day,' he said, 'when thieves had their hands cut off you can imagine what happened to those caught consorting with ladies of joy.'

In those pre-oil days, though the mosque had been an ill-kept ramshackle wooden building, Islamic laws had been cruelly enforced. Today, when the great mosque, a magnificence of white marble and blue tiles, was one of the wonders of Islam, a certain amount of Western decadence was permitted. As long as the Sultan said his prayers daily and contributed millions to Islamic causes the imams were appeased.

The Sultan's second drive was satisfactory: not very long but straight and safe. In good humour he again teased Sandilands. 'Is it not the case, Andrew, that democratic governments often pay little heed to the wishes of the people who elected them?'

Sandilands had to admit that that was the case.

'So it is not really the people who govern but a small clique of men? Perhaps just one man, the Prime Minister or the President?'

Sandilands was not much interested in politics. 'Yes, I suppose so.'

'So what is the difference between a democracy like your country, Andrew, and my country where I am that one man?'

And if that one man was just and benevolent, was not that as good a form of government as any? Didn't historians say that England, and Scotland too, had never been so well administered as under the dictator Oliver Cromwell? Surely the very forming of political parties, each one representing a section of the community, made division and dissension inevitable. It had begun in Savu itself. Abad's People's Party championed the poor and powerless, while the Patriots defended the rights of the rich and powerful.

When the game ended, with victory as usual going to Sandilands, in spite of the ten-stroke advantage he had given his opponent, the Sultan shook hands and solemnly handed over the stake, one dollar. It always amused him that it was so small.

His white Rolls Royce was waiting for him. He got into it and was driven off to his palace where he would have his shower in a bathroom where all the taps were of gold.

His bodyguards followed in a yellow Land Rover.

2

It was now gloaming. In a minute or two darkness would fall. Stars had begun to shine. Creatures of the night were beginning to be heard. The lights would be on in the Old Town. There was a New Town, the Sultan's pride, with tall, gleaming buildings and wide boulevards with masses of bougainvillea, hibiscus, frangipani, and other flowering shrubs. Government House was there and the offices of many famous firms eager to do business with so rich a country.

Sandilands preferred the Old Town with its narrow,

noisy, spicy streets and alleys, its small dark shops that sold everything from stuffed snakes to French champagne, and its bars where Malays, Chinese, Tamils, Filipinos, and Dusuns drank Tiger beers laced with brandy and discussed the affairs of the day, which, so far as he could tell from eavesdropping, seldom included politics. It had always seemed to him that those simple souls ought not to be bothered by politicians. They did not want power, even the infinitesimal part represented by the casting of a vote every four or five years. They were content to make their modest livelihoods and enjoy the company of friends and neighbours whether or not these were the same colour as themselves. Theirs was a fortunate little country where it was never cold and never too hot either, because of the sea breezes; except of course deep in the interior, but only aboriginal tribes lived there.

He decided to go home through the Old Town. He would call in at Mr Cheng's bookshop to see if books he had ordered had arrived. After playing golf with the Sultan he liked to sit in a bar among ordinary folk. He was not sure why. Perhaps it was a kind of penance. In spite of that visit to the Shamrock Hotel he was by birth a Calvinist. His grandfather had been a minister of the Free Kirk of Scotland.

He was pleased to see some of his students in the bookshop. He greeted them and they were, as always, courteous and respectful. They were also that little bit guarded in their attitude towards him. It wasn't him as a person they distrusted, though perhaps distrust was too strong a word; it was him as a representative of the arrogant and greedy West.

He looked for Mr Cheng and found that white-haired and white-bearded old Chinese in a corner behind piles of books, talking to a tall black-haired Asian woman in Western dress – white blouse and blue skirt. His heart began to beat faster. There was no sensible reason why it should, for though the woman was Dr Abad's daughter, 'the beautiful Leila', she was a stranger to him and besides, she was coloured.

In her letters to him his mother kept telling him that if he ever got married it must be to one of his own kind. She meant white. He had replied that she needn't worry. He knew white men who had married coloured women and had seen, in spite of their efforts to keep it secret, how intolerable they found the burden of resentment, shame, and guilt with which they had saddled themselves. He had felt greatly relieved that he was free of that heartbreaking burden.

At the side of Leila's neck was a tiny black mole: it made her skin look quite light. She was wearing a thin gold chain with a crucifix attached. He had heard that Dr Abad was a Christian; so, it seemed, was his daughter. His mother would not have counted that in her favour: being the wrong kind of Christian was worse than not being a Christian at all.

On her way out of the shop she passed him, so close he could smell her perfume. She gave him a smile that had his heart racing. She was the most beautiful woman he had ever seen and had the most intelligent eyes. His own smile was too late and too timid.

He wanted to run after her. He wanted to be with her always. He wanted her to be his. Had he fallen in love?

For a wonder Mr Cheng did not seem to notice any transformation in Sandilands. He gave him his usual friendly chuckle. Sandilands was one of his best customers.

'Good evening, Mr Sandilands,' he said, in English. 'I am pleased to tell you your books have arrived.'

Sandilands was not interested in the books. His mind was on Leila.

'Who was that lady you were talking to, Mr Cheng?' he asked. His voice was curiously hoarse.

'Are you having a cold, Mr Sandilands? That was Dr

Abad's daughter, Madam Leila Azaharri. She is very beautiful, is she not?'

Sandilands felt an absurd jealousy. He wanted her beauty,
tainted though it was, for himself alone.

'And very clever,' added Cheng. 'One day she will be
Prime Minister of this country. In ten years when it has
become a democracy.' He chuckled again but behind the
steel-rimmed glasses his eyes were earnest.

Sandilands was not interested in her as a politician.

'She's a widow, isn't she?'

'Yes, sad to say. Her husband died in Malaya, a year or so
ago. He was young. He was a lawyer like the lady herself.
How is your own lady, Mr Sandilands? Miss Hislop, the angel
of mercy with the yellow hair and the voice that makes lazy
ones tremble.'

He had been a patient in the hospital where Jean Hislop,
the Chief Nurse, had impressed him with her brisk, unsen-
timental efficiency. She had made sure the bedpans were
not only promptly collected and properly emptied, but
scoured too.

She wasn't really Sandilands' lady, though she often
spoke and acted as if she was. Soon the post of Principal of
the Training College would become vacant. As Vice-Principal
Sandilands was favourite to fill it, but there was a snag: the
Principal had to be married. It was not a snag in Jean's eyes.
All he had to do was marry her. She spoke enthusiastically
of the children they would have: two boys and a girl. She
would say it while they were making love. She pointed out
that with his salary and pension as Principal and hers as Chief
Nurse (though she expected to retire as Matron), they would
be able to go home in a few years with money enough to
buy a semi-detached villa in Morningside or Fairmilehead
and send their children to superior schools. With her his
future would be secure but dull. When he woke up in the

morning and saw her pale face and fair hair on the pillow beside him he would feel pangs of disappointment. Suppose it was Leila's darker face and coal-black hair – what would he feel? Shock and dismay perhaps; but also defiant joy.

'Has she any children?' he asked.

'One little girl, now eight years of age.'

'Oh.' In spite of this complication Sandilands' interest was not diminished.

'I think she would like to meet you, Mr Sandilands.'

'Oh. Why do you think that?'

'She asked who was the tall man with the curly hair.'

'Did she?' Sandilands could not keep joy out of his voice.

'When I said you were Mr Sandilands of the Training College she said she had heard of you from your students. She said they all spoke highly of you.'

Then Mr Cheng, still chuckling, went off to fetch the books.

3

Saidee, his Malay amah, small, fat, flat-nosed, and fifty-five years of age, had long since given up her pretence that she was Tuan's lover and now adopted a motherly attitude. When he came home late she would scold him fondly: it never sounded impertinent in Malay; and when he was silent and moody, as this evening, she would try to cheer him up. She didn't wait till he'd had his shower, but poked her head between the curtains, to tell him there had been two telephone calls, both from the woman with the big feet; by which she meant Jean. He was to telephone her at the hospital as soon as he got home.

He wasn't pleased. Jean was capable of inviting herself to

spend the night and he wanted to be alone, to brood about
Leila. His house being isolated, at the edge of the sea with
jungle behind, most of his women friends would not visit
him at night. Jean, though, was not afraid to drive in the
dark. She had once hit a water buffalo asleep on the road.
Her radiator had been burst but her nerve hadn't been
shaken. Luckily the animal hadn't been badly hurt. If it had
been, her friends jested, she would have had it carted to the
hospital and put to bed. Jean got things done.

She would soon rid him of his obsession with Leila.

Did he want to be rid of it?

One minute he did, and his heart sank with relief; the
next minute he did not, and his heart leapt at the prospect
of seeing her again.

As he was eating the telephone rang. He let it ring and
would have gone on letting it ring, but Saidee lost patience
and answered it for him. She then informed him that it was
the woman 'with the loud voice'.

'Where the hell have you been?' asked that voice. 'This
is the third time I've called.'

'I've just got home. I was playing golf with the Sultan.'

'Oh. Picture me bowing my humble head. I'm phoning
from the hospital. A bigwig, the Minister of Something or
Other, has just been brought in, with acute appendicitis. So
I'll not be able to go with you to Jack and Mary's. You
haven't forgotten, have you, that the country dancing's at
their place tonight? God, I believe you have forgotten.'

Yes, he had, completely. But he was in no mood for a
boozy boisterous Eightsome Reel.

'I might be able to look in later,' said Jean, 'but I doubt
it. If you go on your own watch out for that cow Madge.
Three whiskies and she's got her fingers in your flies.'

She guffawed but he winced. He could never imagine
Leila being so coarse.

'I don't think I'll go,' he said. 'I'm a bit tired after the golf.'

'How was His Fatness?'

'All right.'

'Did you get a chance to drop a hint about the Principal's job?'

'No.'

'Well, it's time you did. I can't afford to wait much longer, you know. I'm twenty-eight.' Another guffaw.

She was thirty-four.

'Mention it next time, just after he's sunk a long putt. But I'll have to go. Duty calls. Selamat jalan.'

He went back to his curry. What, he wondered, still wincing, would Jean have said if he had told her he'd fallen in love with Leila Azaharri?

She'd laugh. She wouldn't be jealous. She'd remind him how conventional and cautious he was in his views. If, she would say, he got himself entangled with a black-arsed woman he'd mess his breeks with fright. She'd press his face against her own fat white breasts for a cure.

4

He often praised his students for their courtesy, patience, diligence (in the case of the Chinese only) and contentment, but there were times when he would gaze at those brown, yellow, or black young faces, lit up by bright smiles, and wish that they would show a spark at least of rebelliousness or a frown of disapproval at the way their country was run. It was one thing for peasants, fishermen, street-sweepers, and shop assistants to be content with their lot; it was another for these students who were, after all, the intelligentsia to accept without demur or protest the rule of an absolute monarch. Surely, in the twentieth century, they ought to be demanding some say in the government of their country; instead of which they let themselves be bribed into acquiescence. This Training College, for instance, was probably the best equipped in the whole of Asia and its graduates were assured of well-paid, secure, unchallenging jobs. Some might have to teach aborigines in kampongs in the interior but they would be compensated with generous bonuses.

The day after his encounter with Leila in the bookshop he found himself scowling with impatience at his students. They ought all to be members of the People's Party, eager to help her and her father to bring democracy to their country.

He could not keep her out of his mind.

But, of course, if he had accused them of supine conformity they would have smiled and one of the Chinese might have replied, intending no sarcasm, that he, Mr Sandilands, their esteemed teacher, did not refuse when summoned to play golf with the Sultan but went at once, even if it meant cancelling classes. Was not that showing them an example of obedience to authority?

The truth was, though he liked them he did not really understand them. Once, when discussing *Pride and Prejudice* with them, they had baffled him by not finding Mr Collins the figure of fun that Jane Austen had intended. On the contrary, all of them, Malays and Chinese, males and females, had made it clear they sympathised with the pompous parson. Spurned by Elizabeth he had immediately married Charlotte, thus gaining a submissive wife and at the same time pleasing his patroness Lady de Burgh. That was how a prudent man would act. Elizabeth would not have made him a good wife. She would have ordered him about and worse still would have mocked him. For them meek Mr Collins was really the hero of the novel, not the haughty D'Arcy.

Their own marriages would be arranged. They would not object. They enjoyed reading about romantic love but did not expect it or indeed want it for themselves. In real life love was sensible and came after marriage, slowly but surely as trust and dependence grew stronger. It was therefore very important to marry one of your own kind. He had once taken Jean Hislop to a students' dance. She had been a great success with her blue eyes, fair hair, big bosom, and energetic dancing. She was the kind of woman they thought he should marry. His children could then be loved without shame.

If he had taken Leila to the dance the students would have been embarrassed, though they would have tried not to show it. If he was ever to take her to the Golf Club the embarrassment there would not be hidden. It wouldn't be her political opinions that would bother the members – these they would have sniggered at – it would have been the alien darkness of her skin and her impure blood. The one thing that they would find in her favour was that she had the sense to regard herself as a Malay and not as a white woman.

If he was ever to marry a dark-skinned woman his mother would never forgive him, and his father would pity him as if he had contracted some nasty disease.

These were his thoughts that morning as he stood looking out of the classroom window. The students were engrossed in an exercise he had set them. The College grounds were like a large tropical garden. A dozen gardeners kept it under control. Everywhere one looked there was a luxuriance of bright flowers and shining green leaves. There were many fountains. One could pick orchids off the trees. It was paradisean. Yet, what he was seeing wasn't there in front of him, but in his mind: that tiny black mole on the side of Leila's neck.

A red-and-black Land Rover came rattling up the avenue towards the administration building where the Principal's

office was. It was a police vehicle. Beside the driver sat Alec
Maitland, in his Deputy Commissioner's uniform. Since the
Commissioner, a Malay who was a kinsman of the Sultan,
was a mere figurehead it was Maitland who controlled the
police, taking his orders, it was whispered, not from the
Commissioner or the Chief Minister or even the Sultan, but
from the British Resident. So too did Major Holliday, who
commanded the battalion of Gurkhas. Maitland's policemen,
all of them Malays, with an average height of five feet five
inches, carried guns but had never been known to use them.

Sandilands knew Maitland well. They were both Scotsmen and had once shared ownership of a sailing dinghy
called *Caledonia*, in which they had won races. Maitland's
wife had gone home to look after the education of their
teenage daughters. He had in her absence acquired a pretty
young Malay girl as his amah. Whether or not he slept with
her was a matter of humorous conjecture, but no one dared
ask him. Sandilands thought he didn't. Maitland had a fetish
for cleanliness and took half a dozen showers a day. If he
had been a Catholic he would have wearied his priest with
frequent confessions.

What could have brought him to the College? No place
was more law-abiding. Perhaps he had come to arrange
English lessons for members of his force. He had once
mentioned such an intention to Sandilands.

A few minutes later a servant came to say that the
Principal wished to see Tuan Sandilands in his office.

He left the students to get on with their work. They would
do it quietly and honestly. There would be no cribbing. The
Malays, who were the majority, did not mind having low
marks while the Chinese were too proud to be beholden to
anyone. When the bell rang they would dismiss themselves
and leave in orderly fashion. They were the kind of students
that teachers in obstreperous Scotland dreamed of.

Sandilands was smiling as he made his way to the
Principal's office, with butterflies the size of his hand flutter-
ing about his head. There was a serpent in this Eden. After
a number of years – some said ten, some five – in the hot
and steamy tropics a white man's mind began to rust. He
became slack and inefficient, without really knowing it; after
all, everybody, except newcomers who didn't count, was in
the same plight. The Malays, of course, were born indolent.
Blunders and deficiencies didn't bother them, largely because they never noticed them, and if they were pointed out
to them they just smiled with charming self-tolerance. The
Chinese were exceptions, but then no Chinese was ever
appointed to a top job. Indeed, most of the fifty thousand
Chinese in the country, emigrants from Singapore or Hong
Kong, had not been granted citizenship. Mr Cheng of the
bookshop was an example. Their sons and daughters,
though, born in the country, were legally Savuans.

Sandilands was smiling because one man who strove
ceaselessly to keep the rust at bay was Alec Maitland. Once,
when slightly drunk, he had explained to Sandilands that it
was all very well for a teacher to let his sense of morality
become blurred and lazy; a policeman, especially the top
policeman, must not. He spoke Malay well and worked hard
at improving it, for how could he keep the dignity necessary
to his position if he spoke to malefactors in the language of
the bazaar? He had an obsessive distrust of Communists,
having fought them in Malaya.

In the Principal's office he sat upright, as stiff as if on parade.
His hat and swagger-stick were on his lap. His hair, cut short,
was reddish, like his eyelashes. His face and knees were
freckled. He had the kind of skin that didn't tan but turned
ruddy and sore-looking.

The Principal, David Anderson, was scowling; he always

appeared to be because his left eye was missing and that side of his face was contorted: the result of a blow with a rifle butt in a Japanese prisoner-of-war camp. White-haired and elderly – he was due to retire in a few months – he was amiable and forgiving and much liked by staff and students. He had intended to spend his retirement in the coolness of the Cameron Highlands in Malaya, but his wife had died and now, as he had confessed to Sandilands, he looked forward to nothing.

He *was* scowling, though. 'Sit down, Andrew,' he said. 'It seems we have a little problem.'

'I wouldn't call it little,' said the Deputy Commissioner, dourly.

Sandilands was amused. 'What kind of problem?'

'The Deputy Commissioner has accused three of our students of taking part in subversive activities.'

Sandilands couldn't help laughing. 'What bloody nonsense!'

'That's what I think too,' said the Principal.

'Whatever you gentlemen think,' said the Deputy Commissioner, 'it happens to be true.'

'Our students wouldn't know what a subversive activity meant,' said Sandilands. 'I'm not sure myself.'

'You can't know your students very well then, Mr Sandilands.'

That 'Mr' nettled Sandilands. 'What exactly are they accused of?'

'I am under no obligation to tell you.'

Sandilands got angrier. 'Is this a police state?'

Well, was it? The Sultan ruled by decree. Those decrees were enforced by the police. There was no appeal against them. Wasn't that how it was done in a police state? Savu happened not to be a particularly harsh one: that was, up till now it hadn't been.

'You know Cheng's bookshop in the Old Town?' asked the Deputy Commissioner.

Sandilands nodded. He almost said it was a shop he was in often, unlike the Deputy Commissioner who listened to music but seldom read books.

'There is a back room.'

'Used as a store, I suppose.'

'Used as a meeting-place for would-be revolutionaries, like your students.'

Sandilands was incredulous. 'Revolutionaries? Good God!'

Then he remembered Leila Azaharri talking to Cheng in the corner behind piles of books. Had they been conspiring? No, that was too ridiculous.

'They have been using it as a secret meeting-place for some time,' said the Deputy Commissioner. 'We suspect there are similar cells throughout the country.'

' "They"?' said Sandilands. 'Who are they?' Was Leila one of them, he wondered. 'What do they do in the back room? Make bombs?'

'They discuss ways of subverting the State.'

'How do you know this? From spies?'

'We have our means.'

'What language do these conspirators use?'

'English. They read and discuss books that advocate revolution and sedition.'

'Name one.' Sandilands could not help being sarcastic. This accusation was preposterous.

Then he remembered something. Just a few weeks ago it had been reported in the *Savu Times* that Red China had exploded a nuclear bomb. He had remarked, to his senior class, that it was a pity, for the fewer nations that had those bombs the safer all humanity would be. To his astonishment he had been immediately contradicted by the Chinese in the class. Albert Lo, Captain of the class and most likely recipient of this year's gold medal for the best student, had stood up and said, politely but proudly, that China had as much right to possess nuclear bombs as America and Great Britain.

The Deputy Commissioner was not prepared to name a book.

'Well, surely you're going to tell us the names of the students? And what's going to happen to them? Are you here to arrest them?'

'They are not to be arrested, but they are not going to be allowed to continue with their studies. It has been decided they are not fit to become teachers.'

Who had decided? Was it the Sultan? The Council of Ministers? The British Resident? The Deputy Commissioner himself?

'Their careers will be ruined,' said Sandilands. 'I hope you realise that.'

'I hope *you* realise, Mr Sandilands, and you too, sir, that if it is found that this canker has spread among your students the College may have to be shut down. In the meantime it will be sufficient if these ringleaders are sent away.'

'Can we have their names?' asked the Principal.

The Deputy Commissioner took a sheet of paper from his breast pocket. He had to put on spectacles to read what was written on it.

'Albert Lo.'

Sandilands was startled and could not help showing it. Had he got it wrong? Was it possible that Lo was a crypto-Communist? Come to think of it, with his eager smile and zealous eyes he was very like the youths depicted in Red China propaganda films, brandishing flags and bawling patriotic songs. But wasn't he a Christian? Didn't he go to church every Sunday?

'I don't believe it,' cried the Principal. 'Albert is one of our best students.'

Sandilands was waiting for the next name. Would it be Richard Chia? He and Lo were close friends. Chia drew satirical cartoons for the College magazine.

'Richard Chia,' said the Deputy Commissioner.

'But this is nonsense,' cried the Principal. 'What do you think, Andrew? Can you see Albert and Richard as revolutionaries?'

'Hardly.' But Sandilands had no difficulty in imagining Richard too among those young Chinese in the propaganda films.

The Deputy Commissioner read out the third name. 'Abdul Salim.'

Now *that* really was absurd. Salim, a Malay, was plump, good-natured, indolent, and dim. His English was below standard. He was one of those for whom the entrance qualifications had had to be lowered. He would be allowed to graduate because there had to be more Malay teachers than Chinese. The idea of his being able to take part in political discussions was laughable. A revolution would be too much like hard work for him; as indeed it would be for the majority of his countrymen.

'Abdul Salim?' said the Principal. 'That is a mistake surely.'

The Deputy Commissioner looked again at his little list. 'No mistake,' he said.

'I assure you that when you meet these students face to face you will see how mistaken you are, especially in Salim's case.'

The Deputy Commissioner picked up his hat and stick, and rose. 'I do not intend to meet them. There would be no point. The decision has been made. It will not be changed.'

'This is most unfair,' said the Principal. 'What are we to tell them?'

'Simply that they are to be expelled. They will know why.'

'When have they to go?'

'Today.'

'What has happened to Mr Cheng?' asked Sandilands.

'He has been deported to Singapore where he came from.'

'More than thirty years ago.'

The Deputy Commissioner put on his hat. 'Good day, gentlemen. Thank you for your co-operation.'

Sandilands and the Principal sat staring at each other, listening to the Land Rover drive away.

'When I was in Malaya, Andrew,' whispered the Principal, 'I saw some young Communists who had been captured. They were as young as Albert and Richard. They looked so dedicated. Can there possibly be any truth in this, Andrew? Under the surface is there discontent?'

'Shall we send for them? They'll have to be told.'

'I suppose so.'

5

While they were waiting the Principal took an envelope from a drawer in his desk. It had 'Confidential' stamped on it in large red letters.

'Here's something I think you should see,' he said. 'It came yesterday.'

The letter itself had another Confidential stamped on it. It was from the Chief Minister's office and stated that in

future all posts of seniority were to be filled by native-born
Savuans. This would apply to the post of Principal of the
College. Moreover, from the beginning of next year, the
language of instruction in all schools would be changed from
English to Malay.

'I'm sorry, Andrew,' said the Principal.

What alarmed Sandilands wasn't so much that he might
soon be out of a job as that he might have to leave Savu and
so never see Leila again.

'Did you know this was going to happen?' he asked.

'I don't think anyone did. It's probably one of His
Highness's brainwaves.'

'I suppose it's fair enough. It's their country, after all.'

It was Leila's country, not his.

'Would you carry on here, under a Malay?'

'I might not get the chance.'

'Your Malay's good enough, and you could always appeal
to His Highness.'

'I wouldn't want to do that. Who's likely to get your job,
David. Have you heard?'

'No. Some relative of some Minister, I expect.'

There was a quiet knock on the door and the three
students came in, smiling. They seemed to think they had
been summoned to be commended or given some special
task. Whatever it was they were prepared to carry it out as
best they could.

As always they were neatly dressed in black trousers,
white shirts, and black ties. Their hair was carefully brushed
and, in Salim's case, scented. Their shoes were polished.
Their teeth were white and healthy, especially Salim's. His
smile was the widest and, in the present circumstances,
either the most innocent or the most disingenuous. As a
revolutionary, thought Sandilands, he would walk, not run.
If handed a flag he would soon drop it. The two others,

though, looked as if they would grip it tightly and hold it high.

'Would you like to tell them, Mr Sandilands?' said the Principal.

There were, Sandilands saw, tears in that one eye.

His own eyes were dry. But then, as Jean Hislop had often told him, he was good at hardening his heart, if it was necessary.

It was necessary now.

'We've just had a visit from the Deputy Commissioner of Police,' he said.

They nodded. 'We saw his Land Rover,' said Chia, cheerfully.

None of them looked furtive or apprehensive.

'He came to make an accusation against you three.'

Their surprise seemed genuine.

'He accused you of meeting with others in the back room of Mr Cheng's bookshop to read and discuss books that advocate revolution.'

That was a mouthful. No wonder they looked puzzled, though they kept smiling.

'Do you understand?' asked Sandilands.

Lo chose his words carefully. 'We have met in Mr Cheng's shop and talked about democracy.'

Yes, but in a country like Savu wouldn't talk of democracy amount to sedition?

'What books did you discuss?' he asked.

'*Animal Farm* by Mr George Orwell,' said Chia.

'*The Rights Of Man* by Mr Thomas Paine' said Lo.

Salim just grinned.

As their English teacher, thought Sandilands, I should be applauding their reading of books not on the list of those prescribed.

'Who suggested you should read those books?' he asked.

Lo replied without hesitation. 'Madam Azaharri, sir. She is the daughter of Dr Abad. We are members of the People's Party. It is a legitimate organisation.'

All Sandilands could say or rather mumble was: 'You shouldn't be involved in politics. Not while you are still students.'

He was more worried about Leila. She couldn't be deported like Cheng. Was she at that moment in prison? Had there been a crack-down on the People's Party?

It was unbearable to see the students gazing at him with trust and hope. He was their esteemed teacher. If they were in trouble he would help them.

Self-disgust made him speak harshly. 'The Deputy Commissioner came to say that you are to be expelled from the College.'

'Expelled, sir?' Lo turned to the Principal but found that one benign eye shut.

'When have we to leave?'

'Today.'

Salim was still smiling broadly.

An injustice was being done. All that these youths were guilty of was naivety. They did not deserve to have their careers ruined. Someone ought to speak up for them.

It should be me, thought Sandilands. As their teacher I have tried to encourage them to think for themselves, so I am partly to blame for their predicament. But I have troubles of my own. The post of Principal that should have been mine will go to some feckless little Malay with dubious qualifications. I shall have to decide whether to swallow my pride and stay on or to resign. If I resign do I do it with dignity or with my hand held out for as big a golden handshake as I can wheedle out of them? Do I ask Jean to come with me? Do we buy that semi-detached villa in Morningside, where I shall spend the rest of my life haunted by the memory of Leila Azaharri?

I'm not worthy of her, he thought. She would despise me for letting these young men down. Jean, on the other hand, would approve of my not getting into trouble for their sakes.

'Can you not help us, Mr Sandilands?' said Chia.

'I'm sorry. No, I'm afraid I can't.'

'In your country, Mr Sandilands,' said Lo, 'would this injustice be permitted?'

Yes, it would, but there was a good chance that hundreds of students would demonstrate on behalf of their colleagues. Here there would be only some timid whisperings.

When they had gone to collect their belongings, Sandilands and the Principal couldn't bear to look at each other.

He's an old man, thought Sandilands, he's not well, he could be dead within a year, and he lost heart when his wife died. There are excuses for him. What excuse is there for me? Why am I not lifting that telephone and asking to speak to the British Resident or His Highness himself? Why am I not threatening to let the outside world know what a despotic and unjust State Suva has become. In Britain those who have heard of the place think it is a quaint little kingdom luckily enriched by oil. Shouldn't I make it my business to show it up as being as tyrannical as any Communist state, though it is under the protection of Britain?

But who would care? At best it would merit a small paragraph in the *Guardian*. The rest of the world's press would ignore it. He would have sacrificed his own career for nothing. Better to keep his head down and go on enjoying what benefits were left.

'In the Japanese camp,' said the Principal, with rare bitterness, 'we learned to keep our mouths shut.'

6

That evening, as Sandilands sat on his verandah amidst the orchids, slowly getting drunk, there was a sunset remarkable even in that country of splendid sunsets. Sea, sky, sand, and trees were for a few minutes blood red; so too his hand holding the glass. No doubt his face was sharing the glory as well, or was it the cosmic shame? 'You're drunk,' he muttered, 'and like a true Scotsman you're maudlin and self-pitying with it.' The expulsion of three students, however unjust, was hardly a reason for the whole universe to blush. Besides, who was to blame? Everybody and everything. Therefore nobody and nothing.

As the splendour faded he thought of telephoning Maitland and arguing with him, but it wouldn't have done any good and might have done himself harm. If the authorities could so callously, with a snap of the fingers as it were, deprive him of the promotion that he deserved they could just as easily tear up his contract and order him out of the country, on the grounds that he had interfered in matters that didn't concern him. He had a right to look after himself. Didn't everybody have that right?

There was such a hubbub in the jungle behind him, of frogs, cicadas, and nightjars, and such a buzzing in his ears of mosquitoes, that he did not hear the telephone ringing. Saidee came out to tell him. The way she told him, the peculiar voice she used, let him know the caller was a woman.

It would be Jean Hislop. He felt mean. He would find consolation in hinting to her that since he had been cheated out of the Principal's job there was no need for him to acquire a wife.

But it wasn't Jean's loud, demanding voice that he heard. It was quieter and more sincere. Jean was always putting on an act.

'This is Leila Azaharri, Mr Sandilands. I know we have never met but I hope you don't mind my calling you. I would like to speak to you on behalf of the three students who were expelled today from the College.'

He was so astonished he sounded drunker than he was. 'Me? You want to talk to me?'

She hesitated. 'Yes. Perhaps this is not a convenient time. Perhaps I should call again.'

She meant when you're sober, you slob.

He made a great effort to speak clearly. 'No, it's all right. I know what you're talking about. I'd like to help them.'

'You agree then that they have been disgracefully treated?'

'Yes, I certainly do.'

'They speak highly of you, Mr Sandilands. I intend to challenge the legality of their expulsions and I would be grateful for any help you could give me.'

'Of course.' But there was really no 'of course' about it. Hadn't he decided it was none of his business? Hadn't he just watched the sky blushing with shame? Yet he said it again: 'of course'.

She hesitated again. 'Would you be prepared to testify as to their good character?'

'Yes, I would. They are fine young men. Lo, in fact, is our best student.'

'Would you come to my office tomorrow morning at ten? It's in Kotakinabalu Street, next to the Chuu-Chuu tailors.'

Did he have a class at ten? He couldn't remember. Anyway he could cancel it.

'Thank you, Mr Sandilands. Goodbye.'

'Goodbye.'

Putting down the telephone, he went back out on to the verandah, but though the moon was now shining on the sea magnificently there was no peace for his soul there. Nor would he find it in that office next to the Chuu-Chuu tailors. He might find great joy there but not peace of mind.

7

He always dressed well: short-sleeved white shirts of the finest cotton, tailored white shorts, white stockings, and brown shoes specially made. That morning he wore his best. He took longer showering and shaving. He applied his delicately scented aftershave. He might have been a bridegroom getting ready for his wedding. All this for a woman who probably despised him as a drunken clown. All this for a woman who was dark-skinned.

Driving to the Old Town he passed the British Resident's palatial house, with the Union Jack flying over it. The flag was slightly smaller than that of Suva which flew a little above it, on the same mast. This was intended to signify that it was really the Sultan who ruled the country and not the British Resident, but no one was deceived. It was generally assumed that His Highness took no decision of any importance without having consulted and getting the approval of Sir Hugo. The Sultan might pay for the upkeep of the battalion of Gurkhas stationed in the country but their commander, Major Holliday, took his orders from Sir Hugo who took his from Whitehall. Dr Abad's People's Party wanted not only an elected Parliament but also an end to the British connection. His daughter, a more fervent politician, no doubt wanted that too, even if she was half-Scottish.

He kept telling himself he was mad going to meet her. He should drive straight to the College and telephone her from there, apologising for not keeping the appointment. He would point out that it was a condition of his contract not to engage in political activities.

But when he came to where he should have turned right for the College he drove on towards the Old Town. If he associated with her in this affair of the students he would put himself in danger not only of having his contract cancelled but also of destroying his peace of mind forever. If he let himself fall in love with her he would never again be content. But wasn't he already in love with her? Wasn't the prospect of seeing her, perhaps of touching her, if they shook hands, causing him greater joy than he had ever felt before, even if at the same time greater unease?

He parked his car near the fruit market, under a frangipani tree. Petals would have fallen on it when he returned. It was a pleasant spot, with the shining heaps of fruit and the smiling faces of vendors and buyers. There was, though, a stink of durians in the air: that fruit of horrible smell and sweet taste. Was it symbolical?

He walked slowly. The temperature was already in the eighties and he did not want to arrive in her office sweating. Two native girls, colourful as flowers in their sarongs and kebayas, passed him, with admiring glances and giggles. He often received such homage. It hadn't needed Jean to call him a 'good-looking big bugger' for him to know that he was attractive to women. The whores at the Shamrock had played a game of pretending to be in competition with one another for the honour of serving him; but it hadn't all been pretence. The one he had chosen, a grave beauty from Hong Kong, had handled him as if he was a prince. He had been a little embarrassed but also a great deal flattered. He liked to prove to himself – indeed, it was why he'd visited the Shamrock – that though he was still a bachelor at thirty-six, it was from choice and not because he wasn't attracted to women or women to him. He would marry within the next two years, say, while he was still young enough to have a family, though to be honest the thought of having a family was one of the reasons that he had preferred to stay single. He never felt comfortable with children under the age of five.

These thoughts, though, shrivelled in his mind as he stood outside the Chuu-Chuu tailors. There was an entrance next to the shop. Or a close to use the Scottish term. On a brass plate were inscribed two names: Mrs L. Azaharri, solicitor, and Mr H. Chin, dentist. This was where the poor came for legal help or to have their teeth fixed. It was also where Sandilands might meet his doom.

He hesitated, he thought of turning away, he warned himself that in this close, up these narrow stairs, could lie disillusionment and heartbreak, but still he went in and up, grimacing at the faint smell of excrement. He imagined himself saying to her that this was no place for a woman as fastidious and beautiful as she, she must go with him and find more suitable premises. What he did do was knock nervously on a door that had her name on it.

As he waited he heard what he decided was the noise of a tooth drill and he felt a pang of sympathy for whoever it was, undergoing the ordeal. But had he himself in front of him an even greater test of courage?

He thought of Jean Hislop. At the Golf Club they called him a lucky bastard having a handsome and high-spirited woman like Jean keen on him. His mother would welcome her as a daughter-in-law. He could take her to any restaurant in Edinburgh without having to endure insolent or hostile or, worst of all, pitying stares.

He opened the door and went in. It was an outer office. A chubby young Chinese girl in a yellow cheongsam was seated at a desk typing. She looked up and smiled. Her scent was strong. Was it to overcome the stink of the drains?

'Mr Sandilands?' she asked.

'Yes.'

'Mrs Azaharri is expecting you, sir. Please go in.'

He went in.

Leila was seated at a desk, writing, with her left hand, he noticed; it did not have a wedding ring. She was wearing spectacles. She looked up at him with a smile that, in his confusion, reminded him of the moon shining on the sea. Her hair, black as midnight, would, if let down, fall below her waist. The beauty of her body, he now realised, would be added to and not detracted from by the colour of her skin, not white but far from black; a very delicate shade of brown. She was wearing a white blouse.

'Thank you for coming, Mr Sandilands,' she said. 'Please sit down.'

'Thank you.' He sat down.

On the desk was a coloured photograph of her, a little girl with a pink ribbon in her hair, and a dark-faced man, no doubt her husband. Azaharri was smiling happily. How soon after that photograph was taken had he sickened and died?

Sandilands did not feel jealous. He felt sad. Here was a

man who had had everything to live for and yet had died young.

'I believe you play golf with His Highness,' she said.

'Yes. Sometimes.'

'On his private course?'

'Yes.'

'Quite a privilege.'

'I suppose so.'

'My husband played golf. He was quite an enthusiast.'

The man in the photograph did look as if he would have enjoyed a game.

'Do you play yourself?' he asked, somewhat fatuously. 'I don't think I've ever seen you at the Golf Club.'

Dark skins were no longer barred but they still weren't welcomed. If he were to turn up with her there would be astonished and indignant stares. Some of the stupider women might even try to insult her.

'I have played,' she said, with a smile, 'but not recently. I am also told that you go sailing with Mr Maitland, the Deputy Commissioner.'

'We shared a boat once.'

'I used to love sailing. I take it, Mr Sandilands, you agree that these three students have been unjustly treated.'

'If what they say is true.'

'What do you mean?'

'I mean if all they were doing in Cheng's shop was reading books like *Animal Farm*.'

'What else could they have been doing? I myself sometimes took part in their discussions. They are members of the People's Party, as I am. We need clever young men to help us spread our message and recruit members. We are not revolutionaries, Mr Sandilands. We simply wish to bring democracy to Savu.'

He saw then that, for all her lovely smiles, for all that soft voice, for all those fine brown eyes and that splendid bosom, she could be formidable.

'We have reason to believe His Highness is in sympathy with our objectives.'

He doubted it. The Sultan liked to think of himself as an upholder of human rights, such as free speech; but he was in no hurry to introduce them.

'From what I have been able to find out so far,' she said, 'it appears that Mr Maitland consulted neither the Commissioner nor the Chief Minister.'

'I don't think Alec would act on his own.'

'Not on his own, no. Perhaps in collusion with the British Resident?'

Sandilands could easily imagine Sir Hugo saying: 'No need to bother His Highness with such a trivial matter.'

'I understand Mr Cheng has been deported,' he said.

'And others. Yet I have the impression that His Highness knew nothing about it.'

That was possible.

'I have arranged a meeting with one of His Highness's private secretaries. I would like you to accompany me, Mr Sandilands.'

A part of him wanted to cry out that he would go with her to hell if she asked him to, but another part, one more familiar, warned him not to be a bloody fool. If his reward was to win her as his lover it might be worth the risk, but what if she wasn't even at the airport to see him off after he'd been flung out?

She was waiting for his answer.

'When is this meeting?' he asked.

'Tomorrow morning at eleven in the Secratariat.'

'Would my being there do any good?'

'I gathered from the secretary that His Highness admires you very much.'

'As a golfer.'

Others besides the Sultan admired him for his golfing prowess and for nothing else.

'All right. I'll go.' But he didn't want to have to wait till tomorrow – so long a time – before seeing her again.

'The students are at my house, Mr Sandilands. They would like very much to talk to you. Why not join us all at dinner this evening?'

Strangely, it occurred to him that he would meet her little girl; more strangely still, he wanted very much to meet her.

'I'd like that,' he said.

'Good.'

'What time?'

'I usually eat at seven but come when you like.'

'Thanks.'

He got up. His legs were shaky.

She accompanied him to the door. How gracefully she moved, compared with Jean's sturdy swagger. It must be because she sometimes wore saris. How would it be if she appeared with him in one of those Edinburgh restaurants wearing a sari of red and gold? The stares would not be insolent or hostile or pitying; no, they would be envious.

She put out her hand. He took it and held it longer than was polite, but she did not seem to mind. He squeezed, very slightly, but more than was seemly. Did she squeeze back? Yes, she did. But why? She was no simple soul. In her there were many discoveries to be made. It might take a more intrepid explorer than he.

It was a Scottish custom when you were invited to bring a present. He would bring his most beautiful orchid.

He was going down the stairs when he realised that he did not know where she lived. He had forgotten to ask and she had forgotten to tell him.

He hurried back. The Chinese girl cheerfully gave him directions.

As he went out into the street he found himself wondering what qualities he had that would appeal to a woman like her. She devoted herself to helping others; he'd always looked after himself. 'That's what I like about you, Andrew,' Jean had once said. 'You don't give a fuck for anybody but yourself.' That had been unfair. In his time he had made as many magnanimous gestures as most men, provided always that they had not cost him too much, not in money but in commitment. There in the crowded street, in the warm sunshine, he stood and shivered. Better to stop it now. Better to make up his mind never to see her again.

That was sensible advice, so why did he want to tell these strangers, smiling at him curiously, for he must have looked glaikit standing there, that the greatest joy he could look forward to was holding Leila Azaharri in his arms?

8

As soon as he drove through the College gates he felt something was amiss. There were no students about. The classroom block was deserted, except for a group of teachers on the upper verandah who seemed to be waiting for classes that hadn't turned up. He heard cries from the dormitory block hidden by trees. It could be birds or monkeys but it was more likely to be students. What were they up to? They should have been in their classrooms.

He got out of his car to talk to the teachers above.

'Where are the students? What's happened?'

Mr Srinavasan, white-haired and solemn, who taught

Maths, answered with his usual precision. 'It would appear, Mr Sandilands, that they have all gone on strike. We have been waiting for your return to call them to account. They have all lost their senses, I fear.'

George Baker was a blunt Australian; he taught English. 'They'll get the whole bloody place shut down.' He said it cheerfully. He foresaw massive compensation.

Mrs John was a Tamil lady who taught Geography. She wore vivid saris; the one she had on now was yellow and black, like a butterfly. Small and dainty, she was as black as ebony. Compared to her Leila could pass as white. 'It is because Chia, Lo, and Salim have been chucked out,' she said.

Mr Koh was Chinese and taught Art. Everything about him was correct. His paintings were the most meticulous and the most lifeless Sandilands had ever seen. 'Without permission they have used College materials to make their placards,' he said. 'I forbade them, of course.'

'What do they want placards for?' asked Sandilands.

'They have seen it on television,' said Mr Srinavasan.

'Has anybody been to talk to them?'

'We were leaving that to you, mate,' said Baker.

'That is so,' said Mr Srinavasan. 'As Vice-Principal you are responsible for discipline.'

'And get paid for it,' added Baker, who thought he should have been Vice-Principal.

If the students were demonstrating on behalf of their three colleagues, should I commend them or rebuke them, Sandilands wondered. They would be showing a maturity he had never given them credit for, and also an altruism that was even more unexpected. He wouldn't have called them selfish, it was too crude a word to express their attitude of wishing everyone well provided they themselves fared that little bit better. He would have expected their reaction to be sympathetic, sad, and circumspect. They would have ready some aphorism in Malay or Chinese, such as 'If you provoke a tiger do not be surprised if it bites your head off' or 'He who puts his hand into the fire gets it burnt.' Now it looked as if they were all provoking the tiger and putting their hands into the fire.

'Good God,' cried Mrs John. 'They are marching like hooligans.'

Those on the verandah had a better view than Sandilands, but soon he too could see the procession and its placards.

He stood in the middle of the road, with his hand up.

They stopped but their smiles, though as polite as ever, had a quality in them that he had never noticed before. Those smiles said: We like you, Mr Sandilands, we enjoy your lessons, but you are not one of us. You do not know how we feel.

Their placards were colourful and quite artistically in-scribed. Mr Koh should have been pleased. There were words that many of the students would have had difficulty in pronouncing, such as 'Democracy', 'Tyranny', and 'Justice', but they were all correctly spelled. The English Department should have been pleased.

Another thing he noticed. The young women, brown, yellow, or black, were beautiful. He had always thought them pretty but doll-like. Now their faces were alive. They reminded him of Leila.

The young men were similarly transfigured. They had shed their carefully fashioned masks that had portrayed politeness and submissiveness. Revealed was a pride in themselves. In their eyes, all brown like Leila's, was a view of a nobler future than safe jobs and comfortable confor-mity.

If the Sultan ever allowed free elections he might be in for a shock. His Party might not have the easy victory he expected. The British Resident seemed better informed. Had Sir Hugo not warned him to scotch the snake before it got too big? Democracy, for what it was worth, would come, but the Sultan, advised by the British, would make sure it had only the appearance of power and not the reality.

They were waiting patiently for Sandilands to speak to them.

'Where do you think you're going?' he asked, smiling. 'What's all this about?'

They did not smile back at him. Several voices answered him.

'We are going to stand outside Government House.'

'We want Chia, Lo, and Salim to be released.'

'We want them to return to the College.'

'Chia, Lo, and Salim are not in jail,' he said.

'Where are they?' someone shouted.

'In a safe place, I assure you. Do you know Mrs Azaharri, the lawyer?'

Yes, they knew her.

'Well, she has asked me to go with her tomorrow to Government House to discuss the matter with His Highness's private secretary.'

They were silent, thinking about it. Then someone cried: 'Do not discuss, Mr Sandilands. Demand.'

Sandilands would have expected that from a Chinese, but no, Jerome Dusing was a Malay.

They seized on the word. 'Demand. Demand. Demand.' Half of them, he was sure, hardly knew what it meant.

All the same, he had certainly undervalued them. There must have been meetings and discussions he had known nothing about. They hadn't trusted him. Though he felt hurt, he had to admit that they had been right not to trust him. He was a mercenary after all. He would take his pay and leave. They would be here all their lives.

'Long live Mrs Azaharri,' someone cried.

Others took it up.

Evidently Leila was a heroine to them.

Sandilands was disconcerted. He had been thinking of her as a private person with whom he had fallen in love. But if she was ever his he would have to share her with many others. He remembered Mr Cheng's saying that she would be Prime Minister one day. Would she give up her political ambitions for love? Perhaps, but the man who could inspire such love in her would have to be heroic himself. Sandilands hardly qualified.

'In the meantime please go to your classes,' he said.

They conferred.

At last Jerome Dusing said: 'We shall go to our classes, Mr Sandilands, but tomorrow you will come and tell us what His Highness's secretary has said.'

'I promise,' he said.

9

He drove to the Principal's office. There he found Miss Leithbridge, seething. She was a middle-aged grey-haired Englishwoman who taught primary school methods. She was hostile to Sandilands. 'Because,' Jean had said, 'she really fancies you and you hardly give her a kind look.' He himself put it down to professional jealousy. She thought the Vice-Principal's job should have gone to her.

'I hope you're pleased with yourself, Mr Sandilands,' she cried.

'What do you mean?'

'Weren't you always complaining that our students were

too docile? Haven't you often wished that they would show more spirit?'

He could not deny it.

'Well, I hope you're satisfied, now that you've got the College in danger of being closed. This used to be a very happy place. Look at it now. Demonstrating, with placards! Like students at home and we know what bolsheviks most of them are.'

There were tears of anger and frustration in her eyes.

'Margaret has just been to try and reason with them,' said the Principal. 'Not with much success, I'm afraid.'

'I told them that if they carried on like that they weren't fit to be teachers. They paid absolutely no heed. That politeness of theirs is nothing but a shield to hide their real feelings. They don't really respect us. Not even you, Mr Sandilands, though you've done more than the rest of us to win their favour.'

He refused to let himself be provoked.

'Well, they've gone back to their classes now,' he said.

'I've given Mr Anderson a list of the ringleaders, those that were impertinent to me. I'm going to insist that they also be expelled. There's an element that we should get rid of. This disturbance is a blessing in that it has shown us who the troublemakers are.'

'Surely, Margaret, their aims are laudable,' said the Principal.

'What aims, for heaven's sake?'

Sandilands answered. 'Justice, for one. They think their colleagues have been unjustly treated. I agree with them.'

'Well, I don't. You're more easily taken in than you think. I think Chia and Lo got what they deserved. I was never taken in by those big smiles that flashed on and off. I wasn't surprised to hear that they were plotters and Communists.'

'Nobody's accused them of being Communists,' said Sandilands.

'I'm accusing them. They want to get rid of the Sultan, don't they? They want to run the country themselves, don't they?'

'It's called democracy, Miss Leithbridge.'

'Democracy! What's that but a lot of squabbling, with everybody looking to their own advantage? This country should think itself fortunate. The Sultan rules for the benefit of everyone. Aren't the hospitals free? Do our students pay fees?'

It was annoying to Sandilands to hear sentiments he largely agreed with being uttered by someone stupid and prejudiced.

'If the Sultan was a tyrant I could understand it,' said Miss Leithbridge, getting to her feet, 'but you, Mr Sandilands, better than most of us have reason to know that he is not.'

Would a tyrant have played golf with a teacher and suffered defeat after defeat with a meek smile? Would he not have insisted on trying again after a missed putt? No. His Highness was hardly a tyrant. He did his best to be fair. It was true many peasants and fishermen still lived in flimsy shacks and his own palace had 2000 rooms, and the mosque had cost hundreds of millions, but education was free and there was a good health service. Was a benevolent dictator to be preferred to a squabbling Parliament?

Miss Leithbridge then left, saying she hoped there was a class waiting for her. Didn't Mr Sandilands have one waiting for him?

He had, but first he had to tell the Principal about his visit to Government House tomorrow with Mrs Azaharri.

'Will anything come of it, Andrew?' asked the Principal.

'Mrs Azaharri seems confident.'

'What kind of woman is she? I often see her mentioned in the *Savu Times*.'

Sandilands should have cried, with shining eyes, that she was the most beautiful woman he had ever met, the most courageous, the most sincere, and the most desirable. What he did mutter, with lowered eyes, was that she had struck him as quite competent.

'She's half-Scottish, I believe.'

'Yes. Her mother came from Temple, a small village about a dozen miles from Edinburgh.'

Would he one day take Leila to see where her mother had been born?

'Well, if she is as handsome as they say she is she should have some influence on His Highness,' said the Principal, with a chuckle.

'She's not like that. She's got principles.'

'So has His Highness.' The Principal laughed.

Sandilands was alarmed. Leila was a widow and therefore vulnerable. She would not succumb to the lure of riches, he was sure of that, but what if she thought she could use her influence to persuade the Sultan to introduce reforms? She could have as much power as if she really was Prime Minister.

His disquiet lasted only a few moments. As he made for his classroom he felt joyful. The reason was his secret: he was in love with Leila. He told it to a red-headed bird taking a dip in a fountain, but he would tell it to no human being, in the meantime at any rate, and especially not – here his joy receded with a rush – to Jean.

He had given her no promises. She would have to admit that, but she would claim that his sleeping with her, though it was really her sleeping with him, amounted to more than casual friendship.

His joy soon surged back. In a few hours he would see

Leila again. He would meet her daughter and perhaps her father. He would find out if he was right in thinking that she was as attracted to him as he was to her.

If their love for each other was ever openly declared he would be faced with two choices: either to marry her (defying all the consequent difficulties) or – his heart sank – to sever from her as the song put it and be for a long time broken-hearted, but safe.

It was his mother's fault. As a boy and a young man he had had to listen to her warnings against the cunning and wickedness of women: they were all Jezebels. He had come to realise that she was crazy with religion, but it had made his relationships with women cautious and furtive.

10

The custom was to wear trousers, of tropical weight, in the evenings, with a long-sleeved shirt, and a tie. If it was a formal occasion, such as a party at the British Residency, then a jacket too was necessary, even if, in spite of a dozen fans whirling overhead, the heat was such that even on the ladies' flimsy dresses sweat marks soon appeared under the oxters. Dressing for his visit to Leila's, Sandilands swithered whether or not to wear a jacket. When he visited Jean he did not wear one, but this visit to Leila was very different. She would not, like Jean, receive him wearing nothing but a transparent négligé. Her bosom, as splendid as Jean's he had no doubt, would not be on display, and she would not perch herself on his lap. Jean had habits like a Shamrock whore's.

He put on his best jacket. His tie was the Yacht Club's,

dark blue with a little gold yacht and the letters, S.Y.C., also in gold. He took with him, in its pot, his most prized and most valuable orchid, carefully wrapped in some left-over Christmas paper. It was Saidee's favourite too.

She asked anxiously if he was intending to bring it back. He shook his head and said he was going to give it to the woman he loved. He said it in English so that Saidee only half understood. She spoke in Malay. Was he taking it to the lady with the loud voice and big feet? No, he replied, he was taking it to the lady with the quiet voice.

As for Leila's feet he couldn't honestly say he had noticed what size they were, but he was sure that, like the rest of her, the parts seen and the parts hidden, they would be the most delicate shade of brown. His heart missed a beat or two as he thought that, for though the delicate shade of brown was assuredly more lovely than any pinky-white, deep within him aversion lurked.

Leila's house was on the hill opposite the harbour. He had been surprised to learn that she lived there, for it was where the rich, most of them relatives of the Sultan, had their large architect-designed houses. Even if Leila's was one of the smallest it would still be worth a lot of money. He was pleased for her sake. After all, if she had lived in a one-roomed shack who would have heeded her? Not even the poor themselves.

These were his thoughts as he drove up the spiralling road. The whole hillside was a blaze of bougainvillea. Even the tallest houses could be seen only in glimpses. Below was the lighted town, beyond the sea with its many small islands. He had often sailed out to them, picnicking on the elysian beaches. Jean had sometimes accompanied him. She had swum naked in the lukewarm water. He had worn trunks.

He had been told the number of the house was 18, but

the Chinese clerkess had added, with a giggle, that he would recognise it by the stone monkeys on the gateposts. They were orang-utans.

Orang-utans were natives to Savu. They had been in danger of extinction for many had been kidnapped for zoos throughout the world. The Sultan had saved them by making their export illegal. A Parliament would have squabbled over it for months and perhaps never have come to a decision.

As he drove through the gate up the steep drive to the house he noticed that the garden had become overgrown, which happened quickly in the tropics if there was any neglect. The original owner must have employed a small army of gardeners. Leila, it seemed, had very few, if any. Perhaps she wasn't so rich after all. Perhaps the house had been bequeathed to her by some relative. He had heard that her father's family was distantly related to the Sultan.

The house was magnificent, with a great curved terrace and marble steps. What dilapidation there was was hardly noticeable in the lamplight.

He was glad he was going to see her in this splendid setting. She would have been out of place in a standard P.W.D. house, such as his and Jean's, made of wood, with four small rooms and built on stilts.

She must have been waiting for she appeared at once on the terrace and came down the steps to greet him. She was dressed in a red-and-white sarong-kebaya, with a red flower in her hair and red shoes on her feet; these, he saw with absurd satisfaction, were smaller than Jean's. She had her little daughter by the hand.

The child seemed a good deal swarthier than her mother, but perhaps her white dress and the white ribbon in her hair accentuated her darkness. He knew, of course, that in a marriage of white or nearly white and black or nearly black

the offspring usually took after the latter, often, if they were
females, to their lifelong regret. In Savu, as in many other
places in Asia, women prized paleness of skin. They used
lotions to try and achieve it and kept out of the sun.

'Good evening, Mr Sandilands,' said Leila, holding out
her hand.

He took it and held on to it. 'Good evening,' he said. He
did not want to call her Mrs Azaharri.

'This is my daughter Christina.'

The little girl must have been called after her Scottish
grandmother. She was shy and pressed close to her mother.

Reluctantly letting go Leila's hand he bent down to speak
to the child. Her eyes were brown. Jean was always talking
about the blue-eyed children they would have.

'Hello, Christina,' he said.

She hid her face against her mother. She had not instantly
taken to him. He did not have the knack of talking reasonably with small children. He would have to acquire it.

He looked about him. 'I didn't know you lived in such a
grand place. Is it yours?'

'Yes, but not for long. It's up for sale. It was left to me by
an uncle. I couldn't possibly afford to live here. In any case
it's not suitable for Christina. She loves playing with her
bicycle and that needs flat safe roads. So I've bought a house
near the beach at Tanjong Aru. I believe you live in that
area.'

'At the far end, yes. Plenty of flat safe roads there, and of
course there's the beach.'

Ten miles of it, with only a few dead jelly-fish as obstacles.

'Where are the students?' he asked.

'Playing table-tennis.'

'The other students came out on strike today.'

'In sympathy?'

'I suppose so.'

'Good for them.'

'Does your father live with you?' he asked.

'No. He has a house of his own, in the town. Tell me about the strike.'

'There's not much to tell. They just refused to go to their classes. They went back when I told them about our meeting tomorrow at Government House.'

'If nothing comes of it will they go on strike again?'

'I hope not.'

'You wouldn't approve?'

'I don't think it would do any good and might get the College closed down.'

Then he remembered the orchid and went to his car for it.

The flowers were red streaked with white.

She put her hand on his arm as she admired the plant.

'Is it for me?'

'Yes.'

'Thank you very much, Andrew. Isn't it beautiful, Christina?'

She had called him Andrew, so he could call her Leila.

The little girl was still trying to make up her mind about him. She kept giving him quick glances.

They went up the steps. Sandilands carried the plant.

They were met on the terrace by the three students. Chia and Lo held table-tennis bats.

'Good evening, Mr Sandilands,' they said.

They were cheerful, and why not? They were young men and their benefactress was a lovely woman. Indeed, they looked at her adoringly, so much so that Sandilands felt vaguely jealous. It wasn't only the beauty of her face and body that enchanted them, it was also her courage and passion for justice. Seeing her through their eyes Sandilands was ashamed of his own doubts as to her motives.

'Mr Sandilands was telling me the students went on strike today,' she said.

To Sandilands' surprise Lo was not pleased. 'They should not,' he said, frowning. 'It is too early.'

What the hell did that mean, Sandilands wondered. That there would be a time for strikes and demonstrations, but it had not come yet? That they ought not to be spontaneous and sporadic and so ineffectual, but carefully planned and concerted?

There *was* something going on, he thought. Perhaps Alec Maitland wasn't far wrong.

He soon had something much more personal to worry about. Salim, simple soul, asked him about Jean Hislop. It wasn't done maliciously. He had no intention of embarrassing his English teacher. At the students' dance he had danced with Jean and had never forgotten her yellow hair, blue eyes, and Western exuberance.

They were seated at table, enjoying a Malayan curry, 'not as hot as Indian', which the students had helped to prepare when Salim, in Malay, asked, most unexpectedly, when Mr Sandilands was going to marry Miss Hislop.

Chia and Lo, more sophisticated, and aware that there might be some degree of intimacy between their hostess and her Scottish guest, were amused; especially when they saw how put out that guest was by the ingenuous question.

They all waited for Sandilands to answer.

'Miss Hislop is a nurse at the hospital, I believe,' said Leila. 'My father says she is very efficient.'

'Miss Hislop and I are friends, that's all,' said Sandilands at last.

Quickly he changed the subject. He asked the little girl about school.

She replied warily. She had a friend called Mary, a white girl who lived at Tanjong Aru. When Christina went to live there she and Mary would have great fun on their bicycles.

He could not have claimed that he had won the child's trust. She spoke defensively.

Did he deserve to be trusted? He hadn't lied about Jean but he hadn't been entirely honest either. Nor was he being honest about the students, for he was using them as a means of getting to know Leila. Worst of all, he was being dishonest about Leila, in that, though he was sure he was in love with her, he still had reservations.

When he was leaving, shortly after eleven, with Christina and the students gone to bed, Leila went down the steps with him to his car. She stood so close that her breast nudged his shoulder. The moon shone on her face. A nightjar called. The Chinese wagered on those calls. The man who guessed the right number won. He thought, if next time it calls three times I shall kiss her goodnight. He waited. She was silent. The bird called: one note, two notes, three notes, and then it stopped. She saw the curious expression on his face. She pressed closer. 'What is it?' she asked.

'The bird,' he said, 'the nightjar. Did you know the Chinese make bets on the number of calls?'

'Yes. What of it?'

'I thought if it calls three times I'll kiss her goodnight.'

'And how many times did it call?'

'Three times.'

'Well?'

Her face was held up, ready to be kissed.

He kissed her, on the cheek.

Then in a great hurry he got into his car and drove away.

A kiss today meant very little. Drunk or sober, he had kissed a lot of women and they had forgotten it the next day or even the next minute. But Leila was different. There was that terrifying Eastern chastity. She would kiss only the man she was going to marry. Did he want to marry her? Yes. But what about those reservations? How could he marry a woman involved in political activities that might be sub-versive? What if she wanted him to take part in them?

11

He was close to his house, on the narrow track with jungle on either side, when he heard raucous music, added to the hum of mosquitoes, the croak of frogs, and the racket of cicadas. He hoped it was coming from Saidee's quarters, but alas, parked outside his house was a Mini, its colour lost in the moonlight. He knew it was red and belonged to Jean Hislop. She was making herself at home, though it was half-past eleven. She intended to stay the night. She must have brought the record with her. His, she complained, were either too high-class or old-fashioned.

In a panic he thought of reversing all the way to the public road and spending the night in a hotel, but there Jean was, on the verandah, giving him a wave, with a glass in her other hand. Her face and arms gleamed. She had put on cream to repel the mosquitoes. With her fair hair she had tender skin.

'Where the hell have you been?' she cried. 'Not at the Shamrock, I hope.' She laughed, coarsely.

He had often noticed that though she would parade naked in front of him she nevertheless had a curious shyness in relation to sex. She tried to disguise it with obscene words and gestures. For all her toughness she was vulnerable. If he told her what he had been rehearsing to tell her she might go to pieces.

Did he love Leila that much? More important, did Leila love him that much? She had let him kiss her and, being half-Oriental, she would never have done that if she didn't love him; but, because she was half-Oriental, he could not confidently predict her reactions. It would be ironical indeed if he suffered the unpleasantness of telling Jean that what was between them, whatever it was, was finished, only to find that Leila had been flirting with him. After all, she was half-Occidental too.

He got out of the car and went up the steps to the verandah, slowly.

'My, we're all dressed up,' cried Jean. 'You *must* have been at the Shamrock, or was it Lady Mortimer's? Same difference, eh? Lots of high-class whores there too.'

Though staunchly British, she liked joking about the stuffiness of those who frequented the Residency.

'Let's go inside, for God's sake,' she cried. 'These little buggers are biting my boobs off. There'll be nothing left for you.' Again she laughed.

Was it to his advantage that she was drunk or nearly so? Should he wait till she was drunker still? She mightn't then completely understand what he was saying to her and so her reception of it would be that much less furious or distressful.

She was wearing a thin white dress that hardly covered her thighs: just that, a brassière, and skimpy briefs. The mixture of scent and sweat was aphrodisical. He remembered Salim's slavish praise of her. Golf Club and Yacht Club members envied him having her soft on him. They would be incredulous, and disgusted, if they heard that he had jettisoned her in favour of a coloured woman: for they would not take into account that Leila's mother had been white. Two days ago he would have agreed with them.

Jean poured him a whisky and handed him the glass. She replenished her own.

'How can I sit on your lap if you don't sit down?' she asked.

He couldn't bear the whining banalities of the song.

'Would you mind turning that off?' he said.

'Anything to oblige.'

She did it and hurried back to him.

He didn't want her on his lap but couldn't very well keep standing.

He sat down on a basket chair: he sighed and it creaked.

Jean at once plumped herself on his lap. There were more sighs and creaks. She was no lightweight. Her bottom was soft, warm, and damp. How could he help feeling roused? Especially as she kept squirming and giving him whiskied kisses.

'You've jaloused I'm staying the night,' she whispered.

She knew he liked using old Scots words.

It was his opportunity to tell her she must go. He let it pass.

'Have you heard about the new regulation?' she asked, indignantly. 'I just heard this evening. Only natives to get top jobs in future. So you'll never be Principal and I'll never be Matron. Do you know what I say? I say, go to hell; stick your jobs up your arse. If I met His Fatness I'd tell him to his face. I've been thinking, Andy, why don't we pack it in and go home. Edinburgh's a lot nicer place to live than this hot stinking midden.'

He imagined himself walking along Princes Street with her. He would be given many admiring, envious glances.

Then he imagined Leila as his companion. The glances would be admiring, yes, but perhaps not envious.

His body was intent on betraying him.

She knew it. Those squirms informed her.

'Let's get into bed,' she whispered. 'Would you like to feel how ready I am?'

She took his hand – it went with an awful willingness – and pushed it inside her briefs.

She got up then and pulled him towards the bedroom. He resisted but not so that she noticed.

Even if, he thought desperately, I have sex with her – it could hardly be called making love – it will not commit me. I've done it before and never felt committed. She's the one who's always wanted it. With her in the state she is, and me in the state she's got me in, how can it be avoided and how can I be blamed? And need it have any more significance than the upside-down mating of those chichaks on the ceiling?

It was soon over though she did her best to prolong it.

'Do you know something?' she said, as they lay side by side under the net. 'I stopped taking the pill two weeks ago. I was going to ask you to use a french letter. I brought one with me.'

He was dismayed. 'Why didn't you tell me?'

'I thought if I got pregnant it would get you to make up your mind about us getting married. They all keep warning me that you're the kind that'll never get married. You're a big selfish bugger satisfied with your books, your records, your orchids, and your fly visits to the Shamrock. I tell them they're wrong. They don't know that your grandfather was a Free Kirk minister and that your mother brought you up to hate women.'

The chichaks were making the shrill noise that had given them their name. He imagined they were being derisive.

She went on: 'I could tell that a bit of you was thinking it was sinful, us not being married. To be absolutely honest a bit of me too. I'm Scottish as well, you know. But it will be different when we're married, won't it? It'll be better too.'

That was all very well, but she had cheated by not using a contraceptive. Fair-minded people would say that that absolved him from responsibility.

12

Jean had to be on duty at the hospital early next morning. She got up and had her shower while he was still in bed. She prattled happily to Saidee, saying that Tuan and she were soon returning to Edinburgh where they would get married, but Saidee wasn't to worry, they would see to it that she got a good job before they left.

In the bedroom Sandilands overheard and groaned. He was in love with Leila, he would remember her till he died, but he would have to marry Jean. He just wasn't heroic enough or caddish enough to do otherwise.

After Jean was gone he thought of telephoning Leila to say that he was sorry but he wouldn't be able to go with her to Government House. As far as he knew he hadn't been included in the invitation. His presence might be resented, especially if, as Leila suspected, the appointment was really with His Highness and not with his secretary.

He had the telephone in his hand to make the call but put it down again. There were the students to consider. If his testimony could help them he ought to be prepared to give it. What he should do, therefore, was accompany her to Government House and then, whether or not their mission succeeded, let her know, as discreetly as he could, that their relationship was ended. He owed it to Jean but also, in greater measure, to Leila herself, who might well become an important person in her country, helping to bring about a democracy of sorts. Involvement with a foreigner like himself could be a handicap to her. Savu Town being a small place it was probable they would see each other again but only from a distance, and in any case were not Jean and he going to resign soon and return home to Edinburgh?

These were his thoughts as he shaved that morning, gazing into the mirror. Those were his eyes staring at him, but he did not trust them. They were assuring him that it would be easy enough to give up Leila, for wouldn't he at the same time be giving up the probability of grievous trouble for himself? They were lying, those eyes. He would give her up but it would be the hardest and most painful thing he had ever done. When he was an old man, with grown-up grandchildren, he would remember it with anguish.

As he got dressed, jacket, trousers, and tie, and as he drove into town, he kept telling himself that he had made the right decision.

The Chinese girl looked up from her desk and smiled at him. Was her smile different from those she had given him yesterday? Did it show a more intimate interest in him? Had her employer spoken of him in affectionate terms?

The moment he saw Leila joy vanquished all doubts and scruples. Jean was forgotten. It was like the end of a race, with his boat first past the last buoy. There was the same transcendent sense of triumph, of white sails, blue sky, sunlit sea, and rainbow spray. Her sarl was blue as the sky. Her earrings were blobs of white coral. Her teeth were white as shells.

'You're early,' she said.

It was as if she had said, 'I love you.'

He replied, 'I didn't want to be late,' but what he was really saying was that he loved her.

Was the sari to impress His Highness?

One of her shoulders was fully exposed. It seemed a shade or two darker than he had remembered.

This was strange, this was abominable. He loved her, he wanted her, he needed her, and yet here he was ready to find fault with her. Was there something wrong with him, or did all lovers behave like this?

She picked up a black briefcase from the desk. He took it from her. Their hands touched. They smiled at each other. They were giving promises, the kind that could not be spoken, the kind that he had never given to Jean Hislop.

Going down the stairs he was aware of the stink from the drains, in spite of his companion's perfume. Why had he not noticed it on his way up?

Jean would have cried, 'My God, what a guff!' and held her nose.

Leila might have been walking through a garden of roses.

'Do you never think of moving to the New Town?' he asked.

That was where other lawyers had their offices.

'My clients couldn't afford a lawyer who had an office in the New Town.'

Her father's surgery was in the Old Town; his patients too were poor.

Sandilands' own sympathy for the poor had always been theoretical and distant. He sent cheques to charities.

They walked along the crowded narrow street to where her car was parked. Almost everyone they passed greeted her warmly. This was a popularity that Sandilands was sure she had deserved but somehow it made him uneasy.

'Have you ever met His Highness?' he asked.

'Once.'

'At the palace?'

'At the British Residency.'

'Oh.'

They were then at her car, a white Saab.

'Why don't we walk?' she asked. 'It's not far and we've got plenty of time.'

'All right.'

But he wasn't sure whether to feel pleased or embarrassed when she took his arm. The way to Government House lay through wide streets with not many people in them and those people were professional men not likely to gawk but it was still an ordeal – no, that was ridiculous, how could it be an ordeal to be seen in public arm-in-arm with the woman he loved?

Leila looked happy and carefree.

He despised himself. He was a worthless, humourless, treacherous, hypocritical bugger: how could admirable women like Jean and Leila love him? His only distinction was that he could play golf well, but what did that amount to? The ability to hit a small ball further and straighter than most other men. He was also competent and bold in sailing a small boat, but there were members of the Yacht Club more competent and bolder, and some of them were boozers and lechers.

Government House was a magnificent building, mostly of marble. A city with a population of millions would have been proud of it. For a country with fewer than half a million citizens it was pretentious and grandiose, but nonetheless impressive, with its enormous air-conditioned entrance hall that contained several fountains and real trees, its marble staircase, and its many sparkling chandeliers.

There were armed guards, in red-and-white uniforms and tall turbans. Even so they looked small. Leila was inches taller.

The chief receptionist, to whom they had to report, was dressed in morning coat and striped trousers, as if for a wedding. He was very deferential to Leila, but seemed upset by Sandilands' presence. It indicated that the meeting was indeed with His Highness and Sandilands had not been invited.

A servant was summoned to conduct them to Room 138.

'I'm not supposed to be here,' said Sandilands, as he and Leila went up the grand staircase.

'But you'll stay with me, Andrew.'

'Of course.'

But how could he if half a dozen of those turbaned midgets were ordered to throw him out?

Upstairs Leila stopped at a large imposing door, of mahogany, brass, and leather, evidently the entrance to an important chamber. 'This is where the National Council meets,' she said, scornfully, and pushed it open.

Sandilands followed her in and was astonished, although he had heard that this room was one of the wonders of Savu. He was reminded of the interior of the Taj Mahal; the walls here, too, glittered with semi-precious stones. It was indeed more like a tomb than a debating chamber. No voices would ever be raised here in angry debate. There was a chair like a throne, higher than all the others. It was cushioned in royal purple, they in red. A large portrait of His Highness in resplendent military uniform – where had he got all those medals? – looked down, like a god.

Leila's eyes were glittering too.

'This is where our Parliament will meet one day,' she said.

'Isn't it a bit grandiose?'

'What do you mean?'

'It's a show-place. Can you imagine any serious debates taking place here?'

'Yes, I can: when we have an elected Parliament.'

That was to say, when pigs could fly.

'A Parliament, properly elected, represents the people,' she said. 'It is right therefore that it should conduct its business in appropriate surroundings.'

It was like a bit out of a political speech, pompous and not very convincing.

This was a Leila he had not seen before. He should have known that she existed. He got a glimpse of her as she would be in, say, ten years' time: dominating, self-righteous, ruthless, always on the side of what was right.

She saw the dismay on his face. Smiling, she patted his cheek. 'Don't forget I'm also a good cook.'

So she was able so easily to read his mind. She had more humour than he. She could laugh at herself. All his life he had found that difficult. What had his mother once said to him? 'You're getting more like your grandfather every day.'

They went out into the corridor where the servant was waiting glumly. He led them along what seemed half a mile of corridor that got more and more narrow, into a part of the building, remote and silent.

They came to Room 138. The servant knocked and entered. They followed. It was a small room but expensively furnished. There was no bed but a couch that could have been used as one.

Through an inner door came His Highness's secretary, a small bespectacled man dressed like an undertaker. He gazed gloomily at Sandilands. There had been a hitch: the coffin had been put in the wrong grave. Sandilands should not have been there.

'The appointment was for yourself alone, madam,' said the secretary.

He had what in Scotland would have been called a posh English accent. There it would never have been taken seriously.

'Mr Sandilands,' he added, 'the servant will show you to another room, where you may wait.'

'Mr Sandilands will stay,' said Leila. 'He is Vice-Principal of the College. He knows the students well. He is to testify to their good character.'

The secretary's gloom deepened. He was not interested in the students. He had almost forgotten that they were supposed to be the reason for this meeting.

'Mr Sandilands will be given an opportunity to testify at a later time,' he said. 'Would you be so kind, Mr Sandilands, as to withdraw?'

'No, Mr Sandilands will not withdraw,' said Leila. 'He is not only Vice-Principal of the College, he is also my fiancé.'

It would have been hard to say whose amazement and incredulity were the greater, the secretary's or Sandilands'.

There were bafflement and horror also behind the secretary's big spectacles. The coffin lid had fallen off and there was the leering corpse.

'Excuse me,' he muttered, and hurried back through the inner door, no doubt to pass on the startling news to His Highness.

No one could have been more startled than Sandilands. He supposed that she had told the lie so that he would have a right to remain as her chaperone, but it had taken the coolest of impudence on her part. Where was the fabled modesty of Eastern women? Nor could her extraordinary brazenness be attributed to her Scottish blood. Women in Edinburgh never announced their engagements in this way.

He should keep in mind she was a lawyer, skilled in ruses and devices.

He lowered his voice. 'Do you think he's reporting to His Highness?'

'Of course.'

In the old days, thought Sandilands, into the room would have rushed half a dozen diminutive Savuese warriors with their curved swords and razor-sharp parangs. In a minute he would have been a truncated corpse; the walls would have been splashed with his blood. Eunuchs too would have appeared, to drag Leila off to their master's seraglio. Would she have gone screaming and kicking? No, she would have gone silently and scornfully, determined to bide her time and make the Sultan pay.

The inner door opened and in slipped His Highness, dressed not in flowing Sultanic robes but in white slacks and a dark-blue blazer with, on its breast pocket, the crest of the Royal and Ancient Golf Club of St Andrews.

He sat and stared at them.

It was hard to believe that this chubby little man with the scarce hair and Errol Flynn moustache could, by lifting a telephone and giving a few instructions, throw the world's financial markets into chaos.

It was even harder to believe that, in that blazer, he had come with ravishment in his mind.

'So, Andrew,' he said, as one golfer to another, 'I am to congratulate you.'

Sandilands' smile was like that of a golfer who had just missed a fifteen-inch putt.

'And you too of course, Madam Azaharri.'

'Thank you, Your Highness,' she said, coolly.

'Why did you not mention it last time we played golf, Andrew? You led me to believe that you had never met the beautiful Madam Azaharri.'

'We became engaged very recently,' said Leila.

'I see. Is the wedding to take place soon?'

Not in the least nonplussed she smiled at Sandilands: 'Would you say soon, Andrew?'

Sandilands was dumb.

'Here, in Savu Town?' asked His Highness. He was enjoying himself.

'Yes. In the Anglican Church.'

This was impudence indeed. Sandilands did not believe in God and would never agree to be married in a church. Jean had teased him: 'Should we get married in St Giles, Andrew? I'm told it can be hired for the occasion.'

His Highness laughed. 'And would you like me to give you as a wedding present a bagful of rubies or pardons for the students?'

'The pardons, Your Highness,' said Leila. 'Though we do not think they have done anything wrong.'

His Highness was watching Sandilands closely. 'Do *you* think they have done nothing wrong, Andrew?'

Sandilands was in a quandary. He had to back up Leila and the students but he had also to tell the truth. Since talking to Albert Lo in Leila's house he had wondered just how innocent those book-readings and discussions in Cheng's back room had been. There had been a fanatical eagerness in Lo's eyes: he was the kind of young visionary who, to further his cause, would set himself on fire. Had it, in Cheng's back room, ever been discussed what was to be done if elections continued to be denied them? Had violence been advocated?

'The books they read and discussed were harmless, Your Highness.'

'Don't you think they might have discussed also how to get rid of the tyrant?'

'The people of Savu are the most peaceful in the world,' said Leila. 'Violence is not in their nature.'

Sandilands remembered those cheerful and unresentful men in the bars and cafes.

'That is true, thank God,' said His Highness.

But even so, thought Sandilands, there were the palace

guards, the armed police, the Gurkhas, and the British soldiers ready to be flown in.

'Will the students be reinstated, Your Highness?' asked Leila.

'Why not? Perhaps Mr Maitland acted too hastily.'

On whose orders, wondered Sandilands. Evidently not the Sultan's. The British Resident's? How ironic if the tyrant was more liberal in his outlook and less obsessed by fears of revolt than the representative of the freedom-loving democracy.

'I look forward to reading an account of the wedding in the *Savu Times*,' said His Highness.

'Why not come and see for yourself, Your Highness?' said Leila. 'We would be proud to send you an invitation.'

'Thank you very much.' He then left, laughing.

'So that's it,' said Sandilands.

He was thinking that if there had been a Parliament and an opposition there would have been angry questions and evasive answers. An enquiry would have been ordered and in the end some fudged compromise would have been reached. It would have taken weeks, perhaps months. Here it had been done in minutes.

13

Going down the majestic staircase, Leila, proud as a princess, took his arm, not this time in a humorous teasing of him but possessively, like a bride, or so it seemed to him. She looked very pleased, as she was entitled to, as a lawyer who had won her clients' case, but it was more than that, she was pleased with herself as a person, no, as a woman, who had a man in her possession. He had seen the same thing in other women. He had escaped from them, though in Jean Hislop's case it was still doubtful. But those had been Western women the workings of whose minds he had more or less understood. Not only was it Leila's ancestry that made her incalculable, it was also her own peculiar qualities. What other woman, for instance, Oriental or Occidental, going down these marble stairs, all fifty or so of them, would still at the bottom have made no mention of the astonishing lie that he and she were engaged and were to be married soon? It was as if she had forgotten all about it, or rather as if, since it was a settled thing, there was no need to mention it.

Out on the street, while he was fishing in his own mind for a pretext to bring it up, a white Rolls Royce purred past them. It was the Sultan's. He gave them a wave, thus adding to the unreality of the scene. Where else in the world would a Scottish teacher, with Calvinist forbears, walking arm in arm with a beautiful coloured woman in a blue sari, be waved at by a Sultan in a white Rolls Royce?

'I think we deserve a celebration,' she said. 'Would you like to take me to dinner this evening, in the Gardenia?'

But in the Gardenia any evening in the week there were bound to be friends of Jean's who, the minute they got home, would telephone her to say that they had seen Andrew Sandilands dining with – guess who? – the notorious Mrs Azaharri, widowed daughter of old Abad. Those friends might not even wait till they got home but would telephone from the restaurant. In which case it was not at all unlikely that Jean might turn up, in a rage not so very unreasonable. He could imagine her yelling: 'Would you believe that this big bastard, last night, was fucking me in his bed and talking about us getting married?'

If that happened it would be more dignified for him to bow his head and say nothing, though he could point out that dining in public with a woman hardly amounted to a serious commitment. Most fair-minded people would agree with him.

But what would Leila do or say?

'Well?' she asked, smiling.

It occurred to him that perhaps she meant to include the three students in the celebration. After all they were the ones with most to celebrate. If they were present he would have a plausible explanation.

'No, just you and I. They will have to return to the College.'

She was well aware that being seen with her in the Gardenia would be something of a travail for him. Her attitude seemed to be that if he loved her he would gladly endure it. But he had never said that he loved her. He had kissed her, but that was all; well, almost all. He did keep giving her looks of admiration. But then didn't every man in Savu Town, from street-sweeper to Sultan, give her such looks?

But, yes, he did love her. She melted his heart. Did she love him? Did he melt her heart? He found it hard to believe. What was her game? What was she up to?

He would have liked to ask her point-blank if she had meant what she had said about their being engaged, but he lacked the courage. Besides, he was afraid that she might say yes, she had meant it; and even more afraid that she would say no, she hadn't meant it.

Outside the Chuu-Chuu tailors they parted, she to go up to her office, and he to drive to her house and take the students back to the College.

She patted his cheek, not caring who saw her. 'Where shall we go for our honeymoon, Andrew?' she asked, smiling.

Without waiting for an answer she disappeared into the close.

Seconds later she was back. 'What would you like me to wear tonight?' she asked, and again did not wait for an answer.

He heard her laughing as she went into the close.

His heart, though melted, was still capable of sinking. Was she going to be too much for him?

On his way to her house there was no need to go anywhere near the hospital, but he found himself driving towards it, right into the grounds, and sitting in his car outside the entrance, among other cars, one of them Jean's red Mini.

A woman came out, weeping.

He did not know what he was doing there.

If Jean had come out, in her blue red-lined cloak, he would have run to her, embraced her, and told her yes, they would go home together to Edinburgh; but of course she did not come out, she was too busy inside, perhaps attending to the patient who was dying.

The students were waiting on the terrace. They came running down the steps; at least Chia and Lo did. Salim stayed up on the terrace. He did not seem to be as anxious as they to hear the news.

'Well, you've been reprieved,' said Sandilands, as he got out of the car. 'Thanks to Mrs Azaharri. It was His Highness himself we saw. If you get your bags ready I'll take you to the College. Mrs Azaharri had to go to her office.'

They were silent. He hadn't expected them to shout with relief and joy, but this grim silence surprised him.

'What is it?' he asked. 'What's wrong?'

'It is Salim,' said Chia. 'He is a spy.'

'A spy?' Sandilands looked up and saw Salim looking down at them cheerfully.

'What do you mean, a spy?'

'His brother is a policeman,' said Chia.

'That hardly makes him a spy.'

'We could not understand why he wished to attend our meetings,' said Chia. 'His English is not good.'

'We could not understand why he became a student at the College,' said Lo. 'He does not want to be a teacher.'

Sandilands had wondered about that too. The standards at the College were judiciously lowered so that students of native origin might graduate, but even so Salim would probably fail.

'He reports to his brother who reports to his superiors,' said Chia.

'Did he tell you that?'

'He did not mean to but he told us. He is very stupid.'

Too stupid surely to be used as a spy.

'He should be punished,' said Chia. 'He should have his tongue cut out.'

'That was the punishment in the old days for spies,' said Lo.

No doubt it had been in Scotland too, if you went back far enough.

'For God's sake,' said Sandilands.

They were as solemn as executioners.

'I would think he's more of a sneak than a spy,' he said.

Then, like a conscientious teacher, he had to explain the difference.

They were not convinced.

'We will take care of him,' said Chia.

That sounded ominous. There were many places in the College grounds and in the jungle that encroached on them, where a sneak's body, with or without its tongue cut out, could be safely disposed of.

Would Leila, he wondered, with a shudder, approve of such a disposal?

14

Leila had telephoned the news to the Principal. He had passed it on to the staff who had told their classes. Therefore when Sandilands' car arrived it was mobbed by cheering students. Even timid little girls who had been taught by their parents that ladies never raised their voices screamed with the rest. Everyone looked on this reinstatement of their colleagues as a triumph for right and justice, whereas Sandilands himself saw it simply as a case of authority having the sense to remedy a blunder. All the same, if they could show such enthusiasm for what after all was a fairly small matter how would they react to a matter of importance? Could he imagine them marching with banners through the Old Town? A day or two ago he could not; now he was not so sure.

He noticed that Salim was included in the congratulations and showed no shame. It would be interesting, if an opportunity arose, to try and discover his motives, though probably he did not know himself what they were. This was a country where, not so long ago, the aborigines cut off human heads and decorated their longhouses with them, for religious reasons. The spirits who haunted the jungle would be pleased not only with those who offered them the heads but also with those who, as it were, contributed their heads. Thus propitiation was shared.

Sandilands and the Principal had once made a journey, by river-boat and along leech-infested trails, to visit a kampong where it was said there was a display of heads of Japanese soldiers. The Principal had wanted to see them. It had amazed and perturbed Sandilands that the Principal, so humane a man, should show such persistence to get there and then, when there, exhausted and drenched with sweat, should squint with such satisfaction at the shrunken heads that still, after forty years, were recognisable as Japanese. 'You can still see the arrogance.'

Margaret Leithbridge and Mr Srinavasan were in the Principal's office, drinking coffee. A holiday had been declared. There were to be no more classes that day. The rejoicing of the students could be heard in the distance.

'Well done, Andrew,' said the Principal.

'It's Mrs Azaharri who should get the credit.'

Miss Leithbridge sniffed. 'You didn't by any chance see His Highness?'

'Yes, we did.'

The sniff became a sarcastic snort. 'What was she wearing? A sari? Showing her bare midriff? I thought so. She's cunning, that one, and dangerous.'

Mr Srinavasan liked to agree with everyone but he could not help pointing out other people's illogicalities. 'In what way is the lady dangerous because she wears the dress of my country? My dear wife also wears a sari. Is she also dangerous?'

Mrs Srinavasan was small, fat, and pock-marked, therefore not likely to entice His Highness or any other man.

Miss Leithbridge could not very well say so. 'I merely meant,' she said, 'that Mrs Azaharri should mind her own business and not meddle in politics.'

'But is not the welfare of Savu the lady's business? She was born here, as was her father, and his father before him. She has distant kinship with His Highness, I have been told.'

'Orang-utans are born here, Mr Srinavasan. Would you say the welfare of Savu is their business too?'

He got to his feet, with dignity. 'May I say, dear lady, that I consider that an offensive remark.' He walked out, very upright, so as not to be mistaken for an ape. He was as black as ebony.

'They're so stupidly sensitive,' said Miss Leithbridge, with a sigh of impatience. 'I wasn't calling him an orang-utan. He does say silly things, though. Do you remember, Andrew, when he reprimanded you because the Scots had helped the English to colonise India? When I said, teasing him really, that he should have said civilise, not colonise, he got up and walked out of the staffroom, just as he did now. Oh dear. I suppose I'd better go after him and make my peace. I'm always having to do that. I'm invited to his place for lunch. Curry so hot it scorches your tongue. But they're really a pair of dears.'

When she was gone Sandilands told the Principal about Salim, the suspected spy.

The Principal sighed. 'What's happening, Andrew? This was such a peaceful and friendly country just a short time ago.'

'There are changes all over Asia. Savu was bound to be affected.'

'Are they to be welcomed, these changes?'

'Depends on what they are.'

'This clamour for democracy, I mean. I've heard you express doubts.'

'Because I don't trust politicians. They're in it for their own good, though they pretend otherwise. Take Mr Srinavasan's country. Ruling India must be the most difficult and thankless task on earth. Yet there never seems to be a dearth of contenders. It must be a love of power.'

'Which we are told corrupts. Yes, I've often wondered myself what makes men involve themselves in politics; women too, nowadays. Take Mrs Azaharri. She's a politician. Would you trust her? What are *her* motives?'

What indeed? Sandilands said nothing.

'But in the meantime we should be grateful to her. I shall write and tell her so. But I'm afraid there are more troubles ahead.'

They listened to bursts of cheering.

'You used to grumble at their docility, Andrew.'

'Yes. But it will be all right. If change comes it will happen peaceably. They're that kind of people.'

'Yes, indeed. So polite. So good-humoured. So patient.'

'Yet you're going to leave them.'

'It's the climate, Andrew. The heat. I'm too old.'

'Well, you're going to where it's a lot cooler. You'll live to be a hundred there.'

The Principal closed his eye so as not to let Sandilands see the pain and grief in it. 'You will have to come and visit me, Andrew, before you go back to Scotland, and stay for a while. There's an excellent golf course nearby. And you will bring the dauntless Miss Hislop with you.'

Sandilands smiled and nodded, but he was wondering what his friend would say if he replied that it might not be the 'dauntless' Miss Hislop who would accompany him, but the 'dangerous' Leila Azaharri.

15

Leila was dressed and ready, so unlike Jean whom he had always found in her underwear. She had chosen a long close-fitting white dress that showed off the shapeliness of her figure – indeed gave it a touch of voluptuousness – and accentuated the blackness of her hair; as did the one white flower in it, a child-like touch that caused him to remember Miss Leithbridge's charge of cunning. She was quite stunning. If there were any friends of Jean's in the restaurant their resentment at him and their sympathy for Jean must be muted by involuntary admiration. A favourite saying of his mother's was: what have I done to deserve this? Only she said it if some misfortune had befallen her. He was saying it now, to himself; but it was because of his inexplicable good luck. His mother also said, if she had been fortunate: 'You'll see, I'll have to pay for this.' He felt that he too would have to pay for it, though what form the penalty or penance might take he had no idea.

Her father was in the house, she said. He was reading a story to his grandchild.

'He wants to meet you, Andrew.' She took his hands and gazed at him. 'You're looking very handsome.'

'And you're looking beautiful.' His voice was a little hoarse.

She let go one of his hands and held on to the other to lead him to her daughter's bedroom. They must have looked like an engaged couple. He wondered if that was her intention.

Her father, small and grey-bearded, finished the story – it was in English – closed the book, kissed the little girl on the brow, and stood up to meet Sandilands.

'Father, this is Andrew Sandilands.'

They shook hands.

'I have heard of you, Mr Sandilands, from your students. They are full of praise. What is it they say above all? You do not condescend.'

'Well, sir, we Scots consider ourselves the most democratic nation on earth.'

'If you, Mr Sandilands, and my dear late wife are examples then your boast is justified. Leila's mother was born in Scotland, not far from Edinburgh. She was as gracious to the peasant in his hovel as to the prince in his palace.'

Well, thought Sandilands, so would I be. What, though, of that absurd colour prejudice? Mrs Abad could not have had it, but then her father had been a doctor most of whose patients had been Malays, whereas Andrew's mother had from his infancy filled him with prejudices, most of them out of the Bible, the kind so hard to get rid of. He hated colour prejudice and knew all the arguments against it and yet he suffered from it. So did all mankind, but that was no excuse. Surely Leila could cure him.

The little girl in the bed was gazing steadily at him. She did not frown but she did not smile either. She had still to make up her mind about him.

Lacking natural ease towards small children, but knowing that he must gain her approval, if not her affection, he went over. 'Hello, Christina. Do you remember me?'

She nodded.

'Do you like to listen to stories?'

Still impassive, she nodded again. Perhaps a little distrust had come into her eyes.

'I'd like to read you a story. What kind do you like best?'

'About bicycles.'

He couldn't help laughing. It was the wrong thing to do.

She frowned. 'I've got a bicycle. It's red and white. It can go fast.'

'I hope you're very careful when riding it.'

'I always put my hand out when I'm going to turn.' She demonstrated.

'That's good.'

'And I always ring my bell when there's anybody in front of me.'

Her mother then rescued him. 'That's enough, darling. Mr Sandilands and I have to go. Perhaps Grandfather will read you another story.'

Grandfather still had the book in his hand.

Leila kissed her daughter. Sandilands did not. He could not trust himself to make it look natural. Besides, the little girl did not look as if she wanted him to kiss her.

They went out.

'Has she ever been to Scotland?' he asked.

'No. Neither have I.'

He was surprised.

'My mother died when I was three. I have never met her people.'

'I'd like to take you there.'

'Then I could meet your parents.'

'Yes.' His father would make her welcome but his mother was more likely to rebuff and insult her. He could not hide his disquiet.

Leila noticed but said nothing.

16

They went in her car, the immaculate white Saab, leaving his dusty, untidy Triumph at her house.

'You can drive if you like,' she said.

So he was driving when they arrived in the parking space in front of the restaurant. Two men and two women were getting out of a car. They were in evening dress and were in a party mood, laughing and giggling. They saw Sandilands. 'Hello, Andrew,' cried one of the women, a Mrs Williams. Then she became aware that his companion was not Jean Hislop. She was shocked into silence as she stared at Leila. So were her companions. It wasn't so much that Leila was in Jean's place, as that she was the notorious Leftie and daughter of the demagogue Dr Abad. It was also because she was so stunningly beautiful and so self-confident. A coloured woman as beautiful and elegant as she ought, in the presence of whites, to be humble, or, if that was asking too much, to be at least diffident. Instead of which this woman was holding her head high and smiling at them, as if her smiles were as good as their smiles, though none of them was smiling. One of the men, John Williams, was heard to mutter, 'Good God!' and he didn't mean it as an oath.

Sandilands swithered about introducing Leila to them and decided not to. He took her arm and went with her through the door and up the stairs to the restaurant.

The quartet followed them, but not closely.

The Gardenia was sumptuous. It would not have been out of place in a fashionable part of Paris. Its patrons, especially the expatriates, joked about its extortionate prices but were really proud of being able to afford them. It was thickly carpeted, air-conditioned, and luxuriant with plants. On the walls were paintings of Savu scenes.

The waitresses were little Malay girls, in native dress. The one who led Sandilands and Leila to their table smiled at the latter. It was a shy but grateful salute to her country-woman, who outshone all the white women.

Those white women were not smiling. Those who knew who she was whispered the information to those who didn't. All of them were displeased by her intrusion; not because she seemed to have supplanted their friend Jean Hislop – they did not think of that immediately – but because she was a native and coloured and therefore automatically inferior. That she was said to be a relative of the Sultan made no difference. Indeed, in spite of his immense wealth, he too was inferior, though of course if they were ever invited to his palace they would bow and curtsey, as they would do in Buckingham Palace.

Then those women, and their men, turned to the matter of the intruder's escort. 'It *is* Andrew Sandilands,' a man's voice was heard to say. Incredulity did not quite smother the envy.

They began to conjecture as to why Sandilands was with her and not with his usual companion, Jean Hislop.

'I suppose you know them all?' asked Leila, coolly.

'Most of them. Now what would you like to drink?'

'A glass of water, please.'

He had forgotten she did not drink alcohol. There were many things about her that he had yet to learn.

'You drink whatever you like,' she said.

He ordered a whisky. He must not, so soon anyway, let her change him, even for the better.

They were approached by a man Sandilands sometimes played golf with. Bill Nelson sold expensive cars to the Sultan and the Sultan's rich relatives: his commissions were very lucrative. His wife was in England, seeing to the education of their teenage children. He drank too much. He lived with a native woman whom he called his amah but who was really his mistress. She was a quiet dignified woman with too broad a nose and a fondness for gaudy jewellery. He never took her out or introduced her to his friends. One or two of those friends had written to his wife, telling of his adultery. It was believed that she had written back, sarcastically thanking the sneaks and saying she didn't give a damn who Bill slept with, so long as he kept increasing her allowance. It was suspected that she too might be having an affair.

He patted Sandilands on the shoulder. 'How are things, old man?'

'Fine, Bill.'

He leered at Leila. 'So you're the fabulous Madam Azaharri? Those that said you were the most beautiful woman in Savu weren't lying. I'm Bill Nelson. I play golf a lot with this big bugger and I always lose.'

He held out his hand and Leila took it.

'Don't worry about this po-faced lot,' he said. 'Live your own life is what I say. Don't you agree?'

'Yes, I do.'

'Good for you. Do you happen to play golf yourself?'

'I did once, in Malaya, years ago.'

'Good. Get this character to have you made a member.

There's a big flame-of-the-forest tree that's the glory of our course. Isn't it, Andrew? Well, here's a lady who'd outshine it.'

At last she got her hand back. 'Thank you, Mr Nelson.'

'Bill. Please call me Bill.'

He then staggered off to rejoin his friends.

Sandilands briefly gave an account of him.

She smiled. 'Would you, Andrew, if we were separated for a long time, find another woman?'

He was glad that his whisky arrived then. Not only did it save him having to answer, he also needed it.

17

Questions were being asked at every table.

'What's Jean going to say about this?'

'I didn't know it was finished with her and Sandilands.'

'It isn't. I happen to know that she spent last night, or was it the night before, in his house which meant in his bed.'

'We've all heard her say she and Sandilands were going to get married and live in Edinburgh.'

'Yes, but nobody's heard *him* say it.'

'He's too canny.'

'Look, he can't keep his eyes off her.'

'No bloody wonder. She's tremendous. Lucky bugger!'

'If she's so tremendous why is she interested in him? He's nothing special.'

'Except on the golf course.'

'He plays with the Sultan, doesn't he?'

'Maybe he met her through His Nibs.'

'They say she's related to His Highness.'

'Why then are she and her father, the old doctor, always on about elections?'

'I read an article by her in the *Savu Times* once. Well, I didn't read it all, it was too damned long, but I read enough to realise that she wants to get rid of His Highness and put an elected Parliament in his place.'

'I don't think they want to get rid of him exactly. They want him to be like our queen, a figure-head.'

'I can't see him standing for that.'

'He needn't worry. If there were elections his party would win every seat. Look at all the money he's got to buy votes.'

'What would happen to us if they had a Parliament? We'd all be kicked out.'

'Or kept on with reduced salaries.'

'They'd put their own people in all the top jobs.'

'That's happening already.'

'Our man, Sir Hugo, would have to go if they had a Parliament. I heard him say it himself. It seems old Abad had the cheek to tell him to his face.'

'That's gratitude for you. We open up their oil fields for them, make them one of the richest countries in the world, and then they want to throw us out.'

'They wouldn't throw us out. They're too polite for that. They'd ask us very nicely to leave. Mind you, in next to no time they'd want us back, for left to themselves they'd make a mess of everything. They're charming but God, aren't they incompetent?'

'If they weren't under British protection wouldn't they be in danger from the Japs? I don't mean by war, I mean by buying them out.'

'We wouldn't allow that.'

'Jean's got nothing to worry about. Sandilands would never marry a coloured woman.'

'Has he ever said so?'

'Not in so many words. But it's an impression he gives.'

'Well, there couldn't be a bigger contrast, Jean with her blond hair and that dusky creature.'

18

All this whispering was interrupted by the sudden clattering of a chair to the floor, as a woman jumped up and rushed out, in the middle of her meal. Everyone was startled but no one was surprised. It was just Nancy Turner being outrageous again. They were all sorry for poor Archie. There he was, looking miserable, with his fork at his mouth. He was too nice for his own good. Any other man would have sat there, finishing his meal and drinking lots of wine as a gesture of defiance. Archie, though, got up at once, paid his bill, and hurried after her.

Those nearest to their table had heard no quarrel; in fact they had heard nothing, from Nancy at any rate. Archie's few careful remarks had been unanswered. He was always careful, especially in public, for Nancy was given to bursts of obscenity if thwarted in any way.

She was waiting for him in their car. 'For Christ's sake, what kept you?'

'I had to pay the bill.'

'Well, get going and don't dawdle.'

'What's the hurry? Do you feel ill?'

'I want to be the first to tell that conceited cow Hislop.'

Archie's niceness sometimes made him dense. 'Tell her what?'

'That Andrew Sandilands has thrown her over for that haughty black bitch.'

Archie's thought processes were slow and simple. It seemed to him she had no good reason for saying Sandilands had thrown Jean over; or that Mrs Azaharri had looked at all haughty, and she certainly wasn't black. Also, even if all those things were true, telling Jean about them was none of Nancy's business. As her husband he should be trying to prevent her from stirring up mischief, but he was too afraid of her insane rages.

Still, he had to try. 'It will upset Jean.'

'Fucking right it will. I hope it has her screaming her head off.'

'What harm has she ever done you?'

'She's sorry for me. That's what's she's done. Interfering cunts, all of them, and she's the worst. I've never understood what Andrew Sandilands sees in her.'

Once before, from something she'd let slip, he'd got the impression that she fancied Sandilands, though as far as Archie knew she had never spoken to the big Scotsman.

'She's vulgar. She's got a vulgar laugh.'

Jean did have rather a loud laugh and, if she'd had a drink or two, it could become a bit boisterous, but hardly vulgar. Nancy herself, because of her obscenities, was considered by most of the expatriate women as worse than vulgar.

'I don't think you should telephone her, Nancy.'

She laughed.

'I'm serious.'

She laughed again.

At their house she was out of the car and up the steps before he had time to shut the garage door.

He went up the steps slowly. Not for the first time he let the thought of strangling her pass across his mind. He would do it fondly, for he loved her. He remembered the one child they had had, ten years ago, a little girl. She had died in infancy.

He hoped Jean was out and not available, but no, Nancy was through to her immediately. The telephone system was efficient, thanks largely to him. He was Chief Engineer.

'Hello, Jean. Nancy Turner here.'

He went close enough to hear Jean's reply. 'Hello, Nancy. How are you?'

'Is there a chair handy, Jean? A bottle of whisky? You're going to need them when you hear what I've got to tell you.'

He wished he had the courage to snatch the telephone from her grasp.

Jean was laughing. 'What terrible news is this then?'

'Archie and I were at the Gardenia tonight.'

'You're home early then.'

'Guess who was there.'

'Let me think. His Highness?'

Now and then the Sultan showed himself among the people. He always had bodyguards with him.

'Not *His* Highness. *Her* Highness.'

'One of his ladies, do you mean? With her face covered?'

'No. Azaharri. Mrs Azaharri, Abad's daughter. The lawyer. Her that's always writing political articles in the newspaper. She's a widow.'

'What are you havering about, Nancy? I know who Mrs Azaharri is. What's wonderful about her being at the Gardenia?'

'But who do you think she was with?'

Jean laughed. 'Who the hell cares who she was with?'

'Oh, I think you'll care, Jean, you'll care a lot.'

'Well, tell me.'

'Andrew Sandilands. That's who she was with. Just the two of them. Holding hands.'

'I didn't see them holding hands,' muttered Archie.

If Jean was upset she didn't show it. On the contrary, her tone was sympathetic: the caring nurse's, not the enraged lover's. 'You're not well, Nancy. If you don't get treatment soon you'll end up in a mental institution. Good night.'

Nancy threw down the telephone with a scream, and rushed into her bedroom, slamming the door shut.

Archie heard her weeping. If it had been the heartbroken weeping of a woman in distress, as indeed she was, he would have felt nothing but compassion; but it wasn't that kind of weeping, at least not much of it was – it was the weeping of a woman mad with hatred and jealousy. Was it possible that she was in love with Sandilands herself? He had hardly ever looked at her. Whatever his game was with Mrs Azaharri he always kept clear of women likely to cause him trouble, such as married women. Archie did not know him well. No one did. He didn't let himself be known. But Archie had never heard him say ill of anyone, and had seen him by himself in bars frequented only by Malays and Chinese. He was a lonely decent man and Archie wished him well.

19

If Archie had been an invisible presence in the car as Sandilands and Leila drove towards her house, he would have heard Sandilands' decency being put to a severe test.

Passing Mr Cheng's bookshop they talked about the old man and the others deported with him. They would be invited to return in honour one day, said Leila, when the country was free and democratic.

'How long will that be?' asked Sandilands.

'Not as long as you think, Andrew.' Without a change of tone she added: 'What *is* your relationship with Miss Hislop?'

He had noticed that Eastern women sometimes blurted

out impertinent questions, not realising that they were impertinent. But Leila was not as naïve as that.

Tell her to mind her own business, Archie's shocked shade would have advised him, but Sandilands, the decent man, felt obliged to answer honestly.

'She's a friend; well, maybe more than a friend.'

'I know of her, of course. She's a nurse at the hospital. My father praises her. I have seen her. She has beautiful yellow hair. She is Scottish. I was told you and she are engaged.'

'That's not true. We're not engaged. We've never been engaged.'

'You think so, but does she? Women see these things differently. Have you slept with her?'

She asked it coolly, like a lawyer.

'Yes.'

'Recently?'

Archie would have stopped the car there and then and got out to walk the rest of the way, rather than put up with this insulting inquisition. But he did not know how guilty Sandilands felt.

'Yes,' said Sandilands, meekly.

'Since meeting me?'

'Yes.'

She said no more until they stopped beside his Triumph outside her house.

Sandilands could not bear to look at her. He was sure that his romance with her, if it could be called that, was finished. He was going to say that he was sorry and then leave. They would never meet again. But his affair with Jean was over too. He would go and live in the Cameron Highlands with David Anderson, taking his guilt and regret with him.

'Wait.' Leila took hold of his arm and kept him from

getting out of the car. 'You have a choice, Andrew, Miss Hislop or me.'

This was the height of arrogance, and yet he did not see her as arrogant.

Her grip on his arm was quite painful. She was in a state of great stress, though she did not show it in any other way.

'You heard me tell His Highness that we were to be married. You did not deny it.'

'I thought you said it so that he couldn't send me away.'

'Yes, but surely you saw that I was in earnest?'

This was the East where marriages were arranged, but not by the bride herself.

'Shouldn't there have been a discussion first?'

(Not to mention a courtship of sorts.)

Her grip tightened. 'You kissed me.' She whispered it, tragically.

It hadn't been much of a kiss.

'And I kissed you.'

That had been even less of a kiss.

He had realised, from the first time he had met her, that she was not the kind of woman with whom his life would be safe and cosy, and he had felt qualms. Now he saw that, in spite of her formidable competence, her political ambitions, and her self-confidence, she had weaknesses of a deep-seated kind and needed help. Christ pity her, she seemed to think he could give it.

'Are we engaged, Andrew?'

'Yes.'

He was amazed at himself, canny Andrew Sandilands, jumping recklessly over this wide chasm, with a drop below all the way to infinity, and knowing that there would be more chasms ahead.

She let go his arm and leaned forward to let him kiss her. He did so, with more politeness than passion, but she returned it with sudden desperation. He tasted tears.

He felt tender towards her. He wanted to embrace her but shyness kept him back. He stroked her head.

'Good night,' she said, and got out of the car. She was crying. 'See you tomorrow.'

He got out too and stood watching her go up the steps. At the top she turned and waved. He waved back.

Only then was he aware of the racket of the night creatures, the fragrance of the bushes, and the brilliance of the stars.

20

He had to let Jean know. It was tempting to wait till she got in touch with him, for out of pride she might not, but that would be cowardly. By this time one or more of her friends would have telephoned her, with the titbit of news. She would have been more amused than angry, for she was fair-minded and intelligent, and would place little import-ance on his taking another woman, even one as unlikely as Leila Azaharri, out to dinner. He, though, had to confess to a great deal more than that. Just how culpable was he? He had told the truth when he had said they weren't engaged. He had slept with her, more than once, but always at her instigation. She had noticed his reluctance and teased him about it, attributing it to the influence of his Calvinist grandfather. Even so, it did not exonerate him. Her friends would be justified in saying that he had callously jilted her. She herself would take it bravely. She would not abuse him or seek revenge. She would not go out of her way to avoid him. If they met by accident she would give him a smile and turn away. If he had Leila with him perhaps she might not smile.

Now that he was about to part from her he recognised as never before what an admirable woman she was. No wonder other men had envied him.

No one was to blame. It just happened that he was not in love with her.

Once, a class of his, with whom he had been studying *Jane Eyre*, had been puzzled by Jane's falling in love with Rochester, who was old and ugly and in the end blind. Their own wives or husbands would be carefully chosen for them. Was Jane going to marry Rochester because he was rich and had a big house? That made sense. Giving love as the reason did not. Sandilands, not taking the subject very seriously, had concluded, to their dissatisfaction, that love was a mystery.

Now he had fallen in love with Leila and she with him.

As soon as he was in his house he dialled Jean's number. It was engaged.

Saidee had gone to bed, so he could not ask her if Jean had telephoned earlier. He would have to wait and try again.

A few minutes later the number was still engaged.

Saidee had gone to bed, so he could not ask her if Jean had telephoned earlier. He would have to wait and try again.

A few minutes later the number was still engaged.

What if Jean came to confront him face to face?

There was something he had forgotten or rather had not taken into account. She loved him. God knew why, but she did. It was a great pity in the circumstances.

The third time he got through.

'Jean Hislop speaking,' she said.

She sounded cheerful.

His heart sank. 'It's me, Andrew.'

'I thought it might be. What's this about you gallivanting with a dusky lady?'

Was her cheerfulness a defence? If she was hurt she was not going to let anyone, him especially, see it. Her sneer at Leila as a dusky lady was uncharacteristic. She had no prejudice against people with dark skins. 'How could I have?' she had once said to him. 'Most of my patients are dark. Some of them die.'

'How did you get to know her?' she asked. 'Was it through His Nibs? I believe she's related to him. Me, I'm related to an Edinburgh shopkeeper.'

Her uncle had an ironmonger's business.

She was not as carefree as she was trying to have him think.

'Leila and I are going to get married,' he said.

There was a pause.

'Leila? Is that her name?'

'Yes.'

'Did you say you were going to get married?'

'Yes.'

'I thought that that was what you said, but it sounded so silly. Is this some kind of joke, Andrew? You do have at times a rather laboured sense of humour.'

'It's not a joke.'

'You may not intend it as a joke, but it is a joke all the same. All our friends will laugh at it. How long have you known her?'

'That doesn't matter.'

'Is this Andrew Sandilands talking? Him that walks round every situation, half a dozen times at least, studying it so cautiously, as if it were a putt to win a championship?'

'I'm sorry,' he muttered.

'Is it some kind of marriage of convenience? Does she want to become a British citizen? Is that it? As soon as the ceremony's over, you part company, never to see each other again. Lots of Asian ladies do it. Some pay a lot of money. How much is she paying you, Andrew?'

'It's not like that.'

'Isn't it? Is it you that's paying for it? If you marry a Savu citizen you become one yourself. So you'd be eligible for the Principal's job.'

'No.'

'It's a love match then. Is that what you're trying to tell me?'

'I'm sorry, Jean.'

He put the telephone down. It was cruel but not so cruel as prolonging so painful a conversation.

For the next few minutes he dreaded that the telephone would ring and it would be Jean, weeping.

It did not ring.

21

It rang next morning as he was getting ready to set off for the college. Thinking that it might be Jean, with a question that had already occurred to him, spoiling his sleep, he let it ring several times before picking it up.

The question was: what if I'm pregnant, Andrew? What do we do in that case?

In that case the world would have turned upside down.

It was Leila, sounding elated. 'Good morning, Andrew.'

He remembered last night's tears. 'Good morning, Leila.'

He braced himself. She was going to ask if he had been in touch with Jean and what had happened. But her subject was altogether different.

'Have you seen the newspapers this morning?'

There were two, the *Savu Times* and the *Savu Herald*. Usually he didn't see them till he got to the College. They were fond of big black headlines that dirtied the hands.

'No. Is there anything special in them?'

Such as the announcement of their engagement. No, there wouldn't have been enough time for her to put it in.

'There are to be elections. We are to have our Parliament.'

He almost said: Is that all? It was how he felt but it would have been churlish to say it, since she was so delighted. So he simply said: 'When?'

'In six months. There's to be a commission to divide the country into constituencies.'

He had to be careful how he expressed his scepticism. 'His Highness must be very confident his side will win. He'll get the credit of being democratic without the pain of having to give up power.'

'Is that what you think will happen?'

'I'm afraid so.'

'You underestimate the people of Savu. They are proud of their country. They want it to be their country, not the Sultan's only.'

If they got married was he to sit at home while she was out making election speeches? Even worse, was he to attend her meetings and listen to her speeches? Seeking privacy himself, how could he survive having a wife who sought publicity?

'See you this evening,' she said. 'Goodbye for now.'

No endearments, he noticed. But then he himself hadn't used any. It wasn't a Scottish custom.

Yet, in spite of all his misgivings, he was looking forward eagerly to seeing her again. There was nothing he wanted more. He would tell her how much he loved her and she would tell him how much she loved him. They would convince each other. He would overcome his dislike of politics for her sake and promise to help her in every way he could. As her husband he would have a right, for, as Jean had said, his marriage would entitle him to Savu citizenship. Being involved, he would be better able to console her in defeat, for he had no doubt whatever that her People's Party would be so badly beaten that they would lose heart and break up.

22

In the staffroom the conversation was about the proposed elections, but only Mr Srinavasan was enthusiastic. Savu, he announced, would be the smallest democracy in the world, while his own country was the largest. Sandilands did not have the heart to remind him that the world's largest democracy had the world's worst corruption, poverty, and violence. Mr Srinavasan was now saying that it would be a matter for congratulation when Savu had its own Parliament, provided, of course, it did not too officiously reduce the salaries of expatriates or get rid of these altogether. It was true that those salaries were the most generous in all Asia, but surely that was something the country should be proud of, since it meant that it was able to call upon the services of the most qualified and efficient people. 'Such as ourselves, dear colleagues,' he said, beaming round at them all, without a trace of irony.

Baker, the Australian, rubbed his hands together. He would not mind being kicked out, he said, if he was laden with bags of gold.

'You're all being ridiculous,' said Miss Leithbridge. 'There will be no Parliament to speak of. His Highness knows what he's doing. He knows the people are behind him.'

There were nods of agreement. Their servants, they said,

assured them that very few supported the People's Party. There were large crowds at their meetings but most people went out of curiosity and also, especially in the case of the men, to see Dr Abad's daughter, the beautiful Mrs Azaharri.

'Beautiful!' cried Miss Leithbridge. 'Shameless, if you ask me. That naked midriff!'

Mr Srinavasan wagged his finger. 'You are being naughty again, dear lady. Are Indian ladies shameless?'

'A sari is a traditional Indian dress, Mr Srinavasan, and therefore quite proper when worn by Indian ladies. Mrs Azaharri is not Indian. She has no right to wear a sari. She does it because she is conceited as well as shameless.'

Sandilands had to say something. 'A sari is a beautiful garment. That is why Indian ladies wear it. That is why Mrs Azaharri wears it.'

'Well spoken, Mr Sandilands,' said Mr Srinavasan. 'I would be obliged, however, if this subject was closed. Please let us discuss arrangements for the forthcoming examinations.'

In the classroom block the students were excited and gleeful. Girls, usually so demure, danced and shouted in the corridors. Everywhere students were shaking hands with each other. It was as if the elections had been held and victory won. Sandilands was amused to see Salim, the spy, as triumphant as the rest.

He noticed Chia and Lo by themselves in an empty classroom, talking earnestly. When he went in they stood up, respectful but wary.

'Well, so far so good,' he said.

They smiled and at the same time frowned.

'I mean, elections are fine but they're only one step forward. There's a long road ahead of you.'

'We are patient,' said Lo.

'If you lose will you still be patient?'

'If the elections are free and fair,' said Chia, 'we shall not lose.'

Sandilands remembered that when the elections took place, if they ever did, Chia and Lo might be in exile in the interior, far removed from the centre of things. They would be among ex-headhunters, whose grandchildren were their pupils. It was amusing to imagine these dedicated young Chinese haranguing, in not very persuasive Malay, antediluvian old men about the advantages of democracy, and going from longhouse to longhouse canvassing for votes, with shrunken heads grinning down at them.

'Well, good luck anyway,' he said.

'We do not need luck,' said Chia, 'because we have justice and right on our side.'

'Still, a little luck is always useful.'

He would need more than a little himself.

23

As she came down the steps in the lamplight to greet him she looked so dignified and chaste – he could think of no better word, unfashionable though it was – that lust certainly, and perhaps love itself, was chilled. She seemed to be carrying herself with exaggerated elegance, as if to emphasise how untouchable she was. He was being made to look crude and unworthy. Was that her intention? Did she suspect, from giveaway signs that he himself had not been aware of, that he had an instinctive or instilled prejudice against coloured skins and was challenging him? No, that was absurd. More likely she was simply letting him see that if he married her he would be getting a wife he could be proud of. The trouble was she was doing it too well. Could it be that she was not as self-possessed as she pretended?

She stood close to him. He smelled her perfume, among all the other fragrances of the warm night. She shivered and sighed. He sensed in her – what? Unhappiness? Grief? Despair?

He almost embraced her then.

Instead he showed her the presents he had brought, a record of Scots love-songs for her and an illustrated book of Scottish folk-tales for Christina.

She put her hand on his arm. 'Love songs?' she said, smiling.

'We have some of the finest love-songs in the world, though the world finds it hard to believe.'

'Why does it?'

'Because the Scots are thought to be dour and reserved.'

'I think *you* are a little dour and reserved, Andrew.'

Thanks to mosquitoes he did not have to answer that. They started biting in earnest so that he and Leila had to flee up the steps into the house.

Her father, she said, was at a meeting. Was she letting him know they had the house to themselves?

'Why aren't you at it?' he asked. 'Won't they be discussing the great news?'

'Yes, but I'd much rather be here with you, Andrew.'

It would have been ludicrous for him as a lover to ask her why she preferred to be with him, and yet he would have liked to ask, not because he wanted to hear praise of himself from a woman he loved or thought he loved, but because he really could not see what in him attracted her. It was easy to tell what he found attractive in her: beauty, grace, intelligence, courage, and sadness, but above all mystery. There was so much about her that he didn't understand and perhaps never would. Jean, so different, had revealed her inmost thoughts and feelings as freely as she had her body. Would he be happier or at least more at home with a woman like that?

They went into her daughter's bedroom. Christina was in bed, looking at a picture book.

'Here's a lovely book Mr Sandilands has brought you,' said her mother, in English. 'It's about Scotland. I'm sure if you were to ask him nicely he would read one of the stories to you.'

'Would you like that?' he asked.

She nodded, dourly. After all, she had Scottish blood in her.

He chose a tale set in North Uist where his mother had been born and his grandfather had been a Free Kirk minister. It was about a little girl the same age as Christina herself who, while playing on the beach, had been kidnapped by selchies, creatures half-seal and half-human. They had taken her to their land under the sea. One day, years later, she had returned, strangely changed, with a marvellous account of where she had been and to where she must go back.

Now and then he would look up from the page and see those young brown eyes watching him. She was following the story, smiling at some parts and looking sad at others, but all the time she was judging him, not as a reader of stories but as a person. Had her mother told her he might be taking her father's place? She was old enough to remember her father.

He thought that he would be proud and happy to regard her as his daughter. What if he and Leila had children of their own? Would they all be happy together? There could be more joy and more danger in their marriage than he had so far foreseen.

Leila tucked in her daughter and kissed her good-night.

Sandilands did not offer to kiss the child, nor did she

expect him to. He wished her good-night. She returned it, quietly; not shyly, though. Young though she was, she seemed to have put up defences.

In the dining-room, as they ate, Leila said: 'She's very interested in Scotland. She tells her friends that she's part Scottish. She's sorry she never saw her Scottish grandmother.'

'You'll have to take her there some day.'

'*We'll* have to take her, you mean.'

'Yes, of course.'

'Tell me about your mother, Andrew.'

How could he, telling the truth, say that his mother was bigoted, embittered, vindictive, and unloving? That she would never welcome Leila as her daughter-in-law? That she would write letters full of hysterical vicious screams?

If the truth could not be told, what lie could he make convincing?

All the defences he had built up since childhood were no protection. He felt exposed and desolate. Even that dark beautiful face opposite him seemed inimical, though it was smiling at him with sympathy and love.

'She's very religious,' he said at last. 'Like most of the people on the island. Her father was a minister.'

'You are not religious yourself?'

He shook his head.

'But you would not mind being married in church?'

He minded but would not object if that was what she wanted. He shook his head again.

'Thank you, Andrew.'

In the sitting-room, as they sat on chairs well apart, he looked more like a casual visitor than a lover, and she like a polite hostess. For something to say, he asked if she would like to hear the songs on the record. Let other lovers say for him what he could not say for himself.

She said she would like very much to hear them.

So for the next half hour they sat and listened to the yearnings, griefs, joys, and triumphs of those other lovers of long ago. The Highland chief inconsolable after the death of his Maiden of Morven. Jock o' Hazeldean riding off o'er the border with his English sweetheart. The Borders man lamenting fiercely the death by accident of his burd Helen on Kirkconnel Lea. Leezie Lindsay joyously off to the Highlands with Lord Ronald McDonald, a chieftain of high degree. The poet taking farewell with ae fond kiss. The lovers who would never meet again on the banks of Loch Lomond.

Jean had laughed at his fondness for those 'sentimental' songs of the past. 'For heaven's sake, Andrew, be more up to date.' But the love-songs of today seemed to him by comparison shallow and tawdry.

Leila, he saw, was in tears: thinking of Azaharri, he thought, but he did not feel jealous. On the wall was a photograph of her dead husband. Chichaks lurked behind it. He had died when only thirty-six.

'Would you take Christina and me to the Golf Club on Sunday?' she asked, suddenly.

He could not quickly enough disguise his dismay.

Members' wives sat outside in the shade of the trees, drinking and gossiping, while their husbands played golf and their children built sand-castles. Most were white. Jean's friends would be there. Jean herself might be. Did Leila realise that? Was she deliberately putting him to a test? He had been seen with her in the restaurant. Now he was to be seen with her and her child. Those women, most of them mothers themselves, would be especially interested in watching how he behaved towards Christina. They knew that he never made any fuss of their own children. He was not that kind of man.

'Don't you go to church on Sunday?' he asked.

'Yes. But after the service we could go to your house and then to the Club. Perhaps we could have lunch there.'

It would amount to an announcement of their engagement. There might be unpleasantness. One or other of Jean's friends, who had had too many gins, might shout abuse. But it wouldn't matter. It came to him, as an inspiration surely, that he had a defence against not only abusive women but against the whole world; against Leila even. The child, Christina. She represented everything of value that had been left out of his own life. Even if she never grew fond of him, looking after her would give him strength and comfort.

24

The clubhouse was on the edge of the South China Sea; in front a beach as spacious and splendid as any in famed Bali. Tall casuarina pines gave shade. That Sunday, as usual, it was crowded. Children, near naked, playing on the sand, were as brown as Christina; some were darker though both their parents were proudly white. She saw some of her friends among them and rushed to join them. They were glad to see her and made her welcome.

Sandilands called after her to be careful.

He and Leila found an empty table in the shade.

They were stared at with more surmise than animosity.

'Not playing this morning, Andrew?' shouted one woman.

There was a competition that he would probably have won.

'Giving the others a chance, is that it?' cried another.

'That's right, Marjorie.'

He went in and brought out drinks, beer for himself, lemonade for Christina and Leila. Christina came running up to get hers. She was excited and happy. She gave Sandilands a big smile.

He felt that nothing else would matter if the child trusted him.

Suddenly, though, he grew tense. One of Jean's friends, and then Jean herself, came out of the clubhouse, wearing bathing costumes.

Others saw her. There were whispers. Everyone stared.

'What is it?' asked Leila. Then she too saw Jean.

He had no idea what Jean would do. Had she loved him enough to hate him now and seek revenge in the presence of all these people? But it would not matter. There was Christina happy among her friends. She turned then and waved to her mother and him.

It was at Leila that Jean kept staring, for a long minute, before running towards the sea.

'Isn't she afraid of the jelly-fish?' murmured Leila.

There were Portuguese men-of-war which could cause painful burns. A child had once died.

'My father says she's very brave. It's important for a nurse to be brave.'

'Yes.' He had eyes only for the little dark girl with the yellow ribbon.

'Have you thought about where to go for our honeymoon? I've been thinking myself that we could go to Scotland. I would like to meet your parents, Andrew. But perhaps they'll come to our wedding.'

'No, they won't do that. My mother's not well enough for the journey.'

'So I should go and visit her.'

A meeting between his mother and Leila would be agony

for him, but he would be able to bear it if by that time he had won Christina's love.

'If you like,' he said.

'We could also visit Temple, the village where my mother was born. It's not far from Edinburgh.'

'I know Temple.'

'I'd like to stay in Singapore for a day or two first. I have friends I would like to see.'

Political friends, he thought. But he did not feel displeased.

'We could take Christina with us,' he said.

Leila shook her head. 'No. Later perhaps. Not on our honeymoon, Andrew. My father will look after her. We should have moved into our house by the beach by then, near her friends, where she can play with her bicycle.'

'Is that what she'd prefer?'

'Yes. I've discussed it with her. She says the Robinsons will look after her. Mary Robinson's her special friend. That's her with the white ribbon.'

Mr and Mrs Robinson were seated not far off, with friends. They had already given Leila, and therefore Sandilands too, cheerful waves.

Jean was now splashing ashore. She took off her cap and shook her hair. The sun glittered on her as it would have on a selchie. With what sinister purpose had she come out of the sea?

Anxiously he watched her bend down to talk to the children. She put her hand on Christina's head, beside the yellow ribbon.

He got to his feet.

'What's the matter?' asked Leila.

He could hardly say that he wanted to run down on to the sand to protect Christina. Trembling, he sat down again.

'You don't think she'd do Christina any harm?' asked

Leila. 'I've been told she's fond of children.'

Yes, so much so that she had said she and Sandilands would have three, two girls and a boy. Those children would never be born. Yet was that altogether true? She had said she might be pregnant. If she was and she refused to have an abortion he would be faced with another enormous difficulty. But again his love of Christina and his need of her would help him overcome it.

Jean was now coming towards their table. Drops of sea-water sparkled on her cheeks like tears. Her nipples showed through the wet costume. Her thighs were brown except at the top.

'Do you mind if I join you?' she asked, and sat down.

She was instantly interested in the black mole on Leila's neck. 'Pardon me for asking,' she said, 'professional curiosity, but have you had that long?' She pointed to it.

'All my life.'

'Does it ever hurt?'

'No.'

'Or get bigger?'

'No.'

'Then I'd leave it alone. These things can turn cancerous if disturbed. I believe your husband died of cancer.'

Added to the sunburn there was a blush. She was being mean and spiteful and had not intended or wished to be. She was letting herself down.

'My father's a doctor,' said Leila, quietly.

'So he is. No doubt he'll keep an eye on it. By the way, Mr Sandilands, I'm to be Matron after all, in three months, when Mrs Aziz retires. I've been wondering if you had anything to do with it. Through your influence with His Highness, I mean. As a sort of consolation prize.'

He shook his head. 'I had nothing to do with it. Congratulations.'

'Thank you.' She turned to Leila. 'Perhaps it was you then? I hear you're related to His Highness.'

'Very distantly. I'm afraid I can't claim the credit either.'

'Anyway, it means I'll be staying in Savu for a while longer. Unless of course the People's Party takes over and throws out all the white faces.'

'I don't think we would wish to do that.'

'I've heard it said you would. I've also heard it said you haven't a snowball's chance of taking over.'

'That remains to be seen.'

Jean turned back to Sandilands. 'What's happened to your contempt for politicians? Not to mention that thing of yours about dark-skinned ladies?'

She stood up. The water drops on her cheeks had dried up.

'Is that your little girl with the yellow ribbon?' she said. 'She's very bright.'

Then she walked away. By the jaunty swinging of her buttocks she let them know she wasn't broken-hearted.

Sandilands was left wondering, shamefully, if he would have been happier or at least safer, married to her. But no, for in that case he would have lost Christina.

25

They were married, within six weeks, in the Anglican church. His Highness, regretfully, could not attend. He sent a card, hinting that some of his more devout Muslim subjects might object. But he also sent a present, a very valuable solid gold salver. It was as well that he did not come, with his retinue of attendants and bodyguards, for there wouldn't have been room for them in the small church. Some of Sandilands' students were there, including Chia and Lo. So too were officials of the People's Party, quiet, discreet, purposeful men in dark suits, Malays, Chinese, an Indian or two, and even a few aboriginals or bumiputras. Sandilands had seen some of them in Savu Town where they were business men or shopkeepers. They were all deferential towards Leila, not because she was the bride but because she was the daughter of their leader. Perhaps, thought Sandilands, the Sultan's Party ought not to be so sure of a crushing victory in the elections. These men – there were no women among them – would say little but work hard. They looked very patient. They might not win this time or the next but in the end they would. It was possible that they might establish a true democracy in which the politicians were the servants of the people and not the masters. It would not last long. Corruption would inevitably set in, affecting the best of them, including Leila herself.

Sandilands' parents were not present. He had telephoned. Luckily his mother had not been at home. His father had offered timid congratulations. These he seemed to want to withdraw when told that Leila was part Malay. Sandilands was sure that his father would not inform his mother of the conversation.

Dr Abad gave his daughter away. He did it with his usual mild good nature, though he had not yet given his blessing to the marriage.

David Anderson, the Principal, was best man. He too thought the marriage a mistake. Andrew, he had hinted, lacked the recklessness that would be needed.

Sandilands had been afraid that Jean would show up, not angry or resentful, at any rate not showing anger or resentment, but deliberately radiant, with her fair hair conspicuous among all the black, and her blue eyes among all the brown.

She would want to show him that she wasn't pining. Once, late at night, she had telephoned to tell him that, thank God, she wasn't pregnant.

Two of her friends were present in the church, though not invited. They sat at the back, as unobtrusive as spies. He wondered if Jean had asked them to attend.

If they told the truth they would have to report that the bride had looked lovely in a light blue costume, with a bouquet of orchids in her hand. As for the groom, well, Jean would be pleased to hear that he had looked more anxious than triumphant. She would say that it was because he was getting married and so committing himself for life. It wouldn't have mattered who the woman was.

The spies, though, wouldn't have noticed his glances at the little girl Christina, acting as a bridesmaid with her friend Mary Robinson.

Mary's parents were in the church. They were afterwards to be reproved for it.

A meeting had been held in the Golf Club at which it was decided that, considering how badly he had treated Jean Hislop, no one should accept Sandilands' invitation to the reception in the Gardenia. By marrying Abad's daughter he had let the side down. God knew why he was doing it. Was it ambition? Did he think that the People's Party would win the elections and through his wife's influence he would become Minister of Education? That would never happen, of course. What would happen was that, to use one of his Scotch words, he'd soon find himself scunnered, surrounded by dark-skinned aliens, including, it could be, his own half-caste children. Jean needn't worry. The big bugger had a punishment in store for him that would serve him bloody well right.

One member, rash with drink, had proposed that Sandilands' name be deleted from the list of past captains and also the list of past club champions, on which it appeared six times. This proposal, after much debate, was rejected. After all, he held the course record and, to be fair, he had always conducted himself like a gentleman, even when playing with duffers. Also, through his pal the Sultan he had got the Club a number of useful little privileges.

One member, though, did attend. This was Alec Maitland, in civilian clothes.

All the College lecturers, with one exception, attended both ceremony and reception. Miss Leithbridge sulked at home.

Saidee, Sandilands' amah, was present, looking very proud. When they returned from their honeymoon she was to continue in their service. In the Principal's large house several servants would be needed.

Thomas Harvey, deputy to His Excellency the British Resident, telephoned Sandilands to say that he was looking forward to attending the wedding (although he hadn't been invited) and to insinuate, in his bland oblique English way, that Sandilands, as husband of Abad's daughter, would be in an excellent position to pass on information about the People's Party, if he thought such information would be helpful to the proper authorities. There had been suave mumbles about it being to everyone's advantage to keep subversive elements out.

26

On the plane, trying to sort out his feelings, Sandilands could hardly believe that this beautiful woman beside him, in so many ways still a stranger, was now his wife. Surely it had all happened and was still happening, not to him, not to the person he had known all his life and had often disliked, but to someone else hidden in him. It must have been that other person that Leila had fallen in love with and that Christina at the airport had embraced and kissed. Who was it then, as his elbow touched Leila's, felt this immense and yet humble joy? And who was it remembering the little girl with affection and pride?

Leila had said something. She had to repeat it, with a smile. 'This friend who's coming to see me in Singapore, perhaps I should warn you, has just been released from prison.'

'What was he in prison for?'

'Political reasons. You must not, at your peril, criticise the leadership in Singapore. Nor must you wear your hair too long.'

In spite of the humorous remark, made no doubt to conciliate him, he could not help frowning. This was the familiar Andrew Sandilands. He objected to having his honeymoon spoiled by grubby politics.

'How long was he in prison?' he asked.

'Five years. He has been let out because he's old and very ill. In fact, he's dying.'

The old Andrew Sandilands would have felt a vague sympathy for the old 'martyr' but would have seen it as none of his business. This other liberated Andrew Sandilands, because Leila was involved, wanted to be involved too.

'Is he Malay?'

'No. Chinese. He's really a friend of my father's but I've known him for years. A wise, kind, cultured, hopeful old man.'

'Hopeful?'

'Yes. He thinks that in the end we shall learn to love one another.'

The Sandilands of only six weeks ago would have sneered

at such absurd optimism, which surely was contradicted by history and by the old man's own experience. The Sandilands of now was sceptical but did not sneer. What he did was think of Christina. Love might not be the solution but it was the only consolation.

He looked out at the stars. 'I hope Christina's all right,' he said.

'Of course she'll be all right. The Robinsons are kind people. They'll take good care of her.'

'And your father will keep an eye on her.'

'Yes, but she's not a baby, you know. She's quite self-reliant. They say she's very like what I was at her age.'

He smiled. 'I'm sure she is. But perhaps we should have brought her with us.'

'On our honeymoon?' Leila laughed. 'She understood. She said she'd rather stay at home and play with her friends.'

There was a little incident as they were going through immigration. The Chinese official examining passports looked at Leila's and then at her and then went through the door behind him, saying 'One moment, please.' Seconds later another officer, his superior, came out with Leila's passport in his hand.

'Mrs Azaharri?' he asked, smiling.

She still had her old passport. There hadn't been time to have it changed.

'Now Mrs Sandilands,' she said. 'I was married this morning. This is my husband.'

'Is there anything wrong?' asked Sandilands. 'I am a British citizen. So, therefore, is my wife.'

'She still has her Savu passport.'

'There wasn't time to change it.'

'I see.' He handed Leila her passport. 'Have a pleasant honeymoon.'

'What was all that about?' asked Sandilands, as they moved on to collect their luggage.

'It seems they have my name on their list.'

'What list?'

Of course he knew about those lists that governments had, of suspicious and dangerous characters, but they had meant nothing to him in the past. They had represented a world of mess and misery far removed from his. Now it had come close, in the person of his beautiful wife.

'Don't look so alarmed,' she said, smiling. 'They're letting me in, aren't they?'

Yes, but would they have her, and therefore him too, followed?

He could not help thinking that Jean Hislop's name would never be on any of those lists.

27

Half an hour after they had registered at Raffles Hotel he was telephoning Savu. He intended to do it every evening. He had asked the Robinsons if they would mind. They had been amused, for he was only the child's stepfather after all and besides he didn't have the reputation of being the kind of bachelor who made a fuss of children and was affectionately called uncle by them. Yet here he was fussing over Christina more than her mother.

Leila was lying on the bed. She had taken off her costume and was wearing only white brassiere and briefs. She looked lovely.

He had trouble getting through, but persevered and at last heard Ann Robinson's cheerful voice.

'Good evening, Andrew. We've been expecting your call. Christina's fine. She and Mary are having their shower together. It's a wonder you can't hear their screams. That's what little girls are like, you know. Do you want to talk to her or shall I just tell her you called?'

'Yes, that would do.' But he felt disappointed. 'Perhaps I could talk to her tomorrow night. She's all right, though? Not pining or anything?'

'Good heavens, no. She's really a very happy, independent little girl.'

'So she is. I'll phone again tomorrow about the same time. I hope you don't mind.'

'Of course we don't mind.'

'Perhaps I could talk to her then.'

'I'll have her prepared. Did you have a nice flight to Singapore?'

'Yes, thank you.'

He put the telephone down. 'I didn't get speaking to her. She and Mary were having a shower together.'

'What a good idea.' Leila got up and came over to him. The overhead fan stirred her hair. 'But I've got an even better one. This is our wedding night, remember.'

He remembered, but it wasn't quite the time yet. He had calculated that it would come after dinner, when he had drunk a good deal of wine and felt bolder.

Her offering herself to him prematurely was disconcerting.

God forgive him, he was reminded of the Shamrock whores. They, women of the East like her, had given up their chastity for money. She was doing it for love of him. Yes, but he wasn't worth it.

'What's the matter, Andrew?' she asked, quietly. 'Don't you want me?'

Yes, but he could not have her while he felt unworthy.

It wasn't only his betrayal of Jean, though that counted.

'What have I done?' she asked.

He shook his head. He could never have explained.

'Was it true what Miss Hislop said? Why did you marry me then?'

She turned away, picked up her dressing-gown, and went into the bathroom.

He heard what sounded like her weeping but it could have been a tap running.

There was his suitcase, open but not yet unpacked. He could escape to another hotel. It would mean the ruin of his marriage; worse, it would mean his being cut off from Christina.

He knocked on the bathroom door.

'It's not locked,' she said.

Was there contempt in her voice? There ought to be, for he deserved it.

He went in. She was standing in front of the mirror, staring at her tearful but resolute face.

He stood beside her. 'I'm sorry, Leila.'

'So am I, Andrew.'

'I love you.'

'And I love you. But it's difficult.'

'Yes.'

'We don't know each other well enough. My father said I was hurrying you into marriage. He was right, but then, you see, Andrew, I did not want to lose you.'

'And I didn't want to lose you.'

'Well then, we have each other.'

'And we have Christina.'

She smiled. 'She's important to you, isn't she?'

'Yes, she is.' Though he would have found it hard to explain why.

'And you're important to her.'

'Am I? I hope so.' Again he remembered the child embracing him at the airport.

Christina's love could be his certificate of exemption.

'Since we're here, Andrew, shall we have our shower together?'

28

Next morning at breakfast Sandilands noticed some of the other guests smiling at them, with goodwill; they were being recognised as a honeymoon couple. He did not mind. He was the happiest and proudest man in Singapore and did not care who saw it. Perhaps in the smiles directed at him there was a small element of mockery, in that he was a man of thirty-six or so as delighted as a child with a cherished toy. He remembered Christina's joy in her red bicycle; but in the smiles given Leila there was nothing but amazed admiration. No wonder, for she was astonishingly beautiful, because she was also astonishingly happy.

A servant crept up to say that there was a telephone call for Mrs Azaharri.

'It can't be for you,' said Sandilands. 'You're Mrs Sandilands.'

She kissed his cheek as she got up. 'I'll put them right, whoever they are.'

She was soon back, looking sad. The old Chinese who was to visit her wasn't able to come: he was too ill. If she wished she could go to see him. She had said that she did wish. She hoped Andrew wouldn't mind. She promised not to be long. This was an old man whom she honoured and whom she had known all her life.

'I'll go with you,' said Sandilands.

She was doubtful. Was it possible that she loved him and yet did not trust him? Yes, it was.

'Are you sure you want to?' she asked.

'Very sure.' He wanted to be in her company always.

'It's in a rather run-down part of the city.'

'All the more reason I should go with you.'

'I was warned I might be followed.'

'By policemen, do you mean?'

'Yes. He's regarded here as a dangerous revolutionary. Everyone who visits him will come under suspicion. Even you, Andrew.'

He did not smile. 'Has he, as a revolutionary, ever advocated the use of force?'

'As a last resort, yes, I suppose he has.'

He smiled now, pretending that the question he was about to ask was playful. 'Would you and your father ever advocate force?'

'It would be very foolish of us to do so in Savu, wouldn't it? Look at all the might His Highness could use against us. Hasn't he an understanding with the British? Troops would be flown in. Besides, you've said yourself how peaceable our people are.'

He had to admit it. 'So they are.'

They took a taxi. They held hands. He glanced through the rear window to see if they were being followed. A dark-blue car kept close behind them.

'Mr Lee, like Mr Anderson, was a prisoner of the Japanese,' she said. 'He too was tortured. You will see. Two of his fingers are missing. They were chopped off.'

Just then Sandilands saw on the pavement a group of Japanese tourists, laden with cameras. They were enjoying themselves in the Lion City where they were welcome guests. This time they came with wads of yen, not swords.

Soon they were in a district of tall bleak apartment blocks. Here the car following them was more conspicuous.

At a closemouth a young Chinese man was waiting for them. He reminded Sandilands of Albert Lo. He had the same guarded smile and watchful eyes. He greeted Leila with respect. As lawyers she and her husband had, at risk to themselves, defended dissidents.

Sandilands was given a quick curious glance and then ignored. He was not a comrade.

There was no lift. They trudged up six flights of stairs. The place was clean but sour-smelling. There were no graffiti.

Who was it, thought Sandilands, that said the poor would be with us always? For all the singing there would be no overcoming.

They came to a door, like all the others, painted a dull green. There was nothing to indicate that within, dying, was an old man who had once been a professor of philosophy and who still believed in a time when poverty, war, and exploitation would be abolished.

Their escort knocked cautiously. The door was opened by a Chinese woman with grey hair and tired, stern eyes. She smiled when she saw Leila. They embraced, Sandilands was embarrassed. Here was a Leila he had not known and, to be truthful, did not want to know: a Leila who would never be made welcome in the Golf Club.

The woman was not sure how she should greet Sandilands. Leila introduced him as her husband. She smiled at him then, but not cordially.

The room was barely furnished – no carpets on the floor and no pictures on the walls. It was not a home but a place of refuge, not to be stayed in long. There was a bed. On it lay an shrivelled old man. His eyes were shut and would never, it seemed to Sandilands, be opened again. If he was breathing it was not detectable.

Leila took the old man's hand. Sandilands noticed that the fingers were missing. She spoke, in English, but the old man did not hear her, or if he did was too far away to answer.

The visit was fruitless. Leila might have got herself in trouble for the sake of an old man who was dead or very close to it. At any moment there might come a banging on the door. The rest of the honeymoon might be spent in separate jails.

But there was silence, except for a contemptuous snuffling made, Sandilands realised, with shame, by himself. What he meant by it was that it made little difference to a private man who governed, whether the autocracy was a despot's or a parliament's. All he himself wanted was to be let live in quietness with Leila and Christina. He could not remember ever having voted. He had lived so long abroad that his name was on no electoral roll at home. He had never regretted it. Yet here he was, in this miserable room six storeys up, with secret policemen waiting below, in the presence of suspected revolutionaries.

The young man spoke in Chinese, the woman nodded, and then in English said to Leila that they should go now. If her father awoke she would tell him that Dr Abad's daughter had come to see him. He would be very pleased.

Leila kissed the old man on the brow. It was a kiss that declared her love for him and also defiance of his and her enemies.

Sandilands was shocked by that kiss and by the tears in her eyes. Had she forgotten that she was now his wife?

They went down the stairs in silence.

The taxi was waiting. So was the blue car. Sandilands could see the two men in it. They looked bored. He felt sure they had been talking to the taxi-driver, who seemed nervous.

'What now?' asked Sandilands. 'Would you like to do some shopping?'

Too late he realised he was being insensitive and unsympathetic.

'I'd rather go back to the hotel.'

Only then did he try to understand what a strain it had been on her. It had meant nothing to him but surely, if he loved her, it should have been agony seeing her suffer.

'I hope you don't mind, Andrew,' she said, humbly.

'No, of course not.'

They said very little on the way to the hotel.

29

The Chinese clerk at the reception desk looked grave as he handed Sandilands the key. Was he trying to disguise his amusement at the honeymooners hurrying back for an afternoon of blissful consummation? But Sandilands hadn't been in the room two minutes before the clerk, his voice also grave, telephoned, asking him to come to the desk at once. 'By yourself, please.'

'Why, what's the matter?'

'Come at once, please.'

'All right.' Had the police come looking for Leila?

She was in the bathroom. He called to her that he would be back in a minute.

The clerk did not smile on seeing him. 'Please come into the office, Mr Sandilands.'

Sandilands was sure that in the office there would be policemen. Therefore he went in truculently. But the office was empty.

'I must explain,' said the clerk. 'About an hour ago there was a telephone call for you, from Savu, from Dr Abad, who is, I believe, your wife's father.'

'Yes, that's right. What was it about? What did he say?'

'He said I was to tell you when your wife was not present.'

Sandilands was more mystified than alarmed. 'Tell me what?'

'That you were to telephone this number immediately.'

The clerk showed it written on a piece of paper. Sandilands recognised it, it was the number of Savu Hospital. He had used it often enough when telephoning Jean.

He was alarmed now. Had something happened to Jean?

'I shall leave you alone, Mr Sandilands,' said the clerk, and went out.

Sandilands sat down by the telephone. It might take a while to get through and besides, his legs had turned unsteady.

He dialled the number. Strange sea-like noises were heard: Savu was an ocean away. He tried again. This time there was a shrill whistling. But the third time was lucky, though he had a feeling now that lucky was not an appropriate word.

He asked for Dr Abad.

Then he was listening to a quiet tired voice saying something that turned his blood cold.

'Is Leila with you, Andrew?'

'No.'

'I have bad news, very bad news. Christina is dead. She has been killed in an accident on her bicycle at the roundabout near the airport. The child Mary Robinson is here in hospital. She is very badly injured. The old lady who was driving the car, Mrs Wilkinson, is also in hospital, suffering from shock.'

Sandilands was stunned. He could say nothing.

'Do you know her, Mrs Wilkinson?'

Yes, he knew her. She was at least seventy-five. She wasn't fit to drive a car. They laughed at how slowly she drove.

'You will come home immediately, Andrew.'

'I can't believe it.' He would never all his life be able to believe it.

The old man was weeping. 'I cannot believe it either, and I have seen her. Poor Leila. It will break her heart. But here is Nurse Hislop wishing to speak to you.'

Jean was close to tears. 'Oh Andrew, I'm so sorry. Everyone is. She was such a bright happy little girl. They both were.'

'How is Mary?'

'Badly hurt, I'm afraid. They're operating on her now, but they don't think she'll make it. Her parents are here. It's awful. Mrs Wilkinson's here too. She's in a terrible state. It was her car that ran into them.'

If he had been able to weep or rage against the senselessness of the child's death it would in the end have given him some relief, but he would remain outwardly calm and it would destroy him.

'Your poor wife. Does she know yet?'

'No.'

'Poor Andrew.'

She meant that he didn't have the resources to cope with this situation. He had been selfish too long.

She herself was practical and helpful. 'There's a plane leaving Singapore for Savu at half-past four. You could get that. I'd phone now and book seats.'

It was now twenty minutes to one.

'Yes, I'll do that. Thanks, Jean.'

He telephoned the Cathay Pacific office. There were seats available.

He had then to go back to his room. He went slowly. People were seated in the shade at tables in the grassy compound, having pre-lunch drinks. There was a family with small children. There were shrieks of laughter.

He stood in the sunshine, utterly desolate. Nothing mattered any more. The joy that he had found in Christina was gone for good. He remembered the missing fingers of the old man. He remembered the Japanese tourists laughing. He felt bitter and revengeful when he should have been feeling only pity.

Jean was right. He had been selfish too long.

They were gazing at him curiously. A woman with white hair smiled in puzzled sympathy. He tried to smile back, reassuring her, letting her know that it was all right, the child he had loved was dead and he was about to go and tell her mother.

Leila was relaxing on the bed. She had taken her shoes off. The big fan whirred overhead.

'Where were you?' she said. 'It was a long minute.'

He sat on the bed. All those years of looking after himself and of committing himself to no one had him by the throat. Even if he had known what to say he could not have said it then, not even to this woman whom he had married and whom he was supposed to love.

She sat up. 'What's the matter, Andrew? Why are you looking like that? Is it the police? Have they come?'

So she had been thinking of the threat from the police. The blow, a far more vicious one, had come from another quarter.

'Leila, I've just been talking to your father on the tele-phone.' His voice was so hoarse she could hardly make him out.

Her eyes went wide with wonder and then with fear. She said nothing but waited.

'There's been an accident.'

She still waited.

'Christina and Mary. On their bicycles. A car ran into them.'

'Were they hurt?'

If she loved him surely she would understand that his apparent calm was an indication of how deep his despair was. Despair was silent, sullen, and useless.

He should have been thinking only of her and here he was again thinking of himself. That it was largely self-disgust was no excuse.

'Christina was killed. Mary's badly injured. They think she will die too.'

'Dear God.'

At least she had her faith in God to sustain her. If he had been a believer he would have wanted an explanation as to why God, who oversaw everything, had seen fit to arrange death and serious injury for two happy harmless children. He would not, though, say it to Leila, not now or ever. Let her find what comfort she could in her belief in God's wisdom and love.

'I've booked seats on the half-past four flight to Savu,' he said.

'Andrew, if it is true, I don't think I can bear it.'

It was true and he would not be much use in helping her to bear it. He felt utterly disqualified.

There was a long pause.

'Who was driving the car?' she asked, at last. There was no anger or bitterness in her voice. 'Did my father say?'

'An old woman called Wilkinson. She's in hospital suffering from shock.'

'Poor woman.'

Yes, he supposed Mrs Wilkinson deserved pity but she also deserved censure. She ought not to have been driving the car. She had known that she was not a capable, and therefore not a safe, driver.

He thought, with abysmal stupidity, that when they got to Savu he and Christina together would comfort her mother. He could not bring himself to accept that the little girl was dead.

Leila got up. She had not yet wept. 'I think I would like to speak to my father. Will he be at the hospital?'

'I think so.'

He got through for her. It took ten minutes. Dr Abad had left to visit patients.

She spoke to the senior doctor, McAllister. He confirmed that it was true. He hinted, sadly, that it might be better if the other little girl died too. If she lived she might have permanent brain damage.

Sandilands, close to the telephone, heard.

When such things happened, what did it matter whether you lived in a democracy or a dictatorship?

30

It was a bumpy flight, through a tropical storm. Some passengers were terrified. The plane kept falling hundreds of feet, like a lift out of control. Dishes from the galley clattered on to the floor. The stewardesses, two small Malay girls, kept assuring everyone there was no danger, but their voices were shaky. Once Sandilands, in his despair, found himself wishing that the plane would plunge into the South China Sea far below. What use was his life now? As Principal of the College the students would soon see through him as a sham: he had sneered at them for their craven submission, now they would sneer at him for wanting them to go on submitting cravenly. He himself would go on playing golf with His Highness; he would become more and more syco-phantic. He and Leila must not have children. They might escape accident and disease but not the contempt shown to half-castes or even worse, the toleration.

Leila was whispering to him. He could not hear because of the roar of the engines. She repeated it. 'We still have each other.'

It angered him that she should be looking to him to make up for the loss of Christina. Why did she persist in seeing in him qualities that weren't there? Above all, the ability, the readiness, to put others before himself. Selfish himself, he preferred it if everyone else was selfish too. That was the only kind of equality there would ever be.

She was still waiting for a response. There were tears in her eyes, tears of sadness but of eagerness too.

About to reject her appeal, about to find a sadistic pleasure in rejecting it, as if she was his enemy, he felt instead an overwhelming fondness for her. It was as if a dam had burst, sweeping away all his mean reluctances. He realised, for the first time, what a treasure he had in her. She was beautiful, clever, generous, and brave, and she was his. He claimed her humbly. How stupid to think he had nothing to live for when he had her. How cowardly to want no children because they might be despised by fools. With Leila as their mother they would be beautiful and gifted, like Christina.

He took her hand and pressed it. 'That's right. We still have each other.'

Just then the plane gave a great lurch and a woman screamed.

'I'd be terrified too if you weren't with me,' said Sandilands.

It was dark when they landed at Savu airport. Waiting for them in the arrival lounge were Dr Abad, Leila's secretary Miss Lai, the Anglican minister, David Anderson, and Alec Maitland, in uniform, looking uncomfortable.

The Deputy Commissioner managed a word with Sandilands while Leila was greeting her father. 'I'm very sorry, Andrew. A bloody shame. We'll talk about it later. I've got a car waiting. You'll want to go straight to the hospital.'

'Yes.' But surely escorting them there was not the business of the Chief of Police?

'To tell you the truth I was asked to meet you and take you there.'

'Who asked you?'

'His Highness. In person. He's very upset. He really is. He's fond of you both. So he said anyway.'

Being all-powerful in his little State, and having so much wealth, did not necessarily mean that the Sultan lacked simple, human feelings.

Sandilands was afraid that Leila, after her experience in Singapore, might object to going in a policeman's car.

'Why shouldn't we go in my father's car?' she asked.

'Maitland's here because His Highness sent him.'

'That was kind of His Highness.' She did not say it sarcastically.

'He admires you, Leila.'

'Even though he knows I'm going to take his kingdom from him?'

He was glad she was able to joke, albeit sadly.

'You don't mind then going in Maitland's car?'

'It won't be sounding its siren, will it?'

'Your father can come with us. He'll be brought back to pick up his car.'

'What about Miss Lai?'

'I'll take her home,' said David Anderson.

The clergyman said he would like to go with them to the hospital, but in his own car of course.

He was a small elderly man of mixed blood, whose previous benefices had all been in places as obscure and unprofitable as Savu. No bishop had ever been interested in him.

Since no one else was paying him any heed Sandilands did. 'Thank you for coming, Mr Joomar,' he said.

A grateful smile appeared on the sad, sallow, wrinkled face. 'Thank you, Mr Sandilands.'

In the main hall there was a crowd of people, among them acquaintances of Sandilands and of Leila. They had come out of curiosity no doubt but also, Sandilands saw, out of sympathy. Their faces showed concern.

At the very back he caught sight of Saidee, his amah. He pushed through the crowd towards her. Dressed in her smartest sarong-kebaya, she was surprised, pleased, and embarrassed. She thought she had no right to be there, among all those people who had come in their cars. Yet here was Tuan taking her hand and thanking her. She was too shy to say anything.

'Who was that?' asked Leila.

'Saidee.'

'Saidee?' Leila looked for the tiny amah but could not see her. 'It was kind of her to come.'

'Yes.'

Saidee had been very fond of Christina.

Maitland sat in front with the driver. Dr Abad, Leila, and Sandilands sat in the back. He held her hand. He could feel her shuddering.

They passed the roundabout where the accident had taken place. No one mentioned it.

Sandilands looked out at familiar sights: the kampong

ayer, the water village on stilts in the sea, now lit up; places where the jungle came right up to the road; the cinema where the films were in Malay, Hindi, and Chinese.

This was where Leila had been born and brought up. It was his home now. He might one day return to Scotland, but only for a visit.

They passed a big billboard, brightly lit up. The Sultan's face was depicted on it, with a broad benevolent smile. In Malay it stated that a vote for the Patriotic Party was a vote for His Highness and therefore for Justice and Prosperity.

'They've lost no time,' muttered Sandilands.

'The town's full of them,' said Maitland. 'The whole country, I believe.'

'Do they think they can buy votes?' whispered Leila.

'Do they have to?' But Maitland, never at any time interested in politics, was ashamed to talk about them now.

There were more cars in the hospital car park than Sandilands had expected. They couldn't all belong to the staff or people visiting relatives. Perhaps some were friends of the Robinsons or the Wilkinsons.

They were received by Dr McAllister and the Matron. Jean Hislop was there too, still in her uniform, though she must have been off-duty. She gave Sandilands a woeful shake of her head.

Leila asked to be taken to the room where Mr and Mrs Robinson had been waiting for more than eight hours.

Sandilands went with her. Whatever was in store for her he would share it and let everyone know he was sharing it.

Mrs Robinson burst into tears when she saw them come in. She got up and approached Leila. Would she, in her misery, blame Leila? No, she let Leila embrace her. Both women wept together.

Sandilands and Robinson stood staring at each other, helplessly.

Jean stole up to him. She touched his back.

'How is Mary?' he whispered, hoarsely.

'Still the same. In a coma. They're waiting for a brain surgeon from the U.K. He's coming in a private plane, paid for by His Highness. They're not very hopeful, though.'

Suddenly Robinson, catching sight of Maitland in the doorway, yelled: 'Have you arrested that stupid old bitch yet? She shouldn't have been driving, should she? It was murder, that's what it was.'

Everyone was aghast.

'Poor Mrs Wilkinson's terribly distressed,' said Jean.

'So she should be,' said Sandilands.

'Yes, but it seems it wasn't altogether her fault. Little girls having fun on their bicycles can be careless. Sandy Robinson wasn't fair to her. She's usually a careful driver. She's been driving for forty years.'

The minister was doing his best to soothe Robinson. He wasn't succeeding. Suddenly Robinson burst into tears. He was ashamed of himself but no one there thought him weak or unmanly.

His wife, though, made no effort to comfort him. Sandilands wondered why. He had always thought them a secure married couple. Next minute he was wondering why she should choose *him* rather than her husband to appeal to. Perhaps she was remembering that last night she had given him a happy report of the two girls.

'Oh Andrew,' she said, weeping, 'why did this have to happen? We warned them not to go on the public road where there was traffic. They were so confident, so happy.'

As he tried to comfort her he was listening to Leila, who was asking her father if she could be taken to see Christina.

Dr Abad was doubtful. 'Shouldn't you wait until you're rested?'

They were speaking in Malay.

'No. I want to do it now. Andrew will go with me. Won't you, Andrew? Won't you come with me to see Christina?'

'Yes, of course.' He agreed with her father though, that she should rest first. She was too vulnerable now.

He looked at Jean Hislop for advice and help, but her face was a nurse's, neutral.

All his life he would remember, with anguish, the hollow echoes of their footsteps in the long corridors, and the smell of disinfectant.

When the white cover was removed, how peaceful, how young, how innocent, and how dark was the face revealed. It was her body that had been broken.

Leila bent and kissed her daughter.

Suddenly he was in a panic. He wanted to kiss the child too but he might not be able to make it look natural. All his inhibitions and limitations might be exposed, when what he wanted to show was his love and sorrow.

Leila was looking at him. He had not yet told her about his own difficult, lonely, loveless, dry-eyed childhood, but she understood him well enough to know that it wasn't easy for him to express love or, perhaps, feel it. What she was now asking him, without saying a word, was to show love for her and faith in their future together.

He kissed the child's cold brow. For the first time in his life he shed tears.

31

When they returned to the office Jean took them aside. There were others there above her in rank but the duty had been given to her, because of her friendship with Sandilands.

She didn't find it easy, which was why she addressed Leila as Mrs Azaharri.

'My name is Mrs Sandilands,' said Leila, gently.

'So it is. I'm sorry. I've been asked to give you a message, Mrs Sandilands.' She hesitated. It wasn't like her to be so nervous.

'What message?' asked Leila.

'It's from Mrs Wilkinson. She would like to see you.'

'She's the old lady involved in the accident?'

'Yes.'

Sandilands' first reaction was to scowl and shake his head.

'Was she herself hurt?' asked Leila.

'Physically, only slightly. Her face was cut by broken glass. She's terribly upset, of course. Her son and daughter-in-law have been with her all day.'

'Are they still with her?'

'Yes.'

'Do *they* think I should see her?'

'Yes, but they said they'd understand if you didn't want to.'

Leila turned to Sandilands. 'What do you think, Andrew?'

He was still scowling. The Wilkinsons were among those who had condemned her for marrying him. They thought her too presumptuous. She held her head too high in the presence of white people. She might be more talented than they, more beautiful, and more cultured, but she was coloured (worse than that she was half-caste) and so inevitably inferior. That was their instinctive belief. If she refused to speak to the old woman they would accuse her of arrogance. If she went and spoke sympathetically they would be even more resentful, for her fault in that case would be condescension.

'I think you should wait,' he said. 'You've suffered enough for one day.'

'But so has she suffered.'

'Very much,' said Jean.

'If I can help her, Andrew, should I not do so?'

Sandilands turned to her father. 'What do you think, sir?'

The old man said, or rather whined, 'It would be a godly act.'

Sandilands turned from him in disgust. He could not bear giving any credit to God.

'However it happened it was an accident,' said Leila.

'It will give her nightmares for the rest of her life,' said Jean.

'What do you think it will give Leila?' asked Sandilands, angrily.

'Will you come with me, Andrew?' asked Leila.

'Yes. Yes, I'll come with you.'

'Don't be angry.'

He shook his head. It would depend on how the Wilkinsons treated her.

Mrs Wilkinson was in a private room. Jean asked them to wait at the door while she went in to prepare the old woman.

Sandilands was searching his mind for words of love and support when Leila showed him how easy it could be, by kissing him. He would never have the knack. She was so much more gracious and generous than he. This ordeal she was about to undergo she would endure bravely. She would know what to say and would say it with compassion and dignity. She was, too, heartbreakingly beautiful in her dark-blue costume.

Jean came out. 'She's awake,' she whispered. 'She's been given sedatives but she's conscious enough.'

'Does she still wish to see me?'

'Oh yes. I think she's a bit frightened but she very much wants to see you. Remember she's seventy-five.'

'What about her son and his wife?' asked Sandilands.

He knew Sam Wilkinson, a big burly mechanic who worked at the oil-wells. He had the reputation of being aggressive when drunk and morose when sober. Celia, his wife, was a thin nervous woman notorious for the number of amahs she had hired and fired.

'They're really grateful,' said Jean, and added, 'though they might not be able to show it.'

She opened the door for them. 'I'll leave you to it then. I'll come back in, say, five minutes.'

Three would have been enough, thought Sandilands.

'Thank you,' said Leila, and walked in.

Sandilands followed close behind her.

How did one confront a woman who, even if by accident, had just killed your only child? Sandilands watched it being done and felt humble and inadequate and yet proud too. This tall dark-faced elegant woman who spoke so quietly and with intense feeling was his wife. Getting to know her would be a voyage of exciting discoveries. She deserved a more adventurous explorer than he.

Mrs Wilkinson's face was yellow and shrunken. There was a dressing on her cheek. She kept licking her lips. Her white hair had recently been permed. She looked her age, though, in spite of the neat coiffure and the lipstick. Her hands, outside the bed covers, closed and opened all the time. Their backs were covered with brown spots. Sandilands counted six rings.

Leila took one of those hands in hers. The other became more agitated still. 'How are you feeling, Mrs Wilkinson?' she asked.

Words that anyone could have said, thought Sandilands, but very few could have said them like that.

'I'm the one that should have died,' whispered Mrs Wilkinson.

She did not weep. She had no weeping left.

'Please don't say such things,' said Leila.

Again the words were trite, again the way they were said was very moving.

'You must hate me.'

'Why should I hate you, Mrs Wilkinson? It was an accident.'

Yes, thought Sandilands, feeling more than ever inadequate, let's all leave it at that. Don't anyone say it was God's will.

From the background Wilkinson spoke, churlishly. 'It wasn't my mother's fault. Ask Maitland. He'll tell you.'

'Be quiet, Sam,' said his wife. 'She didn't say it was Mum's fault. She said it was an accident.'

Sandilands noticed how both of them avoided addressing Leila directly. In spite of her magnanimity and her beauty they instinctively saw her as inferior.

'How is little Mary Robinson?' whispered the old woman.

Sandilands thought it time he gave his wife some help. 'She's still unconscious, Mrs Wilkinson,' he said. 'A surgeon's being flown from Britain. He's expected tomorrow.'

'The Sultan sent for him,' said Wilkinson. 'He's paying all the expenses.'

His mother ignored him and Sandilands too. She had eyes only for Leila. 'I've seen you in church, Mrs Sandilands, you and your father.'

'Yes, my father and I attend regularly.'

'Do you pray?'

'Sometimes.' Leila smiled but she was close to weeping.

'Will you pray for me?'

'Yes, I'll pray for you.'

'And I'll pray for you.'

Sandilands was relieved then when a knock on the door put an end to this unbearable conversation.

Jean came in, briskly professional. 'Time to say good night to the patient,' she said. 'She needs sleep.'

Leila put her hand on the old woman's head. There wasn't a trace of condescension in the gesture. 'Good night, Mrs Wilkinson,' she said. 'Try to remember happier things.'

For the first time there was a tremor in her voice. All of them noticed it.

The Wilkinsons hurried out after Leila and Sandilands. He had something to say to Leila. He could not say it graciously. 'Thanks. Not many would have done it, the way you did. They say you're a dangerous Red, but I'll tell them you're all right.'

'We're grateful,' said his wife, curtly. 'Have you got the car keys, Sam? He's always losing them. Good night, Andrew. Let them say what they like but you've got a real lady for a wife.'

Sandilands and Leila watched them walk towards the hospital door. They would be back again tomorrow.

'Take me home, Andrew,' said Leila, at last in tears.

He held her in his arms. How could he comfort her? He did not have the resources. Besides, where was home? He still had his P.W.D. house at the edge of the sea, and Leila had hers near the airport. They would soon be moving into the Principal's house in the College grounds. But no place could be home without Christina.

She dried her eyes. 'Am I a dangerous Red, Andrew?' she asked.

'He was being stupid.'

'Is that really what they think of me?'

He felt bitter. 'They've got a nice little apple cart here. They don't want anyone to upset it.'

32

Maitland took Dr Abad to the airport to pick up his car before taking Sandilands and Leila to the house by the sea. That was Leila's wish. She had said she would like a walk on the beach.

At the airport Maitland held the car door open for Dr Abad. In his uniform he was as deferential as a chauffeur. 'Will you be all right, sir?' he asked.

'Yes, thank you, Mr Maitland. You have been very kind.' The old doctor looked into the car. 'Good night, my pet. Take care of her, Andrew.'

'Yes, I will.'

If he could. He himself was thoroughly exhausted, after that long painful day; but even after he was rested would he be able to comfort her?

God knew how she was feeling.

The car bumped along the track through the jungle. The night was busy and loud with many insects. The rest of the world seemed very far away.

'Do you really like living here?' muttered Maitland.

'Yes. I used to, anyway.'

When he had been content with his own company. It was very different now.

The house was in darkness. As they got out of the car Sandilands thanked Maitland. It did not occur to him to thank the driver too. Leila did.

'You're a brave woman, Mrs Sandilands,' said Maitland, 'and Andrew's a very lucky man. I think you both should go away for a bit. Take her to Scotland, Andrew. It'll be cold at this time of year, but it could be the change you both need. Good luck anyway.'

As the car drove off Sandilands noticed the driver giving Leila a smile and a wave.

The house was now lit up. Saidee appeared on the verandah. She was weeping and felt that she was being impertinent. A small, squat, ugly little peasant woman had no right to weep in sympathy with this tall lady who was a lawyer and the daughter of a doctor, who spoke English as well as she did Malay, and who was related to His Highness.

It didn't occur to Sandilands that poor Saidee needed to be comforted. But that was what Leila did, as if it had been Saidee's child who had been killed.

The telephone rang. He hurried in to answer it. It was Jean, to say that Mary Robinson had died.

33

He waited till after the funeral before suggesting to Leila, one night in their bedroom, that they should take Maitland's advice (the Deputy Commissioner had been among the mourners in the small cemetery) and go away for a while, if not to Scotland, then to any other place she liked. She shook her head. He was forgetting the elections, she said.

She must stay and work hard. Without her her comrades might lose heart.

'Perhaps you should go home, Andrew,' she said, 'to see your parents. How long is it since you last saw them?'

It was at least six years. He had spent all his long leaves visiting places like Cambodia.

'Not without you,' he said.

Nor with her, either. He remembered his mother's hysterical letters.

'It would be only for a few weeks.'

Did she think the elections more important than their marriage?

'A day would be too long away from you,' he said.

'But you're not interested in the elections. You think they're a waste of time, because His Highness is sure to win.'

'Yes. Your father thinks so too. Everybody does.'

'I don't.'

He saw that her hope of victory was somehow bound up with her grief. It was to be part of her consolation. He must be careful not to take it from her.

'You don't know the people of Savu as I do, Andrew. I was born and brought up among them.'

'I've been teaching their intelligentsia for eight years,' he said.

'Yes, but you've said yourself they never let you know their inmost thoughts.'

He remembered how he had laughed at their sensible conception of love.

He couldn't resist saying: 'But, Leila, don't you realise that if there was a miracle and your People's Party won it would really make no difference? His Highness would still have the money. He'd still have the first and final say in everything.'

'It would be a step forward, a small one, yes, but it would be a beginning. You don't prefer dictatorship, do you?'

'I suppose I just don't trust politicians.'

'I am a politician.'

'An exceptional one.'

But she would not let him dismiss it with a joke and a kiss, the one as awkward as the other. 'You are my husband, Andrew. If you were to forbid me to take part in politics I would have to obey you.'

That was preposterous, but he felt tempted.

He had not offered to make love to her since Christina's death, showing the same consideration as he would have if she had had a child recently born and not one recently buried.

She had not offered either.

Tonight he did, half-expecting her to refuse, half-hoping indeed, but no, she was eager. She had one condition, though.

'I want a child, Andrew,' she murmured, 'but not yet.'

He supposed it was because Christina's death was still too painful a wound, and he loved her all the more for it.

'Not till after the elections.'

He felt let down. Irony was needed to make the situation tolerable, but neither he nor she had any, then. She was sweetly serious, he rather sourly embarrassed.

'You understand, Andrew?'

Yes, he understood. Any woman, in a Muslim country, standing up on a platform and addressing a crowd mostly of men would be regarded as shameless. If she was noticeably pregnant she would be doubly condemned.

Had she forgotten that she might already be pregnant? No contraceptive had been used when they had consummated their marriage in Raffles Hotel.

He remembered that she was no shrinking novice, she had been married before and had been made love to dozens, no hundreds, of times. It was stupid being jealous of a dead man, especially one who from all accounts had been worthier than himself, but if what he felt wasn't jealousy, it was worse, it was resentment. For a few mad vicious moments he wanted to hurt her.

'Are you angry with me, Andrew?'

Not with her exactly, and surely not with Azaharri. With whom then? Himself. He saw, far away in the depths of his mind the admission that he had made a mistake in marrying her. He had thought before that he wasn't worthy of her, but it had been part of his love for her. Now, though it was still part of his love, he was afraid it would make their marriage impossible.

He got out of bed. Naked, he fumbled in a drawer for a contraceptive. Seated on the bed, with his back to her, he put it on. Tenderly she stroked his back. That was a trick of the Shamrock whores.

He saw himself in a mirror. Did a man ever look more silly than when doing that? Love-making was always ridiculous; love itself was, sometimes.

That she was willing, and ready, more so than he, was shown by how easy she made it for him. She pressed his buttocks, gently: another Shamrock trick. He should have been delighted and exalted, but instead was dismayed. This lovely fastidious woman ought not to be performing this crude act with someone like him.

He had seen chichaks do it on the ceiling, upside-down.

'I love you, Andrew,' she said, humbly and, God forgive him, gratefully.

'I love you, Leila,' he said.

He meant it, and if reservations made his voice hoarse it wasn't doubt that caused them but fear.

He would one day try to explain to her, but how could he if he didn't understand it himself? Why should he be afraid of committing himself body and soul to this beautiful woman who loved him and wished him nothing but good? There was that aversion to dark skin, so wickedly fostered by his mother, but it couldn't be that, not altogether. For the past fifteen years he had worked with dark-skinned people and surely had got rid of that pernicious prejudice. What was it then? A congenital defect of character? A distrust of happiness? Of love? Inherited from his grandfather perhaps, that fanatical old man with the grey beard and the belief that he looked like God. Or rather that God looked like him.

Part Two

1

Expatriates, especially the British, looked on the elections as an entertainment: a chichak taking on a water buffalo. Dr Abad might be a competent enough doctor – though none of them would have let him treat their dog – but as a political leader he was simply pathetic. Some of them, out of mischievous curiosity, stopped to listen to him making a speech in public. They didn't understand a word for it was all in Malay but they could tell by the reactions of the crowd that he was not being taken seriously. Hecklers, no doubt in the pay of his rivals, shouted questions at him that he tried to answer at length, getting himself into a tangle, so that his audience, though they didn't want to hurt his feelings, had to laugh.

Except for his daughter, his colleagues were no more successful. They were Malays and therefore soft-spoken and easily rebuffed. The Chinese members of the People's Party, more aggressive and resolute, had the sense to keep in the background. In the past few weeks quite a number of them had been discreetly deported to Singapore and Hong Kong: a sensible move of His Highness's. No Chinese was to be trusted. In their hearts they all supported Red China.

Abad's daughter, though now, God help her, Mrs

Sandilands, was not to be laughed at. The crowds at her meetings were large and enthusiastic. That could have been because she looked splendid in her brightly-coloured saris and kebayas and sarongs, but, according to Malay friends, she was a passionate and persuasive orator. The expatriates were not sure what to make of her. They knew about her magnanimous treatment of old Mrs Wilkinson and had to give her credit for it. Of course she was half-Malay, and the Malays as a race, bless them, were good-natured and, to be honest, pretty indolent. They found it much easier to smile than to scowl, to forgive than to seek revenge. They were like their country's climate: black clouds, torrents of rain, and then, minutes later, warm pleasant sunshine. That part of Mrs Sandilands – might as well give her her legal name, though it did sound odd – had been uppermost in her behaviour towards the old lady. It was the other part, the Scotch part, that was actuating her as a politician. Everyone knew that the Scotch were a contentious, discontented lot. What about Red Clydeside?

But, as was asked in the Golf Club and Yacht Club, what the hell did the woman want that she didn't already have? She was a relative of His Highness and therefore an aristo-crat. She was good-looking: even expatriate women granted her that – in some cases with qualifications: wasn't she just a shade on the dark side, and wasn't her backside more than ample? She was clever. George Heddle, the Englishman who was Chief Justice of Savu, had said he admired her skill as a lawyer, though he couldn't understand why she took only cases that paid skimpy fees or none at all.

Whether she was fortunate in having got a white man to marry her was a matter much debated. Sandilands was dour and thrawn (to use his own Scotch words) but he was big and handsome, with a good job and a house damned near as big and well-appointed as the Resident's. He was an excellent golfer, too, and a golfing pal of His Highness's. It was said the silly bugger refused to give His Nibs two-foot putts, but he got on well with him and would probably end up running the Education Department. There was ribaldry as to how he and his dusky bride got on in bed. According to Jean Hislop – who could blame poor Jean for being a little spiteful? – he wasn't whole-hearted in his performance, though there was nothing wrong with his visible equipment. Apparently it had to do with his upbringing. His grandfather had been a minister of the Free Kirk of Scotland, a bunch of bigots who regarded knitting on the Sabbath as sinful. Well, with his Calvinist hang-up and her Oriental coyness it wasn't likely to be a joyous romp, was it?

Would they nevertheless produce a child to replace the one killed? She would want to, but would he want to be a father? It was said he had been devastated by the death of the little girl, though she had really been nothing to him, but then the people who had said it, the Robinsons, had themselves been devastated at the time and therefore not reliable judges. They had since cancelled their contract and returned home.

Many of the expatriates couldn't understand what the fuss was about. They had served, happily and lucratively, in countries run by dictators with reputations for brutality. It had been their experience that those imprisoned and tortured – though perhaps torture was going a bit too far – had brought it upon themselves. Those who gave no trouble were left in peace, more or less. But in Savu it wasn't like that at all. It was rumoured that underneath the magnificent palace were well-equipped dungeons, with blood on the walls; and the penalty for rebellion was hanging, but so it bloody well ought to be. The Ministers of State, most of them relatives of His Highness, weren't what you would call diligent and efficient, but they didn't have to be, their work was done for them by top-class civil servants, most of them British, and behind the throne was the Resident, offering advice that was always heeded. This was surely the best set-up for a small rich country with envious neighbours like Savu. It was reassuring to see, every Sunday, on the padang besar, the big grassy square at the heart of the town, the Gurkha pipe-band playing Scotch tunes. Also, if they were ever needed, reinforcements were only a day's flight away.

Perhaps a little more of the Sultan's vast wealth could be spent on the poorer natives, but as it was there were no better equipped schools or hospitals or more palatial government offices in all Asia, or in all Europe for that matter. Savu was damned near a paradise. Trust a woman to want to spoil it.

2

The elections were well under way, Leila having made at least two dozen speeches in different parts of the country, when an invitation came to Sandilands from the Sultan, to play a game of golf.

'Please do not go, Andrew,' she said, shyly.

She was a little hoarse, a little haggard, and more than a little depressed. She was still missing Christina sorely and every day was becoming more aware of the futility of her arduous and passionate electioneering.

'Why shouldn't I go?' he asked. 'We won't talk politics, I assure you.'

'They will say that while I am making speeches against him or against what he represents, you are playing golf with him.'

'What about it? Let them say what they like. Golf's just a game.'

'Have you ever considered why he, the Sultan, one of the richest men in the world, should want to play golf with you, a teacher?'

He frowned. What was she insinuating? 'He likes golf, that's all. He's fanatical about it. He'd give a million dollars to play well.'

'I do not expect you to help me, for you are not interested, but I do expect you not to make things more difficult for me.'

'For God's sake, Leila, be reasonable. I'm not making things more difficult for you. I'm simply playing a game of golf.'

'You know what I mean, Andrew. You are not being honest with me. And, please, do not blaspheme. You do not believe in God. Do not use His name.'

He felt angry with her and yet at the same time sorry for her. Her father had lost heart. So surely had she, though she would never admit it. He had heard her weeping in the middle of the night. So, because he loved her, he pitied her. But he still had these mad vicious moods when he wished to hurt her, to make her suffer even more. Usually he resisted them and tore them from him as he would have poisonous leeches, but sometimes he gave way to them. This happened when she seemed most vulnerable, and it was then that he loved her most.

'I gave my word,' he said. 'I'll have to keep it.'

She recovered her pride as a woman but kept her humility as a wife. 'Yes, Andrew, I understand.'

He sneered. 'I'm sorry if I'm a disappointment as a husband.'

'No, no. You have been very patient.'

'Too patient perhaps. I've watched you grow thinner. I've

seen you being humiliated. When you suffer, I suffer. You know that, don't you?'

'Then why do you make me suffer?'

He ignored that. 'I won't say I've not been tempted to ask you to give it up. You once said you'd do it if I asked you.'

'Yes, I did say it.'

'But did you mean it?'

'Yes, I meant it. You are my husband.'

He almost cried: 'Then give it up!' But said instead: 'Just don't ask me to give up what pleases me.'

'No, Andrew, I won't, ever again.' She approached him, her eyes sad and anxious. 'We haven't fallen out, have we?'

He should have said that at that moment he loved her more than ever, more indeed than he could bear, but he did not say it. He took a perverse and evil satisfaction in not saying it. He wanted to break her heart and his own at the same time.

If little Christina had lived it would have been different. They would have been a happy family together. What was good and positive in him would have shown, what was malevolent and perverse would have been subdued.

This perversity of his was childish. Like a vindictive child indeed he looked in a drawer for one of the Sultan's badges. He found one and held it up. 'Do you think I should wear this?'

Her reaction too was like a child's. She stared at him in horror.

'Most people are wearing them,' he said.

'Yes.'

'But it doesn't necessarily mean that they're going to vote for him.'

He wasn't being honest. He did believe that those servile badge-wearers would vote for their master.

Suddenly he felt sick with shame. He threw the badge

back into the drawer. The fit of viciousness was past.

He took her in his arms, with his face turned away so that she could not see his tears of contrition and self-disgust. She was trembling, and it was he who had made her tremble. He loved her more than anything else in the world and yet he had never been as cruel to anyone as he had been to her. Love gave him that power.

Love also gave him the power to make her confident and happy. It was for him to choose.

3

His Highness sent a car for him, a white Rolls Royce with royal flags on the bonnet. Students watched it from the verandahs of the classroom block. Previously they would have cheered and waved, pleased that their Principal was being honoured by their Sultan. This morning, however, they were silent. He knew what they were thinking: he was being disloyal to his wife, their heroine. They obeyed his order that politics were not to be discussed in college, but of course he did not know what they said in their dormitories. He had no spies or clypes. There was little irony in them, but some of them must be remembering how he used to taunt them because of their lack of youthful idealism, just as he himself remembered how, though they had seemed to like him well enough, they had always stopped short of confiding in him. Whatever his private qualities he was a man from the deceitful West. Albert Lo and Richard Chia, now exiles in the interior, wrote to Leila regularly and sometimes telephoned, telling her of their experiences and asking her for advice; to him they sent polite regards.

From what he himself had observed and overheard, and from hints dropped by members of his staff, he had become aware that the students, though some of them had attended the wedding, did not approve of his marriage. They thought he had done Leila a great wrong by marrying her. So he had, but for profounder reasons than they would ever know.

His Highness was waiting for him, practising putting with his gold-headed putter. He looked very much at ease. The elections were less of a worry to him than his missing a two-foot putt.

He greeted Sandilands cheerfully and proudly showed him a new set of clubs specially made for him in America. They had shafts made of a new alloy, guaranteed to enable him to hit the ball an extra thirty or so yards.

'But can there be such a guarantee, Andrew?' he asked, wistfully. 'It's not the clubs that matter so much as the way they are used. Is that not so?'

'Yes, but I suppose good clubs do make a difference.'

'But they cannot make a poor player into a good one?'

'No, I don't think they can do that.'

'But they might help a fairly good player to become a better one?'

'Yes, they might do that.'

Sandilands was invited to take a few swings with the new clubs. They were certainly a pleasure to use. They must have cost thousands of pounds.

'You swing beautifully, Andrew, but then so do I, when I am only practising. It is when I have a ball at my feet that my swing becomes – shall we say, erratic?'

That, reflected Sandilands, was the case with millions of golfers.

'They were made specially for me, Andrew, so they do not quite suit you. You are much taller than I.'

And stronger. And more athletic. And not so fat. But it

was the small, stout plump-faced man that these soldiers were guarding. If he gave the word they would shoot anyone on the spot, Sandilands included. In that country he was God, even if he did miss two-foot putts.

'Well, shall we start?' he asked. 'Your honour, Andrew. You won last time.' He laughed. 'But then you always win. Tell me, are you never tempted to let me win, once in a while?'

'You would know it, Your Highness, and be insulted.'

'Yes, so I would. If you had ever played badly to let me win I would never have played with you again. Victory must be honourably won. It cannot be given or bought.'

Did he think, Sandilands wondered, that that applied to politics too?

'Perhaps I should give you more strokes, Your Highness,' he said.

'Certainly not. I get the strokes I am entitled to, according to our respective handicaps.'

Sandilands' drive had the usual satisfactory result.

'Fine shot,' said His Highness. 'You make it look so easy.'

Whether it was because of the new clubs or because he had been practising a good deal, he hit the ball more confidently than usual and had the satisfaction of seeing it alight in the middle of the fairway, not so very far behind Sandilands'.

Every golfer who has hit a good shot feels virtuous and magnanimous.

'I have been hearing good reports about the College since you took over,' said His Highness, as they walked along the fairways towards their balls.

On either side were flame-of-the forest trees, bougainvilleas, frangipanis, and magnolias. The air was warm and perfumed. Butterflies as big as birds and birds as bright as butterflies flew past. The sky was deep blue.

This was how golf in heaven would be played, though perhaps the air would be a little less hot and the players would have in their minds only benign thoughts.

They spoke in Malay, a gentle language fit for the mouths of angels.

'Mr Anderson of course was old,' said His Highness, dabbing his brow with a silk handkerchief, 'and too soft-hearted. Students, and staff, took advantage.'

'He was very well liked,' said Sandilands. 'Not many took advantage.'

'Odd how he never forgave the Japanese. But then they did put out his eye. My father never forgave them either. They killed many of his people.'

The Sultan's father himself had been safe in New York.

'Still, I'm sure we agree, Andrew, that a college should have firm but fair control. It's the same with a country.' His Highness laughed. 'But I do not think you and I are tyrants, Andrew.'

The Sultan, then, reaching his ball, prepared to strike it. He swung slowly, as he should. The ball flew far and straight, almost reaching the green. He had never hit a better shot. He gazed in awe. If Sandilands then had asked him for a million dollars he might have got them.

They walked on towards Sandilands' ball.

'How is the lovely Leila?' asked His Highness.

'Very tired. She still misses her daughter.'

'Yes. It was a terrible thing that happened to her daughter. But she should not over-exert herself. Why is she defending this creature who has committed murder?'

Then His Highness was silent as Sandilands prepared to hit his ball.

He hit it very well. The ball landed on the green, only a yard or two from the hole.

He must have been thinking only of his shot, as golfers

were advised to do. Did it mean that golf mattered more to him than his wife?

'Magnificent,' cried His Highness. 'We both seem to be in good form. By the way, I have a message for Leila. I shall tell you about it later, after the game.'

From then on the conversation was about various subjects. Politics weren't among them. His Highness showed an interest in and knowledge of orchids. He talked about a visit he had paid to Saudi Arabia. He spoke nostalgically of Edinburgh where he had been made to feel at home; not because he was the son and heir of the richest man in the world but because the Scots were an hospitable, warm-hearted, and fair-minded people.

At last the game was over. Sandilands had again won the dollar but not so easily as before. His Highness had played well. He was very pleased with himself.

Before stepping into his car he turned to Sandilands. 'The message for Leila. It is this. After the elections I would like her to accept a position in my government. Why not Minister for Women's Affairs? It is time we had a woman and none could be more competent than she. Please tell her that I have no ill feelings towards her and her father. They are doing what they think is right. They will accept the verdict of the people. You would have no objection to your wife becoming one of my Ministers?'

I would have objections, thought Sandilands, but I would try to keep them to myself. Leila was ambitious, like all politicians. Their marriage was already in danger. It would be destroyed if he stood in her way.

'We must move forward in Savu, Andrew, but not too fast. That is the advice that Sir Hugo keeps pressing on me.'

Laughing, he got into his car and it drove off, closely followed by the two Land Rovers carrying the caddies and bodyguards.

Sandilands' own driver dared not look up at him. This Tuan was too great a man to be stared at or even smiled at by a mere chauffeur. Had he not played golf with His Highness and had not His Highness spoken to him like a friend?

4

Leila came home that evening, hours later than usual, looking tired and unhappy, which was customary these days, but also despondent, as if she was at last on the point of giving in. Her beauty was quite blighted. There was a coarseness he had not noticed before. What extra burden, he wondered, had been placed on her? Would the Sultan's offer give her hope or would it depress her more? Should he withhold it?

In the sitting-room after dinner he was reading that day's issue of the *Savu Times*, or rather was pretending to: Leila's face was really what he was studying. She lay back in her chair, her eyes closed, as if she did not want to reveal her thoughts. She was wearing European dress, a white blouse and short skirt. She often wore it nowadays, thinking that he preferred her to. She was wrong, he liked her better in native dress, but could not bring himself to tell her so. She was not wearing stockings or tights: few women did in the tropical heat. Her legs were long and shapely and not any darker than Jean Hislops' which the sun had tanned. She was his lovely and dutiful wife. When he wanted to make love she never refused. Instead she co-operated with a passion and willingness that did not altogether please him. He wanted her to be passionate and willing, but he also wanted her to be shy and modest. He kept raising the standards that he expected from her. It was as if he wanted her to fail.

Just as he had decided to mention the Sultan's offer she spoke, still with her eyes closed. That day, she said, she had acquired a new client: a woman, middle-aged, wife of a fisherman, had killed the new bride, a girl of seventeen, that he had brought into the house. She had hacked off the girl's head with a parang. She would be found guilty and hanged.

For Christ's sake, he thought. He did not believe in Christ's divinity, but how else to express horror and pity, and love?

From behind a picture on the wall a chichak darted out and took a bite out of the wing of an unwary moth,

His voice was harsh. Yet he felt an overwhelming love for her. 'Must you defend her? Can't somebody else do it?'

But why should anyone bother, if she was sure to be hanged?

There was a gain here though; Leila was again being made to see that in the end politics were of little importance. She had seen it before when Christina was killed. This time surely she would be convinced.

'I have to do it. She asked for me.'

'I'd have thought you were too busy.' That was a sneer, though he did not want it to be. He was so ashamed of it that he followed it with another. 'You'll ruin any chance you ever had of being elected. There's not a man in Savu who won't want her hanged.'

'That is why I must defend her.'

'What good can you do? Has she confessed? Was she caught red-handed?'

He imagined the bloodstained parang in the bloodstained hands.

'I can try to comfort her.'

He wanted then to rush across and take her in his arms, and tell her that whatever she chose to do he would support her.

Instead he sat where he was, sneering, hating himself. Because he knew it was the worst time to give her the Sultan's message he gave it to her, not seriously, but as if it were a joke. 'Minister for Women's Affairs, was what he said.'

He remembered old Cheng's prophecy that she would be Prime Minister one day. It wasn't impossible. It might well amuse His Highness to have a woman Prime Minister.

'I would have to abandon my principles.'

Well, Leila, you wouldn't be the first or the last politician to do that for the sake of high office.

Again he felt that surge of love for her, that desire to help and comfort her, but again he sat where he was, smiling obtusely.

He was as guilty as the miserable woman in the prison cell and his crime was more heinous than hers. *She* had killed a rival whom perhaps she had reason to hate. He was martyring someone he loved and who loved him. The murderess would be tried and hanged. He would be made Director of Education.

He realised then what was happening to him. He was making Leila represent everything that was mean and perverse in himself. It wasn't her he wanted to make suffer, it was himself. When she was in distress so was he.

'I'm sorry I'm causing you so much trouble, Andrew.'

She meant it, she was not being ironical.

He was the one who should be apologising. In so many ways she was a better person than he, but in one particularly: she cared for other people, she had compassion, she spent her life trying to help others.

He could not remember his ever having made a sacrifice

of any consequence for someone else's sake. It would have meant his having to become too involved. Now and then he sent cheques to charities but he could easily afford it.

Why had she, so shrewd a judge of character, married him? Why had he, afraid of being found out, married her?

Because they loved each other.

Love. He remembered how he had laughed at the students because of their traditional distrust of love as a reason for marrying. They had foreseen that Charlotte and Mr Collins, who had married for sensible practical reasons, would be happier than Elizabeth and D'Arcy who would marry for love. Love, he now knew, could exalt and give great happiness, but it could also debase and cause profound misery.

It was a toss-up, heads he would overcome these evil impulses in himself and learn to cherish Leila as she deserved and as he profoundly wished, tails he would give way to those impulses and make her suffer for his own weaknesses.

In his imagination he watched the coin spin up and land at his feet.

I must be mad, he thought. I'm gambling with our futures.

Her face, in shadow, was dark, but she was smiling at him with love, and, it seemed, understanding. There was no coarseness. She had never looked more beautiful and more desirable.

She came over and crouched beside him, taking his hand. 'I love you, Andrew.'

God knew why, but it was as if she did understand all his difficulties – call them that – and if he let her would help him overcome them.

Outside in the jungle there was a scream. Some animal had been seized by a predator. He thought of the woman in the prison cell.

He put his hand on Leila's head.

'If you want,' she whispered, 'I'll give it up, the elections, my work as a lawyer. I'll stay at home and look after you as your wife. That will be my happiness. We shall have children.'

So the coin had come down heads.

'I'm the one who should be sorry,' he said. 'You'll give up nothing. You'll win the elections and you'll do everything you can for that poor woman, and I'll help you all I can.'

Of course she would not win the elections and she would not be able to save the woman from being hanged, but he would help her and when she failed comfort her; and they would have children.

5

Next morning Sandilands was in his office when he had a telephone call from the Residency. It was Sir Hugo himself, at his most suave. 'Good morning, Andrew.'

'Good morning.'

There was a sly, diplomatic chuckle. 'Are you alone?'

'Yes, I'm alone.'

Though not for long. Through the window he could see Mr Srinavasan approaching, with a flower in his hand, on his way to the office, probably with another complaint. According to him the standards of the College had grievously fallen. The students neglected their studies and forgot their respect for their teachers, because of these confounded elections. 'Confounded' was a favourite word of Mr Srinavasan's. He had once heard a royal personage say it on a railway platform in India. He had another reason for the decline: the proper person for the post of Principal, himself, had been passed over.

'I would be obliged, Andrew,' Sir Hugo was saying, 'if you could come to the Residency for a little chat; well, to be honest, for a rather important discussion.'

'Am I to bring my wife?'

There was an upper-class peculiarly English chuckle: it meant you're not to bring your troublesome bitch of a wife. 'Well, no. It's a men-only affair.'

'May I ask who else will be there?'

Another chuckle, meaning no, you impertinent Scotch bastard, you may not ask. 'Shall we see you at seven, this evening? It is rather urgent really.'

Then, as Sandilands put down the telephone, in bounced Mr Srinavasan, with the flower at his nose, as if its scent would overpower the stink of injustice and favouritism.

'Good morning, Mr Sandilands.'

'Good morning, Mr Srinavasan.'

'May I sit?'

'You may.'

Mr Srinavasan sat down. He tittered. 'Are you aware that we have trespassers on the campus? I call them that. Perhaps I should use a more sinister word.'

'Do you mean monkeys?'

Mr Srinavasan laughed. 'More mischievous creatures than those, I fear.'

'Tell me about them.'

Mr Srinavasan became coy. 'Just half an hour ago I came by chance upon a group of students in a place among the trees where they could not be easily observed.'

'But you observed them all right?'

'It was their voices that directed me to them, though they were not speaking loudly. On the contrary they were speaking so quietly as to cause me to become suspicious. I succeeded in observing them without myself being observed.'

As a good spy should. 'Who were they? Did you recognise them?'

Mr Srinavasan looked cross. 'They were Chinese.' And therefore, to him, indistinguishable from one another.

'Were they speaking in Chinese?'

'Yes. What an abominable obscure language it is.'

'So you couldn't tell what they were talking about?'

'No, but from their manner which was most secretive I am convinced it was something nefarious.'

'But you said trespassers, Mr Srinavasan. If they were students surely they were not trespassers?'

'I was referring to two of them, Chia and Lo, who were expelled for subversive activities.'

Sandilands was surprised but took care not to show it. 'They were reinstated, Mr Srinavasan. But how could you tell they were Chia and Lo? Do not all Chinese look alike to you?'

'Lo is one I could never mistake. His eyes, Mr Sandilands. Those of a fanatic. And Chia is much taller than the rest of his race. Why are they here in Savu Town? Were they not sent into the interior, among the aborigines? Who gave them permission to leave their posts? It is most intriguing, is it not?'

Mr Srinavasan had a belief, frequently expressed, that one day there would be a bloody coup in Savu, instigated by Communists.

'Should the police not be informed, Mr Sandilands?'

Sandilands would have liked to have known why Chia and Lo had come to Savu Town. Had Leila known they were coming? But he was certainly not going to inform the police.

'Why should former students not visit their college?' he asked.

'But this is a most critical time, is it not? Beneath the surface dreadful things may be brewing that we know not of.'

He would dearly have liked to accuse Leila. More vehemently even than the whites of the Golf Club he thought her a trouble-maker. He had once been heard to say that nature did not favour those of mixed blood.

It was time to get rid of him.

'I believe you have a class waiting for you, Mr Srinavasan.'

Srinavasan got up slowly. 'Thank you for reminding me, Mr Sandilands. I seem to remember that when you were a humble teacher like myself you were not always on time for your classes. Hypocrisy, sir, pervades the world.'

He then sauntered out, leaving the flower like a menace on the desk.

6

When Leila came home in the evening, exhausted and quiet, he told her first of his summons to the Residency.

'That's what it amounted to, a summons.'

They were having a drink before dinner. Leila took a small sherry. To that extent he had already corrupted her.

'Did he say what it was about?' she asked.

'No. Important, he said. Urgent. Men only. I didn't actually say I would go.'

'But you must, Andrew.'

'Why must I?'

'You are a British subject.'

'So are you now, as my wife.'

She smiled. She would always regard herself as a Savuan.

'If I go,' he said, 'I'll warn him before he says anything that you and I have no secrets from each other.'

'Haven't we, Andrew?' How intelligent and how honest were her brown eyes; and also how humorous.

There had been that monstrous secret of his, that the more he loved and needed her the more he had wanted to hurt her. But that was safely past; no need therefore for her ever to know.

'Another thing,' he said, and told her about Mr Srinavasan's having seen Albert Lo and Richard Chia in the College grounds talking to students. 'Did you know they were coming to Savu Town?'

She shook her head. 'They spoke about it but I advised them to stay where they were.'

'Well, they don't seem to have taken your advice. Very foolish of them.'

'Yes, but they're desperately keen to help us win the elections. It will be a terrible disappointment for them if we lose.'

Of the thirty-two seats being contested twenty of them were in Savu Town itself.

'It must be hard for you to understand, Andrew, how these young men feel. You've lived in a democracy all your life. They've never known anything but dictatorship. They feel ashamed.'

Sandilands said nothing. He was thinking that the most terrible disappointment that could come to Chia and Lo and other young hopefuls like them wouldn't be the loss of the elections, but what would follow if the elections were won. They would soon find that the Utopia they dreamed of was as far away as ever. Leila herself would be frustrated by timid, cautious, self-serving, corruptible colleagues.

She suddenly changed the subject. 'I went to see Mrs

Daya today, Andrew. She has a daughter the same age as Christina.'

'Was the girl with her?'

'Yes. They were both weeping. I'm afraid so was I. A good lawyer does not cry with her clients.'

'I think I might have wept too.'

That scene in the prison cell was reality, the elections with their promise of democracy was illusion.

'Will you come with me next time, Andrew?'

There would be too much self-revelation for him in that prison cell, but he said that he would go with her.

She gazed at him with unambiguous love – what he himself was so far incapable of – and said, softly, 'Have you got over it, Andrew?'

He was startled. Over what? Had she guessed? Had she seen it in his shifty eyes? Better not to ask, better to leave it unspoken, not only now but for the rest of their lives.

7

The Residency behind its high walls was guarded by British soldiers, seconded from God knew where and for what purpose. There might be monkeys skulking in the trees and bushes but never assassins.

The soldier who challenged Sandilands at the gate was a Scot, from Glasgow by the sound of him.

'Mr Sandilands, sir?' he asked, with a grin. 'Could I see some identity, sir?'

'What the hell for?'

'New orders, sir. But in you go. I was told you were Scotch.'

Well, it was an accent known and respected in countries even more remote than Savu.

There were already two cars in the compound, a Mercedes belonging to Thomas Harvey, the Resident's deputy (rumoured to be a member of the Secret Service) and Alec Maitland's Ford. So it was security that was to be discussed. Were students again under suspicion? Was it known that Chia and Lo were back in Savu Town?

In the big marble-floored hall the Queen was gazing down glumly at Sandilands and he was looking back at her dourly when Sir Hugo himself came in, dressed in white as if for cricket, except for the red silk cravat.

'Thank you for coming, Sandilands,' he said.

On the telephone it had been Andrew. This of course was the Resident's own midden-heap – a thing of marble and mahogany – where his crowing was loudest. He would have liked Sandilands to bow and salute but did not expect it. He was expecting, though, to be addressed as 'sir'. Sandilands was damned if he would. He felt Leila had been slighted. What a pity the People's Party had no chance of winning. How pleasant it would be to see this polite, pompous official being sent home to his polite, pompous masters.

The meeting was held in the study, where the walls were lined with leather-bound books so imposing that they were probably never disturbed, or read. Harvey and Maitland were seated in armchairs, drinking whisky. The former looked at ease, the latter anxious. Both were wearing jackets and ties. Sandilands was glad he had come in an open-necked short-sleeved shirt. Leila had not approved.

'Please sit down,' said Sir Hugo. 'What would you like to drink? Whisky?'

'Yes, thanks.'

But why was Sir Hugo himself dispensing the drinks? There were at least six servants, all Savuans. Was Sir Hugo afraid there might be a spy among them? If there was, Sandilands hoped he or she was more competent than Salim, whose guilty grins had given him away. Now a sergeant in the police he still grinned, but no longer guiltily, whenever he saw Sandilands in town. Indeed, he let Sandilands park where others were prohibited.

'The Commissioner will put you in the picture,' said Sir Hugo, 'but I would like to make it clear that Dr Abad, leader of the People's Party, is in our opinion, and in the opinion of His Highness too, well-intentioned and sincere, if somewhat naïve, in his desire for some degree of democracy. As citizens of one of the oldest democracies in the world we can scarcely find fault with that.'

'Does this apply to the doctor's daughter?' asked Sandilands.

Disconcerted, Sir Hugo looked at Harvey, who nodded, with a sly smile.

Alec Maitland was gazing up at the chandelier, glittering playground of chichaks.

'When your wife was in Singapore some weeks ago,' said Harvey, 'she visited Dr Wong, though she must have known him to be a notorious Communist sympathiser.'

Keep calm, Sandilands told himself. This is a bastard trained never to lose his temper so that he can tell lies with conviction. 'She knew him to be a professor of philosophy.' he said.

'Dismissed and disgraced for the dissemination of pernicious doctrines.'

'Dismissed for speaking out for democracy. I believe his students demonstrated against his dismissal. I take it you know that I went with my wife to see him?'

'Yes, we know that, Mr Sandilands.'

'I expect the secret police who followed us told you.'

'We have our sources of information.'

'Do these include secret police here in Savu itself? Were you informed that this was an old man, over eighty, a friend of Dr Abad's, whom my wife had known since childhood? When she learned that he was dying should she have refused to go and see him?'

'Let's say it would have been more prudent.'

'Let's say it would have been bloody callous and cowardly, and my wife is not callous or cowardly.'

Sir Hugo now appealed to Maitland. 'Commissioner, perhaps you had better explain to Sandilands.'

Maitland brought his eyes down from the chandelier.

'Andrew, Sir Hugo asked you here so that you could pass on a warning – no, wrong word, a piece of information, shall we say? – to Dr Abad, as leader of the People's Party. We have reason to believe that there is a faction, small but desperate, in his party, which has no intention of accepting the people's verdict in the elections. It sees an opportunity or excuse to provoke an uprising against the Sultan's rule. Chinese, most of them. Young fanatics. Your former students Chia and Lo are among them. If you remember, they were expelled for subversive activities.'

'Just a minute,' said Sandilands, angrily. 'They were expelled for reading books like *Animal Farm*; a charge so bloody stupid that they were immediately reinstated. I know Chia and Lo. I've taught them. They're no friends of Red China. (Though they did think that that country had as much right to have nuclear bombs as Britain and America.) Their trouble is they have too idealistic a view of democracy. They're Christians, for Christ's sake. The idea of their taking part in an armed uprising is idiotic.'

'There have been break-ins at police posts,' said Maitland. 'Guns and ammunition were stolen.'

'It wasn't in the newspapers.'

'No.'

'If it ever happened then it certainly wasn't Chia and Lo and their friends who were responsible.'

'You seem very sure of that, Andrew.'

'I am very sure. My wife knows and trusts these young men. You're not accusing her of being in the plot, are you?'

'Your wife is a very ambitious woman,' said Harvey.

'What the hell do you mean by that?'

Harvey shrugged his shoulders.

'Anybody who tried to provoke an uprising here would be bloody mad,' said Sandilands. 'The Savuans are not that kind of people. They hate violence. They like a quiet life. And they're not stupid. They'd know they'd have against them the police, who are armed, the palace guards, the Gurkhas, and British troops who could be flown in in a day or two. They'd be massacred.'

'That could be the intention,' said Harvey, 'to gain sympathy.'

Sandilands got to his feet. Protocol demanded that he must not leave without permission. Fuck protocol. 'Are you sure *your* intention isn't to provoke an uprising as an excuse to call off the elections? Could it be you're not all that certain your side – the undemocratic side, remember – will come out on top?'

'There is no need to adopt that tone, Sandilands,' said Sir Hugo.

'Good evening.' Sandilands marched out.

Maitland came hurrying after him.

They stood by Sandilands' car.

A soldier whistled cheerfully. A bird joined in. The stars were brilliant. Yonder was the Southern Cross.

'If I may say so, Andrew, you didn't handle that very well.'

'I don't trust those buggers. If it's a choice of siding with them or with Leila do you think I'd hesitate for a minute?'

'No, but let me say this as a friend, as a fellow Scot, and not as a policeman; you don't know Leila all that well, do you? You can't. Her background's so different from yours. You got married so suddenly.'

'What are you trying to say, Alec?'

'I don't really know, Andrew, to tell you the truth. But here's my advice. Take some leave – they'll give it to you like a shot – and go and stay with David Anderson in Malaya for a week or two, till these damned elections are over and done with. Take Leila with you. You're her man. She'll do what you tell her.'

'I couldn't ask her to do that. Besides, she's got this woman to defend.'

'Aye, so she has. She'll not be able to save her, though. And the penalty here for murder is hanging. For rebellion, too; only in that case it's done in public. Good-night.'

Maitland then turned and ran up the steps into the house.

It was the Glasgow soldier who opened the gate for Sandilands.

'I heard on the wireless it's snawing in Scotland,' he said, 'but whit wouldnae I gie to be walking doon Sauchiehall Street wi' my muffler up ower my ears.'

8

He was so eager to get home, to take Leila in his arms and tell her how he had stood up for her, that it was a bigger disappointment than it should have been when he found that she wasn't there to welcome him. Saidee, reluctant clype, said that she had gone off in her car with two young Chinese men. That had been half an hour ago.

He found himself trembling. It was stupid, there was no reason for it. As he poured himself a whisky he whistled jauntily, or tried to, but his hands were shaky. He stared at himself in the mirror, despising what he saw there, and asking what kind of love it was that was so willing to find fault. She had taken the youths to Lo's home. That was it, the simplest of explanations. Yet doubts, black as leeches, clung to his mind, sucking out trust. Why had they not waited till he came home? Were they deliberately avoiding him? Had he not remarked once, more or less facetiously, that Lo in particular was the kind of idealistic young Chinese who would have accompanied Mao on the Long March and considered it an honour to be allowed to wash the great man's feet?

Into Sandilands' mind then, sucked dry of trust, came a vision so horrible that he could not bear it, though he could not get rid of it either: a row of bodies dangling from ropes, Leila's among them.

It could happen. No special mercy would be shown because she was a woman.

The Resident would be shocked in his gentlemanly way but he would do nothing to save her. The British government would express regret but point out that since Savu was no longer a colony it had no authority to intervene. One or two Members of Parliament, eager to sustain their liberal reputations, would ask questions but would easily be put off with the polite evasive answers.

But it would never happen. There was no secret band of suicidal rebels. Leila was in no danger. She was more likely to become a member of His Highness's government.

Misgivings and doubts, though, persisted. Only Leila could rid him of them. Why was she not there to do it? What was keeping her? In the past few weeks whom had she associated with, behind Sandilands' back? No, that was unfair. They had agreed that it would be better for him, a foreigner after all, not to be seen taking part in the elections. Therefore she had conferred with men whose trustworthiness he had had no opportunity of judging.

He sat out on the verandah, among his orchids, heedless of mosquito bites. Because of the din the cicadas were making he did not hear her car until it was almost at the house. He did not, this time, hurry down the steps to open the door for her and kiss her as she stepped out.

She came up the steps slowly. Was it simply because she was tired, or was she hesitant about facing him?

She was wearing a red kebaya, with sarong to match. Though tired, she was as affectionate as always.

She came over and kissed him on the head. 'You're back earlier than I thought,' she said, smiling.

'Yes.'

He should have been on his feet, embracing her, but he sat there dourly.

'For goodness' sake, Andrew, let's go in,' she said.

She took his hand and pulled him into the house. 'You're covered with bites. Is anything the matter? What had His Excellency to say?'

'Where were you?' he muttered, more huffily than he'd intended. He was in danger of losing control of himself.

'At my father's. Albert and Richard came to visit me. I took them to my father's.'

'Lo's people live here in Savu Town. Why didn't you take them there?'

'They've got hold of a small printing press. They're turning out leaflets for us.'

The three printing firms in Savu Town had refused to print leaflets for the People's Party. According to Leila they had been threatened with having their businesses shut down.

'It's very warm tonight,' she said. Sitting under the fan she took off her kebaya. 'I expect Saidee's gone to bed.'

'Yes.'

She pulled her sarong up over her knees. Her legs were bare. 'Am I not shameless?' she said, laughing. 'Could you please get me a drink of cold lemonade, Andrew?'

He went into the kitchen.

'Aren't you going to tell me what was said at the Residency?' she called. 'Or were you sworn to silence?'

He came back with her drink. 'I gave no promises,' he said.

'Who were there?'

'Harvey, Alec Maitland, and Sir Hugo. That's all.'

'Ah. So it wasn't just a social meeting. What important and urgent matters were discussed?'

'Harvey said it was very imprudent of you to visit Dr Wong in Singapore.'

He had never seen her so haughty. 'What business is it of his whom I visit?'

'That's what I told him.'

'Did you, Andrew? Thank you. I suppose those secret police told him.'

'Yes.'

'We've got secret police here too. Not very secret really, for we know who they are. They attend our every meeting. There were two outside my father's house. Do they think we're a gang of dangerous terrorists?'

'Yes, that's what they think.'

'You're joking.'

'No. Maitland said there had been break-ins at some police posts. Guns and ammunition were stolen.'

'What posts?'

'He didn't say.'

'Because it was a lie. Why wasn't it reported in the newspapers?'

'That's what I asked him.'

'And what did he say?'

'Nothing. He didn't seem comfortable about it.'

'Because he's an honest man and it's a lie. They must be desperate. They must realise they're going to lose.'

'I don't think that's it. He said Chia and Lo were implicated.'

'What rubbish! What despicable rubbish! You see how easily Savu could become a police state. It is almost one already, and the British government approves. What about me? Was I accused? And my father?'

'Not your father.'

'But I? Did they accuse me of being involved in a plot to steal guns?'

'Maitland said you probably didn't know anything about it.'

'So if I'm not a terrorist I must be a credulous fool? And what did you say, Andrew? Did you defend your wife?'

She undid her brassiere and dropped it on the floor.

What did it mean? Were her breasts to be witnesses of her innocence? Was she reminding him that he was her husband to whom she had given herself body and soul, because she loved him and because she thought he loved her?

He remembered Maitland's advice to order her to give up politics. Would she obey him? For a few shameful moments he was tempted.

Then, in a moment, all doubts vanished and he felt wonderfully cleansed and happy.

There were no words to express his relief and love.

He went over and, on his knees, kissed her breasts.

Her haughtiness was gone; humour took its place. She laughed. She pressed his face against her breasts.

'Now that the elections are so close,' she said, 'and I don't

have to consider my figure, we could have a child. What do
you say?'

9

The day before the elections a public holiday was declared
throughout the country. To encourage a carnival atmo-
sphere beer was free in the bars between certain hours: His
Highness was meeting the considerable cost. It was not a
bribe, no one was to think that, it was simply a gesture of
appreciation for the interest that his people had shown in
his elections, for he always spoke of them as his. Luckily the
alcoholic content of the beer was low, otherwise half the
male population might have been drunk, though never
quarrelsome, before the fireworks display in the evening.

What most impressed the foreign journalists who had
flown in was that, on that day before the first free elections
in the history of the country, nobody seemed to be bothering
about politics at all. This could have been because the result
was known in advance – triumph for the Sultan and anni-
hilation for the People's Party – but it was obviously also
because the people, though a mixture of Malays, Chinese,
Indians, Filipinos, Dusuns, and Muruts, were too mild-
natured and too well-disposed towards one another.
'Civilised' was the word that occurred to the journalist from
the *Guardian*. Nowhere was to be seen a bitter scowling face,
or to be heard angry words.

The town was thronged with happy smiling people.
Women wore their best clothes, kebaya-sarongs of various
bright colours, with necklaces, bangles, anklets, rings (in
noses as well as on fingers) and earrings. The older men wore

native dress, long white tunics and baggy white trousers, with round tasselled hats. Younger men, more European in their taste, wore white shirts and dark trousers; their oiled black hair shone like helmets and attracted insects. Children, like flowers in their gaudy clothes, delighted the foreign observers with their mannerly behaviour.

Entertainments were put on all day in the padang besar, the great town square. The Gurkha Pipe Band gave two recitals of Scottish tunes, both stirring and sentimental, one in the morning and one in the evening, just before the mosquitoes came out. Native bands played their gongs, and slim rapt men and women performed native dances, so stately and slow as to be almost somnolent; in great contrast to an exhibition put on, at His Highness's special request, by the Savu Scottish Country Dance Group, whose hectic performances of the Eightsome Reel and the Duke of Perth amazed the spectators and exhausted the participants.

Some descendants of head-hunters were brought from the interior to give an exhibition of shooting darts through blowpipes. Their accuracy seemed to indicate that they still kept their hands in. Taking heads in the old days, the reporters were told, had really had been a religious act, to appease the spirits of the jungle. Well, those spirits still lurked in the trees and had to be appeased. Were heads still hunted? Savu was indeed, thought the journalists, a strange country, where a man might one day be out hunting heads and the next queueing to vote in a democratic election.

As one of their nimblest dancers Sandilands was asked to take part in the Country Dancing, but had to decline because he had promised to take Leila for a sail to one of the off-shore islands. She wanted to get away from the excitement.

Dressed in a red top and white shorts, she attracted the attention of some British journalists who had been invited to the Club by members. Drinks in hand, though it was only

ten in the morning, they watched from the verandah as
Sandilands and Leila, with the help of some local youths,
struggled to launch the G.P.14. As there was no jetty the
boat had to be pushed into big breakers that kept pushing it
back. It took nerve and skill, as well as determination.

The members discussed them.

'He can handle a boat. You have to give him that.'

'He's a lucky big bugger.'

'The fellow in the boat, you mean?' asked one of the
reporters.

'Yes. That's Sandilands.'

'In what way is he lucky?'

'Well, he's a great golfer. Six times champion of the Club.
Holds the course record.'

'Gets invited by His Highness to play with him.'

'Principal of the Teachers' Training College, a cushy job
if ever there was one. Hard-working well-behaved students,
not like the louts at home.'

'You should see the house that goes with the job. Huge.'

'And the grounds are like a tropical garden.'

'He speaks Malay fluently.'

'And has some Chinese.'

'But above everything else he's got that marvellous
woman as his wife.'

The reporters had been taking turns at looking at Leila
through binoculars.

'She's a beauty all right,' said one.

'Who is she?' asked another.

'You must have heard of her. She's Leila, Dr Abad's
daughter, the brains of the People's Party.'

'Ah, so that's who she is. She's half-Scottish, isn't she?'

'Yes. She's a lawyer. Brilliant, they say.'

'They say too the Sultan's offered her a job in his government.'

'But isn't she on the opposite side?'

'Sure, but everybody knows the People's Party hasn't a hope. She's ambitious, our Leila. She could end up as Prime Minister.'

'And she'd do this country a lot of good.'

'What she sees in Sandilands is a mystery.'

'She could have been the Sultan's missus if she'd wanted.'

'She'd have had to share him with a dozen others. She would never have stood for that. Can be as haughty as hell.'

'Be fair. She can also be damned gracious. Remember how decent she was to old Mrs Wilkinson.'

'In what way was she decent to Mrs Wilkinson?' asked a reporter.

'Her kid, a little girl of ten, was killed by a car driven by the old lady. She was married before, you see. Her husband died young. Leila was magnificent.'

'We'll all drink to that.'

They drank to it.

'This Sandilands chap that's married to her, is he involved in Savu politics?'

'What politics?'

There was loud laughter.

'No, he isn't. Sensible of him, really. The result's a fore-gone conclusion.'

'You all think so?'

'Damned right we do. It's just as well.'

'You want the Sultan to win?'

'Too bloody true we do.'

'But he's an autocrat, the other lot are democrats.'

'They'd either boot us out or lower our salaries.'

'And they'd bugger up the country in no time.'

'Mind you, even His Highness would like to be able to manage without us. He put out a decree a while back. All top jobs were to be filled by native Savuans or Malays. He had to withdraw it of course, but it showed the way his mind is shaping.'

'I would say we've got another five years and then we'll be booted out.'

'A golden boot, though.'

Again there was loud laughter.

'But this fellow Sandilands that's married to Leila, he'll not be booted out.'

'No. He's here for good.'

The yacht was now far out, well on its way to the islands.

'He *is* lucky,' muttered the journalist who was then looking through the binoculars.

10

Sandilands knew how lucky he was and had never felt more humble or grateful or happy than during that sail to the island with Leila. She threw overboard all her cares as politician and lawyer and became an agile and cheerful sailor. As she sat in the stern, holding the rudder, with her hair streaming in the strong but odorous breeze, he just could not believe his luck that this strange woman was his, well, no, not quite his, for if ever a person belonged to herself it was she, but his, in the sense that as his wife she was more his than anyone else's. Those watchers on the verandah would be thinking and probably saying that they couldn't understand what she saw in him. He couldn't understand it himself, but if he was to deserve her he must from now on show all his best qualities. That lightening of his heart, that cleansing of his mind, must have been a religious experience of some kind.

There was no one else on the little island. They were alone
with lizards, crabs, and birds. They swam, naked, in water
that sparkled and was lukewarm. They climbed to the top of
the hill and looked towards Savu Town, two miles away, far
enough for the buildings and the derricks of the oil wells to
seem like parts of the jungle.

After their picnic, shared by some small red-breasted
birds, they lay side by side in the shade.

'Have you ever noticed, Andrew,' she said, in a teasing
tone, 'how we dusky ladies like to keep out of the sun? We
do not want to become any duskier, you see. Among us it is
considered more beautiful to be pale.'

'That's nonsense,' he said, rather weakly.

'You must have heard Mrs Srinavasan lamenting how
black she is.'

'I've heard her lamenting about a lot of things.'

'She told me, in confidence – but you are my husband
and exempt – that Mr Srinavasan got her cheap because she
is so black.'

'He's pretty black himself.'

'Ah, but it doesn't apply to men.'

He was becoming vaguely aware that this conversation,
so lightly engaged upon, was serious. Leila must know of,
must have divined, his instinctive – she would charitably
think of it as that – aversion to dark skin, though she had
never mentioned it before. Now in this oblique, humorous,
loving way, in this lonely place, she was drawing the poison
out of him.

He turned on his side and stared at her. 'You have the
most beautiful colour I have ever seen.' He was able to say
it with conviction for he believed it.

She turned on her side. 'I hope all our children have blue
eyes.'

'I don't. I want a little girl with brown eyes like you.'

'Do you, Andrew?'

'Yes, I do.'

They both remembered Christina.

Then, still smiling, still speaking lightly, she said something that threatened to revive his worst qualities and destroy his happiness which moments ago had seemed indestructible.

'There is one available, Andrew, a little girl with brown eyes like mine.'

'What do you mean?'

'Mrs Daya's daughter. Her father does not want her and her mother cannot have her. I would like her, Andrew.'

He was appalled. Half an hour ago he was swimming joyfully in the clear uncontaminated sea. Now he was plunged into the murky bitter waters of his own inadequacies.

'She is very intelligent and brave, Andrew.'

'Are you serious? About adopting her?'

'Very serious.'

'Does your father know?'

'It has nothing to do with my father.'

'But you think he might not approve?'

'I hope he would approve.'

'But, Leila, for God's sake, have you considered –'

'That her mother has committed a terrible crime? Yes, Andrew, I have considered it. The child herself is blameless. Is that not so?'

He was silent.

'Is it not so, Andrew?'

'Yes, but the world won't think so.'

'What matters to me is what you think, not the world.'

'What's going to happen to her mother? Won't she be hanged?'

'If they are not merciful.'

'And they won't be.' But if they were and the poor

wretch was shut away for life would they be expected to take her child to see her regularly? He would never be able to do it.

'You would have to give your consent, Andrew.'

He was being asked to do something that was beyond him. Even with all his best qualities on display he just wasn't good enough.

What would those cynics on the verandah say? With guffaws they would say, what a joke, a selfish cunt like Sandilands being asked to face up to something that a saint would turn away from.

But Leila could face up to it, if he did not prevent her.

He felt great shame. It was no consolation or excuse that out there, beyond this ocean and all the other oceans, were millions as selfish and limited as he.

He began to see, vaguely at first, that he might be able to do it, with her help. Was he not looking for a chance to show that he deserved her?

'What about the child herself?' he asked. 'Is she willing?'

'Yes. Will you come with me to see her?'

'Where is she?'

'A friend of mine is looking after her.'

It was a reminder that he did not know her friends. To that extent, yes, she was still a stranger.

'She has seen you, Andrew, the little girl, I mean. You came to her school to inspect your students. She liked you. She said all the children liked you. You made them laugh. Christina liked you too.'

Tears came into his eyes.

'You'll come with me then?'

'Yes.'

'And you'll think about it?'

'Yes.'

'Thank you, Andrew.'

Then, taking him by surprise, though it shouldn't have, she burst into tears.

How grand the sky was, how splendid the sea, how busy these little crabs, how beautiful these flowers fallen from the tree above them, and how necessary Leila's weeping for her dead daughter.

After a while he consoled her.

11

The day of the elections was also a holiday. From early morning there were queues of patient smiling men and women at all the polling stations in Savu Town and elsewhere in the country. It was assumed that this eagerness to vote was because they were the first elections in the country's history. They were therefore a kind of celebration. When asked where they had put their crosses, whether opposite the water buffalo that represented the People's Party or the tiger of the Sultan they had politely declined to say. 'Is it not confidential, sir?' they replied, with secret smiles.

Sandilands and Leila drove into town in the morning to do some shopping. They met Mr Srinavasan and his wife outside Huat Lee's Cold Storage.

Mr Srinavasan had been to watch people voting. 'Such simple souls,' he cried, laughing. 'They go into the polling station as if it were a holy temple. We know what that portends, do we not? They are seeing it as an opportunity to show their loyalty and gratitude for their esteemed ruler. It is not a good omen for you, Mrs Sandilands. Prepare, I am sorry to say, for humiliation. Your Party, alas, will be fortunate to gain a single seat. I do not think that in Mr Huat Lee's emporium you should purchase a bottle of champagne.'

He went off, giggling.

'Just for his bloody cheek,' said Sandilands, 'we will buy a bottle of champagne, the best in the shop.'

'What will we be celebrating, Andrew?'

'Ourselves.'

That afternoon they were going to visit the child that Leila wished to adopt.

She held his arm tightly as they went into the shop.

It was a favourite meeting place for white expatriates. They met several. The men particularly were friendly and sympathetic towards Leila.

'So this is the big day, Mrs Sandilands?'

'Don't be too disappointed.'

'Democracy's a concept beyond most of them.'

She smiled. 'You are going to get a big surprise.'

They laughed. She was almost British, they thought, in the way that she could take it on the chin and still smile.

Sandilands backed her up. 'Look, we've got the champagne ready.'

'Well anyway, we're going to be in the Town Hall tomorrow night. See you there.'

Tomorrow night the results were to be declared in the Town Hall. The voting papers were being brought by helicopter from the remote parts. They were to be counted in public by impartial tellers brought from Malaya. The Sultan wanted everything to be fair and to be seen to be fair. The results would be flashed up on a large screen. They would be announced from the platform by the Speaker of the National Council, wearing his official wig. There was to be free food and drink. It was going to be a celebration party. His Highness might attend. Though the Town Hall was grand and spacious it was thought that there wouldn't be room for

everyone. Arrangements had been made to relay the results
to the crowd outside.

Sandilands and Leila had been invited to lunch at her
father's house. A number of the People's Party's candidates
were to be present. Sandilands was curious to see them. He
had wondered where in Savu were there enough men of
education and experience to form a government, even of a
country whose population was just half that of Edinburgh.

He mentioned it in the car as they drove to Dr Abad's.

'They'll be a lot more competent than the Sultan's
appointees,' she said, scornfully.

'Yes, but the Sultan's got the backing of the British
government. Wouldn't your People's Party get rid of the
Resident?'

'We would, immediately.'

'And the Gurkhas?'

'They'd go too.'

'Who would protect you then? Would you have an army
of your own?'

'We don't need an army. Who's going to attack us?'

'Someone might, for the oil. What about the expatriates?
They fill most of the top jobs. In a sense they run the
country.'

'We'd keep those we considered necessary, but we'd see
to it that Savuans were trained to take their places.'

'That might take a long time.'

'We're patient people.'

'What about the Principal of the Teachers' Training
College? Would he be replaced by a Savuan?'

'Isn't he a Savuan himself? By marriage?'

He laughed and pressed her knee. 'Yes, he is. What do
they do for a living, these colleagues of yours?'

'Teachers, accountants, lawyers, business men. You'll
find them intelligent and concerned.'

So he did, but what impressed him most was their good-natured confidence. They did not boast, boasting not being in the Savuan nature, but they talked quietly of victory. That was surely stupid, and yet none of these well-dressed prosperous men looked or sounded stupid. They pointed out that they knew the people. Besides, they added, teasing him, did they not have his lovely wife on their side? Was he aware that she was the most trusted person in Savu?

He was convinced that there was no faction likely to resort to armed rebellion.

When he asked a group of them what they would do if they lost they assured him they would try another time. But what if there was no other time? What if His Highness decided that they had been given their chance and the people had rejected them, once and for all. What would they do in that case?

A white-bearded Chinese replied that they would leave it to their children or grandchildren. Another, a plump Malay, added, not at all ironically, that their children would be better educated, thanks to Mr Sandilands' excellently trained teachers.

Chia and Lo were present, acting as waiters. Sandilands had a brief private word with them. They said that they didn't regret having left their jobs: winning the election was much more important. In any case, their jobs were safe: their headmasters were supporters of the People's Party. Whether the elections were lost or won they had promised to go back. There was valuable work to be done, educating the children of the interior.

'The verdict of the people must be respected,' said Chia, solemnly.

Alec Maitland's spies must have been exaggerating or lying.

12

Leila's friend, Mariam Muji, lived in Tawau, a village six miles from Savu Town. A tarred road led to it but ended there; beyond, it became a jungle track. His Highness had spent years as a child in Tawau, in one of his father's palaces, now disused. He had told Sandilands that he had once thought of making a golf course there but had given up the idea because, Tawau being several miles from the sea, there were no cooling breezes as there were in Savu Town. No white expatriates lived there but they often drove to it on Sundays, to picnic.

Mariam Muji was Headmistress of the school. This was unusual, for the other three teachers were men. Sandilands had heard, though not from Leila, that she owed her prefer-ment to services rendered to the Sultan in bed when he and she were young but, according to Leila, she had been pro-moted on merit, being cleverer than most men. She had been trained in Malaya and had taught for some years in England where she had learned modern methods of teaching, now, though she refused to admit it, out of date. Sandilands' students did not do any of their teaching practice at her school. Therefore he had never met her.

'Do you think it's true she and the Sultan had an affair?'
he asked, in the car.

'They say *I* had an affair with him. That is not true either.'

'But wouldn't it be a great honour to have an affair with
His Highness?'

'Some women might think so. Mariam Muji would not.'

'Why did she never get married? Did His Highness forbid
it?'

'She does not have a high opinion of men. You should
know why. You have been in Asia long enough to know
that men here consider women to be inferior creatures.'

Not only in Asia, he could have said; all over the world;
among Eskimos too, no doubt.

'Why doesn't she adopt this child herself?'

'As an unmarried woman she would not be allowed to.'

'I see.' It was, he thought, a convenient get-out.

They drove into Tawau under a banner exhorting the
people to vote for the Sultan, whom Allah favoured.

It was a peaceful prosperous little place. The school was
indeed like a temple, with a domed roof. People were going
in and coming out, like worshippers, as Mr Srinavasan had
sneered. Every one of them, Sandilands was sure, would
vote for the Sultan. They had no more idea of democracy
than the headhunters who had once lived here. They might
be able to buy electric toasters in the shops but they still had
their innocence.

The Headmistress's house was next to the school.
Brilliantly coloured parrots sat on the roof.

'Is she a member of your Party?' he asked.

'I cannot answer that, Andrew.'

He knew why. After the results were declared, with His
Highness safely triumphant, he might well wish to punish
all those in his employment suspected of voting against him.

Mariam appeared on the verandah. Years ago she must

have been voluptuous; now she was just fat. Unfortunately
she was wearing her kebaya and sarong much too tight,
emphasising the fatness of her breasts and buttocks, and too
gaudy, giving her a resemblance to the birds on her roof. She
jingled and glittered with jewellery. She stared hostilely at
Sandilands, as if she would have liked to punch him on the
nose with her fist massive with rings like knuckle-dusters.

They sat on basket chairs on the verandah, drinking cold
lemonade. It was very hot. She explained that the child was
playing with friends in an adjacent house.

'So she has friends?' said Sandilands.

The conversation was in Malay and therefore courteous,
though sharp things might be said.

'Why should she not have friends? She is a human being,
among other human beings.'

'Do they know about her mother?'

'No. Not yet, so far as I know.'

'If they did know would they still be her friends?'

'Yes, until their parents poisoned their minds. Children
acquire prejudices from their parents.'

True, but also from their human nature.

'Surely, Andrew,' said Leila, 'most people are fair-minded
enough not to blame the child.'

'I would like to believe that, Leila.'

It gave no pleasure seeing humanity as stupid and unjust,
though it might be true.

'She's seen Andrew before,' said Leila, 'when he visited
her school.'

'Yes, so she has said. She seems to have good memories
of you, Mr Sandilands. Of you, Leila, I am sorry to say, not
so good.'

Leila was hurt and disappointed. 'I have tried to be kind
to her.'

'Yes, but look at you, Leila, beautifully dressed as always, rich (by her standards at any rate), a lawyer, a woman of importance. How can you expect a child brought up as she has been not to be overawed by you? You know my opinion. Have you discussed it with Mr Sandilands? I am sure he agrees with me.'

'What is your opinion?' he asked.

'That it would be foolish for you and Leila to adopt this child. Pay some respectable family to take her. Pay them well. Not here in Savu. In Malaya perhaps, far enough away for them never to know about her mother. I have connections there and could help to arrange it. What do you say, Mr Sandilands?'

He wanted to say that it made good sense. The child would suffer, in a distant place, among strangers, but then nothing could ever be done that would save her from suffering.

'Have you spoken to her about it?' he asked.

'No. Why bother? She will do what she is told to do, she will go where she is told to go. What else can she do?'

They heard children's voices. There was laughter.

But the child on the steps, coming up slowly, gazed at them with utmost seriousness.

She was about the same size as Christina but with coarser darker features. She was wearing white, dress, socks, and ribbon.

She had been dreading this interview but was going to confront it bravely: so much so that Sandilands found his heart missing a beat or two. This was a child he could learn to admire and even love.

But there were difficulties. He did not know if he had the courage to overcome them.

Suddenly she smiled at him. Then she glanced at Leila anxiously and, it seemed, with some distrust.

He smiled back.

She went over and stood by his chair. God help her, he thought, she trusts me. I am the kind gentleman who came to her school and made them all laugh.

'She remembers you, Andrew,' said Leila, in English. She put out her hand. The girl took it, hesitantly.

'Be honest with her,' said Mariam, sharply, also in English, 'and with yourself.'

Holding Leila's hand, the child was not at ease. Was she remembering the scene in the prison cell when she, her mother, and Leila, had wept together? How genuine had been Leila's tears?

'Make no decision now,' said Mariam. 'Give her, and yourselves, time.'

Yes, but he did not want to leave it to Leila to explain. He too did not altogether trust her. He could not have said why.

'This lady is my wife,' he said, in Malay.

The girl nodded. She was intelligent. She knew what was going on. She was even more aware of the difficulties than he.

'We would like you to come and live with us,' he said.

'For a little while,' added Mariam.

'Would you like that?' he asked.

She looked neither at him nor at Leila but at the sky. What she saw in her mind God knew, but it must have been painful. Her mouth moved as if she was about to cry but she did not cry. She closed her eyes but opened them again immediately. This terrible situation had to be faced.

He wanted to help her face it but he could not. His help would have to come later.

Then, freeing her hand from Leila's, she went back to him. He put his hand on her head.

'Either she's very sly,' said Mariam, in English, 'or she's taken a liking to you, Mr Sandilands. But of course it could be both.'

'I wouldn't call it slyness,' he said. 'I'd call it a brave acceptance of circumstances.'

13

As Leila said, trying to make a joke of it, it wasn't so much his having adopted Mary – this was the name they had decided to give her, her native name being considered unsuitable – it was more her having adopted him; like a stray dog, Leila said. She followed him about, taking care to keep out of everybody else's way, especially Leila's. With an effort of imagination that he would have thought himself incapable of, he put himself in the child's place and saw through her eyes. He understood then why she was so unsure of Leila, in spite of the latter's determined Christian kindness. She sensed that she was being asked to take Christina's place – she had been shown photographs of Leila's dead daughter – and, young as she was, she knew that she could not do it. She was not resentful, she was not sophisticated enough for that, but it troubled her. Shown Christina's room and told that it was now hers she just nodded, causing Leila to think her either stupid or ungrateful, but he realised that, on the contrary, gratitude was overwhelming the child. Later, if there was to be a later, she would learn to show it in a way that would convince Leila and unite them all.

He noticed that to Saidee she was a mystery. Saidee did not yet know who her mother was but could see that she was one of the poor like Saidee herself. The mystery was why she was being treated by Tuan and the mistress as if she was part of their family. She couldn't be a relative of Tuan, for she was too dark-skinned, nor of the mistress, for she was too common. There were many like her in Savu, among the poor, so why was she in particular being shown so much favour? The mistress could hardly be looking on her as a substitute for Christina. She was nothing like the dead girl who had been beautiful and lady-like.

When Saidee and the other servants found out that Mary's mother was the woman who'd committed murder they would not praise Tuan and their mistress for adopting her. They would think it foolish and harmful. Most people of whatever class, colour, or religion, would agree with them.

That night, in bed, as they lay in silence, Leila suddenly said, in a strangely bitter voice: 'I think we should wait till we have a child of our own.'

'Wait? What do you mean?'

'I mean we shouldn't adopt her.'

'Why not?'

'You know why not. There are many reasons. You know them as well as I do.'

'You were keen only a day or so ago. Why have you changed your mind?'

'I was never keen. I thought it was something I should do.'

'As a Christian?'

'If you like, as a Christian. I felt sorry for the child. She's worth saving but perhaps someone else would be better able to do it.'

'No one else would even try.'

'You said yourself it would be too great a risk. Her mother's mad. That's what we're going to plead in court. It won't save her, though. She'll be hanged.'

'We knew all that.'

'For God's sake, Andrew, the child of a woman hanged for murder!'

'Didn't you say the child wasn't to blame?'

'Neither she is. But she saw it done. It's a wonder she's not having nightmares and screaming.'

They listened. They heard the racket of the jungle, but no screams.

'It will be with her all her life, Andrew. Can you imagine it?'

He could and it turned his blood to ice, with horror but also with pity.

'We'll have children of our own. What kind of influence would she be on them?'

He thought, a very good influence. But he could be wrong. Most people would share Leila's fears.

'It's not too late,' she said. 'We told her it was only for a little while. Mariam warned her. We've given no promises. Nothing's been signed. Her father's been paid nothing.'

'Didn't you promise her mother that you would look after her?'

'Look after, yes, but not adopt. The woman was hysterical. I had to say something to calm her down. What would your mother say, Andrew? She'd never accept her as her granddaughter, would she?'

His mother wouldn't have accepted Christina either.

'You're saying nothing, Andrew. That's not fair. You should tell me what you are thinking.'

Among other things he was thinking that the result of the elections, to be declared tomorrow night, was more irrelevant than ever; to him at any rate. He felt depressed and disappointed.

'We'll talk about it tomorrow,' he said and turning his back on her prepared to go to sleep.

But it was a long time before either of them slept.

In the morning she told him she did not want to talk about it.

14

In the evening he went with her to the Town Hall for the counting of the votes.

All that day she had been more gracious than kind to Mary, who seemed to understand the difference. Once the child came close to Sandilands and in a whisper asked him whose house it was. When he replied that it was his, she looked relieved. She was willing to be beholden to him but not to Leila. Later she asked him when she was to leave.

'Don't worry about that now,' he said.

'Wouldn't it be better if I left now?'

'Where would you go?'

None of her relatives wanted her. She represented disgrace and bad luck.

Perhaps that family in far-off Malaya would have to be found. They would want to be well paid. Even so, the child would be treated by them as a servant, not as part of the family. She would have a miserable life.

'We'll talk about it later,' he said.

When he and Leila were setting out for the Town Hall Mary watched them from the verandah, from behind the orchids.

'Why is she always spying on us?' asked Leila, irritably.

'She's not spying. She's interested in us, that's all.'

'Interested in you, you mean. I've seen her whispering to you. I hope you've not been giving her false hopes.'

He felt a great fear then that their marriage would not succeed.

Cities with populations of millions did not have Town Halls as grand as Savu's. The ceiling, lofty, was a magnificence of colour, cornices, and chandeliers. The floor was of marble, as were the huge columns, which reminded Sandilands of those in St Peter's in Rome. This evening it was laid out with seats, all gilt and red plush, as if a coronation was about to take place. There was a platform bedecked with Savu flags, red, green, and black; above it a large portrait of His Highness in military uniform. Alongside him was the screen onto which the results were to be flashed. In front of the platform was a long table on which were boxes, solid and secure enough to contain a pirate's treasure; what they contained were the voting papers. Some of the counters were senior students from Sandilands' college. Others had been flown in from Malaya.

The Sultan's wish for a splendid end to his elections was being carried out.

Food and drink, non-alcoholic, was set out on other tables. As the building was air-conditioned, there were no flies or mosquitoes. Perhaps an odd cockroach could have been spotted, by anyone on the look-out for one.

But who would have looked for cockroaches when on display were such self-important persons as the Chief Minister and his colleagues, all of them in European evening dress, for there was to be a party in the palace afterwards, to celebrate?

Also to be seen, for the first time together in public, were the candidates and officials of the People's Party, gathered

round their leader, Dr Abad. His daughter, in kebaya and
sarong, in the Savu colours, was the person most looked at
and most talked about. She was in a brilliant mood, laughing
and gesturing to friends.

She did not gesture to Sandilands who was seated well
apart, nor did he to her.

It was rumoured that His Highness might appear briefly,
to thank the voters.

Alec Maitland was there, in uniform, keeping an eye on
his numerous policemen, small men in khaki uniforms, with
big pistols in their holsters.

He came and sat beside Sandilands, in the front row.

'Not expecting trouble, are you, Alec?'

'You never can tell.'

'I haven't seen anyone with a parang or blowpipe.'

'Now you mention it, Andrew, neither have I.'

'Nor with a stolen gun.'

Maitland grinned.

'I'm told you have the building surrounded.'

'Lots of bigwigs here tonight.'

'Is it true His Highness is thinking of showing up?'

'We've been warned he might.'

'It all seems well arranged. What do you think's going to
go wrong? Will the air-conditioning break down?'

Maitland laughed.

Savuans themselves jested that they never quite got
everything right. But they didn't morosely seek out someone
to blame. They just smiled and let it go. Why fuss? Partial
success was good enough for mortals.

'They're the best forgivers I've ever come across,' said
Maitland.

Yes, but they would not forgive Mary's mother.

'Your wife's the belle of the ball.'

'Yes.'

'From what I hear she's going to come off all right, whatever happens. Hasn't she been offered a job in the government?'

'She hasn't accepted it yet.'

'Well, she couldn't, till the elections were over. But she should. She'd do very well and it's time they had a woman.'

The seats were now all occupied. Some white expatriates had sneaked in. Behind Sandilands sat Sam Wilkinson and his wife.

The mood of the audience was festive.

'They're so bloody good-natured,' said Maitland.

'Yes.'

'Is it the heat, as some say? Too hot to be bothered?'

'It doesn't seem to affect us whites that way,' said Sandilands. 'Have you ever been at an enquiry after a yacht race?'

Maitland laughed. 'Just the same I'll miss those enquiries.'

'When is it you're off?'

'In three months.'

'Home to Perth?'

'By the silvery Tay.'

'Among the sullen Scots?'

'You, I take it, are here for good.' Maitland spoke lightly but his glance at Sandilands was shrewd.

'Who can tell?' said Sandilands, also lightly.

'My God, Andrew, they're all saying you're the luckiest man in the kingdom. Students who just want to work hard and succeed. A golf handicap of two. Handy in a boat. A pal of His Highness's. A house as handsome as the Resident's. And a wife as remarkable as any woman in the world.'

Yes, I'm lucky, thought Sandilands. Should I let little Mary spoil it? As an experienced sailor shouldn't I just jettison her?

Maitland looked at his wrist watch. 'Five to seven. They

should be opening the boxes shortly. I'll have to be on hand, to see that there's no pochling.'

Sandilands smiled at the use of the Scots word.

Maitland's place was taken immediately by the *Guardian* journalist.

'You're Sandilands?' he said.

'Yes.'

'I hope you don't mind my saying I don't think I've ever seen a more beautiful woman than your wife.'

Sandilands felt a tap on his shoulder. Turning, he saw Sam Wilkinson grinning at him.

'We mentioned her name,' said Wilkinson. 'She came and got us in. We wanted to come and wish her luck.'

'She deserves it,' said Mrs Wilkinson.

'My mother mentions her in every letter,' said Wilkinson.

'She's a lady,' said Mrs Wilkinson. 'I haven't met all that many but she's one. You should be proud of her.'

Sandilands remembered Leila weeping on the island. He wanted then to rush off to her, but to do what? To tell her he loved her? To say that it didn't matter about little Mary?

The counting had begun. It would not take long. There had been a large turn-out of voters, over ninety per cent, but they did not amount to a large number. Some of the constituencies in the interior had only a hundred or so voters. Their results would be declared soon.

'A crafty move on the Sultan's part,' said the *Guardian* man. 'He gets the credit of introducing democracy but still holds on to power.'

Sandilands then saw Leila giving him a wave. His heart broke.

'But aren't they well-off as they are?' asked the *Guardian* man. 'I was shown through the hospital. More up to date than most hospitals at home. I paid a visit to your college too.'

'I didn't know that.'

'I was told you were too busy. A very pleasant place. Lovely grounds. Magnificently equipped classrooms. I had a chat with some of your students. Charming young people. They sang your praises, Sandilands, but – I know you won't mind – they sang your wife's more enthusiastically, She's their heroine. I'm not surprised. If I was a student here she'd be mine.'

There was consternation among some of the counters. The Chief Minister was talking to them. He looked angry.

'It looks like a result he can't believe,' said the *Guardian* man.

Not only Tun Mustapha couldn't believe it, neither could the majority of the people in the hall, when it was flashed up on the screen.

In the constituency of Labuan, where, as it happened, Albert Lo was a teacher, the People's Party had got ninety-five votes and the Patriots only sixteen.

'Labuan?' said the *Guardian* man. 'That's in the jungle, isn't it? We were flown over it in a helicopter. Savu flags were flying from every longhouse. So what's happened?'

'I'll tell you,' said Sam Wilkinson. 'They've voted for the buffalo, not for the tiger. You can eat buffalo, you can't eat tiger. I've said all along His Highness was making a mistake taking a tiger for his symbol. Didn't I?'

'You did, Sam.'

Leila and her colleagues were congratulating the successful candidate. He was a Murut, that was to say, of the same race as those who lived in the longhouses.

Soon more results, from similar small constituencies, were declared: all victories for the People's Party.

'What the hell's going on?' asked the *Guardian* man.

Most of the audience were on their feet, shouting. They were like a football crowd, whose team, bottom of the league, playing the champions, had just scored a goal.

Dr Abad was being congratulated by his followers. They knew it was still early, defeat was still possible, but it was not going to be a rout and a humiliation.

At least not for the People's Party. It was, though, for their opponents. Every seat, except one, went to the People's Party. Even the Chief Minister lost his. Dr Abad and Leila had huge majorities.

The counters looked frightened. They were blameless but they might be blamed. Democracy would seem to have triumphed but there were still those dungeons under the palace.

The Chief Minister and his henchmen were conferring frantically. One kept slipping out, no doubt to telephone the results to the palace.

Sandilands noticed the Editor of the *Savu Times* hurrying away. Tomorrow morning there would be the biggest and blackest headlines in the paper's history. He might be hanged for it but he would dangle happily.

'Extraordinary,' said the *Guardian* man.

'Worth a paragraph in the News in Brief column?' asked Sandilands.

Maitland came up to them, looking bemused. He had been talking to the Chief Minister. 'They're blaming me, would you believe it?' he said, indignantly. 'I should have arrested the whole bloody lot of them, I've just been told.'

'Shouldn't you be putting a guard on Dr Abad?' asked Sandilands. 'He's the new Prime Minister.'

'He's not Prime Minister yet. If I was you, Andrew, I'd get my wife home as soon as possible.'

'Why? What do you think's going to happen?'

'Don't ask me. This is a boat that's capsized. We're all in danger of drowning.'

Leila was pushing her way through the crowd to Sandilands.

She embraced him. 'Isn't it wonderful?' she cried.

He had never seen her happier.

'We're going to my father's house to celebrate.'

They were all abstainers. They would toast their victory in lemon tea.

'Will you come, Andrew?'

'No. I'd better continue to look neutral. But I'll go home and drink the champagne.'

'But you're glad we won?'

'Yes, of course.'

Was he? As the wife of a mere teacher, as a lawyer, as a private citizen, as a Christian, Leila might have been persuaded to adopt the daughter of a murderess, but hardly as a Minister of the Government, especially if her ministry was that of Justice.

15

Next morning the people spontaneously awarded themselves a holiday. In their best clothes they flocked onto the streets and greeted one another with the old affection but also with a new respect. They had brought democracy to their country and so had become the equals of the Americans and British. They could be seen happily getting their fingers blackened by the huge headlines in the *Savu Times* and the slightly smaller ones in the *Savu Record*, whose Editor was not quite so reckless. Policemen were offered flowers and accepted them sheepishly. Children danced hand-in-hand in the streets and let off fire-crackers. It was said that in the interior the shrivelled heads had been taken down and reverently dusted, with spiders scuttling out of the eye sockets. In the Yacht Club and the Golf Club there could hardly be rejoicing for it was feared that Shangri La had come to an end. The boys who helped to launch the yachts or who caddied on the golf course, now citizens of a democracy, priced themselves higher accordingly. They demanded and got an increase in pay. In their homes white memsahibs were taken aback to find that their amahs, cooks, and gardeners had overnight acquired a dignity that should have looked impertinent or even comic, but did not. On the telephone those white ladies cautiously praised Mrs Sandilands. If it hadn't been for her the People's Party would never have persevered. Well done, Leila, was their verdict. She might be a half-caste, she might be dark-skinned, she might have become a bit too uppity, but in a country where for generations men had been contemptuous of women she had shown herself superior to the lot of them. They could have named another country where women were still not given their due.

The students congregated outside the Principal's house, playing guitars and singing songs in homage to the Principal's wife. But it wasn't as the Principal's wife that they were honouring her, it was as the future Prime Minister of their country. When she appeared on the verandah they gave a cheer that was heard in the teachers' flats a good three hundred yards away.

In those flats, which had a good view of the scene at the Principal's house, Mr Srinavasan was paying one of his sneaky visits to Miss Leithbridge who lived next door.

Miss Leithbridge's verandah was small. Mr Srinavasan had to stand close to her. She was looking through binoculars.

Mr Srinavasan prophesied doom for the lady at present being exalted. 'You will see she will come a cropper.'

'Why do you think that, Mr Srinavasan?' Miss

Leithbridge asked, aware that he was closer than he needed to be but not yet prepared to push him off. She liked to play a game of waiting to see how far the 'sneaky black prick' would go. The description was not hers, but Baker the Australian's. She thought it apt.

She rather liked the spicy smell of Mr Srinavasan's breath. It was quite sexy.

'She is too big for her boots.'

'She never wears boots.'

'I speak metaphorically. Does she think in her foolishness that the Sultan will abide by those ridiculous results?'

It hadn't occurred to her that the Sultan would not abide by the results. She was sure it had occurred to no one but Mr Srinavasan. 'Why shouldn't she think that?' she asked. 'He gave a solemn promise to accept the people's verdict.'

'That was before he knew he had lost. Is he not a mighty man? Is this not his kingdom? Can he not, with Allah's consent, break any promise?'

'But what reason could he give?'

Miss Leithbridge was genuinely curious, though there was the distraction that Mr Srinavasan was now not so much nudging as thrusting, and he was not using his hand. Her bottom too was thinly protected with only a cotton dress and skimpy panties.

'He will say they cheated.'

'Cheated? How could they cheat? There were impartial observers.'

'He will say that though women were given the legal right to vote they ought not to have voted. They should have stayed at home, like decent Muslim women.'

Miss Leithbridge was still interested, but he really had to be deterred. His thrusting had become too obvious and too urgent. He was panting as if he had just run up a flight of stairs.

As if casually, with no particular intent, she swung the
heavy binoculars behind her with some force, and hit him
where she had hoped to hit him. He gasped, squealed,
withdrew, clutched himself, and, as she saw from a quick
glance round, turned greenish, which was odd considering
how black he was.

Using the binoculars now for their proper purpose, she
saw, with surprise, that Sandilands had brought out a little
girl, a native from the look of her. Who could she be?

Mr Srinavasan, usually a source of information, was not
yet fit to be consulted. Besides, tears of pain were blurring
his vision.

'He's holding a little girl in his arms,' she said. 'Who can
she be? She's not white. She can't surely be the daughter of
a servant? That would be ridiculous. Look, Mr Srinavasan.
Have you any idea who she can be?'

With shaky hands he took the binoculars and looked
through them. 'Perhaps she is Mrs Sandilands' daughter.'

'But Mrs Sandilands' daughter was killed in the car
accident.'

'This could be another daughter, hitherto concealed.'

She thought his mind was deranged. 'Why on earth
should she be concealed?'

'Perhaps her father is the Sultan.'

Now *that* was worth considering. 'Do you think so?'

'It is said he wished to add her to his harem of wives.'

Miss Leithbridge took the binoculars and looked through
them, concentrating on the child in Sandilands' arms.

'No, she can't be,' she said. 'Too common-looking. Too
shy. If the Sultan was her father she'd be unbearably proud.'

'Perhaps she is the bastard of our esteemed Principal. I
have been told he consorted with loose women. This child
could be a consequence.'

Miss Leithbridge had sometimes wished she was one of

those loose women Sandilands had consorted with. 'You are being silly, Mr Srinavasan.'

Mr Srinavasan groaned.

'I think you should go and see if Mrs Srinavasan is awake now and waiting for you to bring her tea.'

He crept away, as if, she thought crudely, he had wet his pants. Perhaps he had. She had read once in a woman's magazine that that was the most tender part of a man's anatomy. If a woman was being raped, the writer had said, she should seize the villain by the testicles and squeeze them hard.

She wasn't angry with him, though. She had got some of her own back, not just on silly Mr Srinavasan, but on all men, especially conceited Andrew Sandilands.

16

He had not asked Leila's consent to bring Mary onto the verandah, to be seen by the students; nor had he asked the child's. He could not have said then why he did it, and afterwards he regretted it. Perhaps he had been provoked by the students' gleeful faces and Leila's so pleased and triumphant, while the child crouched on a chair at the back of the living-room, terrified.

She had not been willing to come with him. She was in tears as he held her up.

The students were puzzled, particularly as they saw that Leila was annoyed.

'What on earth do you think you're doing?' she whispered.

He couldn't have told her. He wasn't trying to shame her

into keeping her promise to the child, nor was he intending to show that his concern was more genuine, and more Christian, than hers.

'This little girl is called Mary,' he cried.

They waited for further explanation but he stopped there.

None of them had seen this child before. To quite a few of them occurred the same suspicion that Mr Srinavasan had suggested to Miss Leithbridge, that the girl was Mr Sandilands' daughter and her mother some Savuan woman. That would explain why he seemed so defiantly fond of the child and why his wife was refusing to smile at either of them.

Soon the students went off, discussing the little incident, but not letting it spoil their mood of celebration.

In the house Leila confronted Sandilands. Mary had run off to hide in a small retreat she had discovered. There she stood with her hands over her ears.

Even if she had been outside the living-room door she would not have understood. They spoke in English, Leila angrily but quietly. Sandilands hardly spoke at all.

'Were you trying to shame me out there, Andrew?'

He thought that she had for the time being at least lost her beauty and distinction; but he still loved her.

'I would never do that, Leila.'

'But that is what you did. The poor child was terrified.'

'I'm sorry about that.'

'I was humiliated. Are you sorry about that too?'

'Yes. I didn't mean to humiliate you.'

'Surely you realised you were putting me in an impossible situation. For the sake of a child like that!'

'Like what, Leila?'

'I'm sorry. I shouldn't have said that. If you were the kind of person, Andrew, who liked people I could understand and sympathise, but you have the reputation of being aloof and self-centred, and you deserve it.'

'Why did you marry me then?'

'I was warned you might ruin my career. My father warned me. I should have listened to him.'

'Perhaps you should.'

'Last night I could see you grudged me and my friends our success. Now you are trying to spoil it for me.'

Had that been his motive? He did not think so. He was glad she had succeeded.

'I love you, Leila.'

'If you do you will help me, not make things difficult for me. Will you agree to Mariam's arrangement? It is really no business of yours, Andrew, but you are my husband and I would like your agreement.'

'Why send the child to Malaya, so far away?'

'If your mother was to be hanged for a brutal murder would you not want to be as far away as possible?'

'She's only ten.'

'When she's twenty she will be grateful to us.'

'I would like to talk to her father and to her mother's relatives.'

'I have talked to them. They do not want her. They have disowned her.'

'But she's not to blame. Didn't you tell them that?'

'I did but it was no use. In their eyes she is as much to blame as her mother.'

'That's bloody nonsense.'

'So it is, but that is how they see it.'

'I should still like to talk to them.'

'Please yourself. I don't think they'll want to talk to you.'

'Whereabouts in Malaya? Shouldn't we go and see the people she was being sent to? I would like to write to her

and perhaps visit her. I could ask David Anderson to keep
an eye on her.'

'That is what you think now, Andrew. In time you will
think differently. You will have our own family to think of.
You say you love me.'

'I do love you.'

'Then help me. I admit I did give the poor child some kind
of promise. I shouldn't have. I was distressed at the time.
But surely I am entitled to avoid that promise, and as my
husband, who loves me, you will help me to avoid it. Will
you help me, Andrew?'

He nodded.

'Explain to her. She likes you. She trusts you.'

'If I was her I would trust nobody.'

'She's a child. She needs to trust someone. She will
believe what you say to her.'

'I will have to be very truthful then.'

17

He found her in her hiding-place.

If he had come with a whip to lash her he could not have
felt more guilty and ashamed. Before he could say anything,
while he was searching his mind for words that would
destroy her hopes without causing her hurt – no such words
existed in any language – she said that she would leave now
and, excusing herself, slipped past him and went to
Christina's room.

He stood at the door watching her put her few belongings
into a green plastic bag. She had very little: her old clothes
had been burned and he noticed that she was taking none

of Christina's except those that she was presently wearing. There were two small books, with tattered covers; a ballpoint pen; a small red handbag; a necklace of coral; and a handful of coloured sea shells. Packing took her less than a minute. She stood there holding the bag, ready to go. There was no self-pity on her face; no accusation; no emotion at all. If she had wept he might have known what to say or what to do. Surely he would have embraced her or taken her hand. This refusal to beg or blame made him helpless.

'I would like to go now,' she said.

If he would please get out of the way, she meant.

'Where will you go?' he asked, though he had no right to ask.

'To Nirmala's,' she said, after a slight hesitation.

'Is she your friend?'

'Yes.'

'Where does she live?'

'Kampong Ayer.'

A fishing village about two miles from the College.

Since he was turning her out of his house it would have been an impertinence to ask if she was sure that Nirmala's parents would take her into theirs.

'What does Nirmala's father do?'

'He's a fisherman.'

Like her own father. Poor therefore. With a house, a hovel, already overcrowded. A more hospitable man than Sandilands, though? And was his wife a kinder woman than Leila?

'How will you get there?'

'I'll walk.'

'No. I'll take you in my car.' He would want to see this place where she would find the welcome that she had not found here. He would want to speak to Nirmala's father and offer him money.

She was shaking her head. 'I'll walk.'

She still would not ask him to get out of her way. She had too much dignity.

He wondered where Leila was; somewhere keeping out of sight. He felt angry and disappointed. What would the people who had voted for her think of her rejection of this child? Most would commend her, for in her place they would have done the same.

A ludicrous thought occurred to him. He would give up his job here, adopt Mary on his own, and take her to Malaya, to the Cameron Highlands, to join David Anderson.

He stepped out of her way.

She thanked him politely as she passed.

He stood on the verandah watching her go down the steps, walk with head up among the flowers and bushes to the road, and there stride along bravely, swinging her bag. She did not want anyone to think that she was afraid or unhappy.

Was she thinking of her mother?

She did not look back. Three students, girls, spoke to her. She replied but did not stop. They looked after her and then they looked towards his house. He skulked behind his orchids.

Soon Mary was gone out of his sight.

The students were debating as to whether they should come and tell him about Mary. Perhaps they thought that she was running away and he did not know.

Leila came out onto the verandah. She looked tired and unhappy. Perhaps she was remembering Christina.

'She's gone,' he said, continuing to speak in Malay.

Leila chose English. 'Gone? Gone where?'

'To a friend's house, in Kampong Ayer. The girl's father is a fisherman.'

'Was she sure that they would take her in? Had they promised?'

'She wasn't sure. I don't think they'd promised.'

'Why did you let her go then?'

'Wasn't I supposed to tell her to go, that she couldn't stay here? That we wanted to get rid of her?'

She winced and turned away. 'Not get rid of her,' she murmured.

'That's what it amounts to, Leila.'

'You could at least have offered to drive her there.'

'I did, but she preferred to walk.'

There was a pause. Leila sighed. The beauty had gone out of his orchids.

'We must find out where this friend of hers lives,' said Leila.

'Why? We've no right to interfere. We've washed our hands of it.'

'Don't speak like that, Andrew. I don't like sending the child away any more than you do. She could not have stayed here. Don't you see that? It would have been misinterpreted.'

He wondered what she meant by that but he would not ask.

'I shall be ashamed all my life,' he said, and was ashamed of saying it. If he had had the dignity of the little girl he would not have said it. Like her he would have kept quiet.

'But, Andrew, we can still see to it that she's well looked after.'

By offering money? That it would be needed and gratefully accepted would not make the offering of it any less shameful.

In the world there were many children unluckier even than Mary; at least she wouldn't starve. To ease his conscience about those children he had sent cheques to Oxfam. With the same tainted generosity he could give money to the family looking after Mary; that was, if they were looking after her. Suppose they too were afraid that their kindness would be misinterpreted and had turned her away?

Another ludicrous thought occurred to him: why not appeal to the Sultan?

18

The time soon came when an appeal had to be made to the Sultan, about a matter more important than the disposal of a child.

For long anxious days Dr Abad and his colleagues waited for a summons from His Highness and a request from him to form the new government of Savu. That was how they thought the transfer of power would be effected, since there was no constitutional method of doing it. It had never occurred to the Sultan or his National Council or his adviser the British Resident that such a situation might one day arise. If he had thought for a moment that his Party would lose so disastrously he would never have sanctioned the elections. It was as simple as that, and it was just as simple that since he had lost so humiliatingly he would pretend that they had never taken place. So Dr Abad and Leila and the rest of the successful candidates waited, holding private meetings at which they lamented about injustice and considered ways of having it redressed, such as an appeal to the Queen of England (as they styled her), the United Nations, or the President of the United States, the self-proclaimed defender of democracy throughout the world.

Days became weeks. At last a deputation went timorously to the palace but found the gates locked and guards with guns. Another, which included Leila, went to Government House, intending to occupy the Council Chamber for an hour or so as a symbolic gesture, but they were prevented from entering by armed police. They had a grievance but how to have it remedied, indeed how to get it widely known in Savu itself, as well as in other democratic countries? The British press was not interested. The tabloids had never mentioned it. In the *Guardian*, in the News in Brief column, there had been a paragraph of six lines.

The British Resident's help was respectfully sought. Sir Hugo as always was courteous and evasive. With urbane mendacity he pointed out that it had nothing to do with him or with the government of the United Kingdom. Savu was no longer a colony: it was a sovereign State. The Sultan was its sole and supreme ruler. Since it was he who had proposed the elections and had paid for the conducting of them, surely it was for him to say whether the results should stand or be set aside? Dr Abad as an educated man must recognise that; and what was more – here Sir Hugo let a little sharpness come into his voice – Dr Abad must take steps to report to the authorities any of his associates raising their voices in protest or, worse still, their fists. There were no legal grounds for protest. What the Sultan ordained became instant law. Regarding the elections he had changed his mind, as he was entitled to do. Sir Hugo conceded that it might seem at present to be a little unfair but the sense of grievance was illusory and would soon fade. No one could prevent anyone from protesting in private, but public protests of any kind would be unlawful and rigorously punished. If force was used there could be executions. Sir Hugo himself was too sensitive to mention hangings but his deputy, John Harvey, did it emphatically.

Leila came back from the mission to the Residency trembling with anger.

'We are to do nothing,' she cried, with passion. 'We are to suffer in silence one of the most iniquitous injustices ever perpetrated.'

Sandilands could not help smiling at such hyperbole. 'What else can you do?' he asked. 'It's the law.'

'You will see what we can do.'

He didn't, not then, feel alarmed. This was Savu, whose people were renowned for their good nature and complacency. They would grumble but they would laugh as they grumbled. All that bother about elections, just to have them cancelled. They would make jokes about it. The white expatriates would chuckle. His Highness, they would say, had certainly dished them.

One expatriate, though, was not amused. At the Yacht Club Alec Maitland spoke angrily to Sandilands. 'I like to be in the right if there's trouble.'

Still, if ordered to use force to quell protestors he would obey, that being his duty. That they were in the right and he in the wrong would vex but not hinder him.

At last the suspense was ended. The Sultan had made up his mind. One morning in the two Savu newspapers, with appropriately bold headlines, he announced his decision. The recent elections were declared null and void, because of irregularities; these, though, were not specified. He expressed regret and disappointment. Perhaps in the future, when the people were more mature in their political opinions and understood better the responsibilities of democracy another attempt might be made. In the meantime the people were to go about their business as before. Public demonstrations of dissent would not be tolerated.

Leila was indignant with Sandilands because he took it so coolly.

'But, Leila,' he said, 'it was always likely. I'm surprised that you're all surprised.'

'We are not surprised. We suspected this would happen, but we like to trust people, even despots. He gave his word. He gave it often.' She had documentary proof in her hand.

'Put not your trust in princes.'

'Don't laugh at me, Andrew. If I had been attacked or raped would you laugh? Well that is how I feel. I feel violated.'

Openly he sympathised, but was he, deep in his mind, relieved that there was to be no new government, with her a prominent member of it? She would now reject the Sultan's offer of a post in his government. Probably it had been withdrawn. He would have her to himself.

There was still the matter of the trial of Mary's mother. He had hoped that she would hand over the case to another lawyer. She would have done so if the People's Party had formed the new government. She would have been too busy with other duties.

The matter of Mary herself had been quickly settled.

19

When Mary had left, Sandilands and Leila had driven to Kampong Ayer that evening. They had stepped carefully, in lamplight, along the wooden walkways on stilts that served as streets. Children shouted out to them where Nirmala's parents lived and followed them to it. People came to their doors to stare at these strange visitors. There were smells, of fish being cooked, of ordure, of salt water, and of engine oil. Leila had been there before, briefly, when campaigning in the election. This time her mood was subdued and she was dressed to suit in dark blue. Nevertheless she had suggested that Sandilands should leave the talking to her. These people were her compatriots. She knew them better than he ever could. His Malay might be adequate, as far as meaning went, for their vocabulary wasn't extensive, but it could not reach their feelings. They would assume that he considered himself superior, for didn't all white Tuans think that? Moreover, with no children of his own, why was he so interested in a Savu girl of ten? Virgins of that age not so long ago had been bought and sold, though not usually by white men, it was fair to say. So, though his intentions were honourable, if not altogether clear, even to Leila herself, these simple folk might look on him with suspicion if he offered money. Besides, they knew Leila as a leader of the People's Party and had probably voted for her. Also she was known as the lawyer defending Mary's mother.

All that she had said in the car.

'All right, Leila,' he had said, 'just so long as you let Mary make the choice.'

'I won't try to dissuade her, if that's what you mean.'

'She's not sure of you, Leila. You're too grand for her.'

'Whereas you, a white Tuan, aren't too grand for her?'

'She trusts me.'

'Really, Andrew?'

'Yes. God knows why but she does.' So, he could have added, had Christina.

Nirmala's father and mother, forewarned by the shrieks of children, had put on their best clothes and tidied their house. This had two rooms. They received Sandilands and Leila in the larger one, while the rest of their family, including Mary, hid away in the other.

Mr Andau was small and skinny, with rotten teeth; his wife was fat, with greasy hair. They squatted on the floor, wearing long skirts, white in his case, red in hers. His shirt was also white but grubby. Her blouse was green, with glittering buttons. There was fish cooking in a black pot on a stove. A mangy cat mewed. Children giggled behind the partition. The lamp flickered and gave poor light.

Sandilands and Leila were given rickety cane chairs. Leila sat on hers as if it were a throne. When she was unsure of herself she became haughty and grand.

Even so, they were honoured to have her, the famous daughter of Dr Abad, as their guest. Her frowns pleased them more than Sandilands' smiles.

To be fair to Leila, and himself, it was easier for them to befriend the child. She was in the same social class as themselves. They had few possessions and few responsibilities. They had no position of importance, no reputation to preserve.

It still remained true that they would need compassion and courage to give shelter and protection to a child whose mother had committed a horrible murder and whose relations had disowned her. They had too their own superstitious fears to overcome.

Leila explained, calmly and lucidly; more like a lawyer in court, he thought, than a concerned human being.

He waited, ready to intervene.

They listened humbly to the beautiful, rich, perfumed lady.

She understood, she said, that they were poor, with their own children to feed – they had seven – so she and Tuan, her husband, were prepared to pay them thirty dollars a month if they agreed to look after Mary. She would benefit from it as well as their own children.

Mrs Andau kept glancing at Leila with sad, anxious eyes. At last she interrupted, shyly, to ask if it was true that Leila's own daughter had been killed by a car.

Yes, said Leila, it was true.

Mrs Andau said that her little boy, aged six, had died of a disease.

There was silence then. Water slapped against the piles on which the house was built. The cat scratched itself.

'We will give the child a home even if there is no money,' said Mr Andau.

His wife nodded. 'She is a good child.'

'But we think,' he went on, showing his bad teeth in a sad grin, 'that it would be better for her if you were to take her to your house. Look at where we live.' He waved his hand at the bare room. He wrinkled his nose to show that he was aware of the stinks. He patted the thin cat. 'She told us about the wonderful house you live in.'

His wife sighed. There was little envy in it but great wonder.

Leila looked at Sandilands, begging him to tell them why it was not possible for her and him to adopt a child who would be out of place in their 'wonderful' house.

He shook his head dourly. He would not make it easy for her. He himself was willing to take the child, whatever the consequences.

Behind the partition the children were strangely silent.

'What does Mary herself want?' asked Sandilands.

Leila had her eyes closed. She seemed to be praying.

Mr Andau grinned ruefully and scratched his neck. He meant who in her right mind, even a child of ten, would prefer his hovel to their mansion.

'Shouldn't we ask her?' said Sandilands.

Leila opened her eyes. 'But, Andrew,' she said quietly, in English, 'won't she feel obliged to say that she'd rather stay here with her friends. So as not to offend them, I mean.'

'But isn't that what you want, Leila. Wouldn't that please you?'

She astonished him by saying, in some agitation: 'No, it isn't what I want.'

'Are you saying that you want her to come back with us?'

'Yes, that is what I'm saying.'

'Are you sure?'

'Yes, very sure. Don't be angry with me, Andrew. I was wrong, very wrong.'

Was it the prayer that had changed her mind? There was so much about her that he had still to learn.

'You tell them, Andrew?'

Did she think his Malay was adequate? He hated himself for the question, though it hadn't been spoken.

He addressed Mr Andau, speaking slowly and carefully. 'If Mary says that she would like to come back with us would you be offended?'

The skinny little man and his fat wife laughed at the Tuan's foolishness. They were fond of the child. If good fortune came to her they would be pleased, not offended.

Mr Andau called her name.

As they waited Leila took Sandilands' hand and squeezed it.

Mary came in, shy but resolute. She smiled at Sandilands and also, less hopefully, at Leila.

'We've come to take you back with us,' said Sandilands, and added, 'This time for good.'

'For good' meant while he was alive, a promise stretching out for thirty or more years. Would he be able to keep such a promise? If there was any doubt should he have given it?

Leila was smiling in a way that he did not quite trust; somehow it wasn't personal enough. She was pledged to save the whole country, not simply one little girl.

Both of them waited for Mary to answer.

It was to Sandilands she looked and spoke: would her friend Nirmala be allowed to visit her?

Yes, he replied, and any other friend she wished.

20

One evening, after Mary had gone to bed, Leila looked up from some papers she was studying which had to do with the forthcoming trial, and said, with a smile, that there were to be demonstrations next Tuesday, to protest against the annulment of the election results. They would take place all over the country but naturally that in Savu Town would be by far the largest: hundreds would take part. They would gather on the padang besar and then march to Government House where a petition signed by thousands of people would be handed in by her father, to be forwarded to His Highness.

Sandilands was surprised and a little dismayed. He had thought, had hoped, that they had put behind them their anger and disappointment. Her forecast of hundreds, he felt sure, would prove to be a great exaggeration, but he kept his cynicism to himself. As her husband, though, he had to voice his concern for her safety.

'Aren't public demonstrations against the law?' he asked.

'Against a dictatorial decree.'

'But still the law. There could be arrests.'

'It will be a peaceful demonstration but we are prepared for arrests.'

Arrests would make good publicity; if, that was, anywhere in the world anyone was interested.

'Will you be taking part?' he asked.

'I shall be at the front,' she said, proudly.

'Will there be other women?'

'Are you suggesting that because I am a woman I should stay at home?'

'I would certainly prefer you to stay at home. I don't want you arrested. I don't want you hurt. I love you.'

'Could you go on loving me if I sat at home like a coward and left my friends to face the danger?'

'So you admit there might be danger?'

'There's always danger, but don't worry. There will be laughter, not anger.'

If so it wouldn't be very effective as a protest.

'If there is trouble,' she said, 'it won't be us who will cause it.'

'I'd like to go with you.'

'No, Andrew. This isn't your struggle.'

'If it's yours then it's mine too.'

If he forbade her would she obey him? She had once said that she was bound to, by her marriage vows.

'There's one favour I'd like to ask you, Andrew. Please don't forbid your students to take part.'

'I wouldn't have any right to do that. They're not children and this is their country.'

'Thank you, Andrew. Don't look so glum. It will be all right. We might even succeed. His Highness might change his mind again when he sees so many of his people pleading with him.'

It was possible. The Sultan was a golfer. Golfers were accustomed to accept their mistakes and try again. But the

demonstrators would have to be peaceful: no insults, no
threats, no blows. It was as well that Savuans were pacifists.
Even the headhunters of the past had borne no ill-will
towards those whose heads they had cut off.

Next day in his office Sandilands had a telephone call
from the Deputy Commissioner.

Maitland's voice was gloomy. 'Hello, Andrew. Maitland
here. You'll have heard about the demonstration arranged
for next Tuesday.'

'Yes. A peaceful demonstration.'

'I've no doubt Abad and your wife intend it to be peaceful,
but there could be others with different ideas. Anyway, even
if it's peaceful it will be breaking the law.'

'Not much of a law, Alec.'

'Maybe not, but the law just the same. They've been
warned that the leaders will be arrested.'

'Wouldn't that provoke trouble?'

'I'm a policeman. I don't make laws. I uphold them. That's
what I'm paid for. Anyone arrested could be in jail for years.
The reason I've telephoned is to advise you to keep your
wife at home. This is serious, Andrew.'

'How can I keep her at home?'

'Order her to. You're her husband. She'll obey you.'

'Not in this matter. Anyway, I think they've got a right
to demonstrate.'

'I hope to Christ you're not so stupid as to take part
yourself.'

'I'd like to but Leila says it's none of my business.'

'Good for her. I like her. I respect her. You know that. If
I was you I'd lock her in a room next Tuesday.'

'Are you serious?'

'Never more so in my life. It could all go wrong. Keep her
at home, Andrew.'

Then he hung up.

Sandilands told Leila of the conversation. All she said was: 'If he was given a order to shoot unarmed people would he feel obliged to obey it?'

21

If it had been Scotland, Tuesday would probably have been a day of wind, rain, and cold, and the demonstration would either have been called off or attended by a handful of shivering disgruntled diehards. Since it was tropical Savu, the day like all other days was brilliant and warm. There could well be hundreds assembled on the padang besar. It would have this advantage, demonstrators and police alike would be in tolerant holiday mood. Sandilands saw it for himself when his students, carrying large banners, set off from the College, cheering and singing. They had not asked his permission and he had not gratuitously given it. He regretted the banners as being provocative, though the inscriptions on them were unobjectionable or should have been: WE DEMAND JUSTICE, in English and Malay. They were in high spirits like students everywhere escaping from their classes and taking to the streets to reform the world.

Leila dressed in national costume, kebaya and sarong, in the national colours, red, black, and orange. She was excited and laughed at his misgivings. This was going to be a historic day for Savu. He would be proud of her.

A car called for her early. In it were Chia and Lo. The driver, a Malay, was unknown to Sandilands. All three were polite to Sandilands but made it clear that as a foreigner he was of no account on this occasion. They looked upon Leila with devotion. Like her they seemed to think that they were about to venture upon a glorious exploit, not a mere amble through the streets of the town. They did not carry weapons, as far as he could see, but these of course could easily be picked up. He was greatly tempted to beg her for the last time not to go, but contented himself with kissing her, anxiously. She waved to Mary who had come out onto the verandah in her nightgown.

The car, a blue Ford Granada, roared off. He did not know to whom it belonged. This, a trivial thing surely, increased his anxiety and foreboding.

Mary came over to him.

'Where is she going?' she asked.

They had yet to decide what the child should call them.

'To meet some friends.'

'Do you not want to meet them?'

'They're her friends, not mine.' That, he realised, was true. There was still a distance between them.

'Is it to do with my mother?'

It was the first time she had mentioned her mother to him.

'No, Mary, it's got nothing to do with your mother.'

She smiled and went back into the house.

All his life he would remember that smile.

After taking Mary to play with some friends on the beach, Sandilands went to his office out of habit but did not stay long. He stood outside, among the fragrant bushes, and listened, but he was too far from the town to hear the loudest shouting. He heard birds calling, yesterday exhilarating sounds, today not so. He was not aware of how great his sense of dread was until he found that he had infected the whole scene with it, the sky, the flowers, the trees, a butterfly that fluttered by. He could not shake it off. He should have gone with her. He remembered Maitland's warnings of arrest and imprisonment.

He walked slowly back to his house. To his annoyance

Mr Srinavasan was seated on the verandah.

'Ah, Mr Sandilands, sir, as you see I have taken the liberty of asking your servant to provide me with this glass of excellent cold lemonade. I hope you do not mind.'

Sandilands minded very much but did not say so.

Mr Srinavasan had come to talk about the demonstration but there was another subject of interest to him.

'Where is the child, Mr Sandilands?' he asked. 'I do not see her about.'

'She has gone to play with friends.'

'Ah, so she has friends?'

'Why shouldn't she have friends?'

'The schools are closed today, I believe.'

'Hers is.'

'So that the teachers can participate in this fruitless protest march. I hope they keep their faces well hidden. Otherwise they will find notices of dismissal on their desks tomorrow morning. The authorities will charge them, incontrovertibly in my opinion, with setting their pupils an example of lawlessness and disobedience.'

A tiny fly with blue wings had fallen into his lemonade. He rescued it with his pinkie. It could not fly but it crawled across the table.

'All life is sacred,' said Mr Srinavasan, with a giggle. 'Is that not so, Mr Sandilands?'

He had splendid white teeth, now revealed in a gloating grin. Sandilands remembered Mr Andau's rotted stumps.

'That being so,' said Mr Srinavasan, 'what do we, as reverent men, propose should be done to the child's mother who has committed murder? Mrs Srinavasan, not so reverent as we, alas, has no doubt. She thinks the miserable wretch should be hanged forthwith.'

The fly, its wings now dry, flew off. Mr Srinavasan seemed genuinely pleased.

'I'd rather not talk about this, if you don't mind,' said Sandilands.

'But it must be talked about, Mr Sandilands. We cannot close our eyes and pretend the problem does not exist. Suppose though, she is hanged, what then is to happen to her daughter?'

'My wife and I intend to look after her.'

'May I ask, for what reason? Is it because you have guilty consciences?'

'Why should our consciences be any more guilty than yours, Mr Srinavasan?'

'Mrs Srinavasan, a woman without philosophy, says that the child should be condemned to make amends for her mother. She should be made to serve in some menial capacity all her life, with long hours of painful toil, with small wages, indeed with no wages at all. Does not the Bible suggest such punishment for the children of miscreants?'

'I doubt if the Bible demands that a child of ten should suffer for what her mother did.'

'You are presuming that the child is innocent.'

'I am not presuming it. I'm stating it.'

Sandilands was beginning to lose his temper. He was too worried about Leila to be patient with this devious fellow.

'Give me leave to doubt her innocence, Mr Sandilands. In a sense we are all guilty when a dreadful crime has been perpetrated. Does not the bell toll for us all? But I fear this poor child's guilt is greater far than ours. We are mere bystanders. She saw the deed done. Did she try to prevent it? Did she assist in it? For what reason was she present? Out of a depraved loyalty? Or because of innate wickedness? As Christian men, Mr Sandilands, we believe in evil, do we not?'

'I am not a Christian, Mr Srinavasan.'

'So I have been told. Yet you were married in church.'

'My wife's a Christian.'

'Yes, indeed. I have seen her in church, praying. Yet where is she at this moment? Taking part in an impious demonstration. I saw her being driven off in a big car. Those young criminals, Chia and Lo, came for her, did they not?'

'They are not criminals. You have good eyesight, Mr Srinavasan.'

'I made use of Miss Leithbridge's binoculars. You were unwise to let her take part. It is inevitable that the ringleaders will be arrested. She is a ringleader, is she not?'

'Why should they be arrested?'

'Because they are wilfully breaking the law and inciting others to break it too. Your wife may be imprisoned, Mr Sandilands. That would be a great pity. I would regret it very much. An unfortunate consequence would be that you could scarcely expect to continue as Principal of this college, if your wife and your father-in-law to boot, were in prison for breaking the law and defying authority. You might even be expelled from the country, even if you have played golf-ball with His Highness.'

He was grinning like a jackal. Sandilands was tempted to strike him.

'You are silent, Mr Sandilands? You have nothing to say? There is nothing you can usefully say. I have sympathy for you but really, sir, how can you as a person from the West understand the minds of Oriental students? Does not Kipling say, never the twain shall meet?'

Sandilands then lost his temper. 'Do you know what the students think of you, Mr Srinavasan?'

'Their opinion of me is irrelevant but I have reason to believe they hold me in high esteem.'

'Well, I have reason to believe that they look on you as an ill-disposed, condescending, envious, lustful, little shit.'

'Lustful!' Apparently he was prepared to forgive all the other accusations except this one.

'They have noticed, everyone has noticed, how you are always ogling the pretty female students.'

'That is professional slander, Mr Sandilands. Take care lest I bring you before the courts.'

'It is possible, as you have so shittily pointed out, that my wife may be arrested and put in prison and I may be dismissed and expelled, but I can assure you that you are the last person in Savu who would be put in my place. The students would go on strike. All the staff would resign.'

He expected Mr Srinavasan to get up and slink off, snarling, like a jackal repulsed, but no, he sat there looking woeful and taking another sip of lemonade. His brown eyes were bloodshot. From them trickled some tears.

He then began a recital, wistfully uttered or rather whined, that disconcerted Sandilands, it was so mournful, so self-pitying, and, though in some ways comic, totally humourless.

'It is easy for you to abuse me Mr Sandilands. You have a beautiful wife. My own wife, as you have seen, is ugly. She is fat, her bottom is immense and yet not voluptuous. Once a carpenter had to be summoned to saw her out of a chair. All that I could forgive for her dowry was substantial to compensate for her uncomeliness, but what I cannot forgive or overlook, what disgusts my soul, is that –'

Sandilands had to try and stop him. 'Mr Srinavasan, you should not be saying this to me.'

'I have been longing for a long time to say it to someone, and you, Mr Sandilands, are a suitable confidant, not because you are a sympathetic person, for you are not, but because your wife is so beautiful. Making love to the magnificent Leila . . .'

'Just a minute, Mr Srinavasan!'

'. . . must be an experience of heavenly bliss. My Kamala in the act chews betel nuts; her mouth looks bloody. Who can with fondness kiss a bloody mouth? She chatters about inopportune things: the length of cloth to make her a sari, the house she lived in when a child, a fellow she was fond of when she was fourteen.'

Was it possible to feel pity, revulsion, and amusement all at once? Sandilands felt them.

'If I suggest that she caress my member, which in wedlock is permissible, she seizes it with impatience, and her hand is sharp with rings. I have been lacerated. Is it any wonder that we have no children? Is it any wonder I have become – what did you say – ill-disposed, and envious?'

If ever there was a rhetorical question that was it.

'You are saying nothing, Mr Sandilands.'

'I'm afraid I don't know what to say, Mr Srinavasan.'

'I am not finished.'

'I don't think you should say any more.'

'I have a confession to make.'

'I don't think I want to hear it.'

'It is your duty to listen to it. It concerns members of your staff, myself and Miss Leithbridge.'

'Miss Leithbridge?'

'I have made an immoral proposal to that lady.'

Sandilands nearly smiled. Miss Leithbridge was quite capable of dealing with any immoral proposal, especially from Mr Srinavasan.

'I invited her to make love. No, let me be truthful. I implored her to allow me to make love to her. On my knees I implored her. I was in her house borrowing her binoculars. Kamala was having a nap. I often borrow her binoculars, to spy on this house, in the hope of seeing beautiful Leila.'

Sandilands stood up. He had had enough. 'You are a

member of the Anglican church, Mr Srinavasan. Why don't
you have a talk with the minister?'

Srinavasan stood up too. 'No, I shall go home and murder
my wife. I shall cut her throat.'

While Sandilands was wondering, with some alarm, if the
demented fellow meant it there was heard the roaring of a
motor bicycle. In a few moments it stopped outside the
house. Its rider was Baker, the Australian.

He got off and ran up the steps. He was hot and dusty.

'I've come from the town,' he cried. 'Christ, could I do
with a cold beer!'

Sandilands called to Saidee to bring it. 'Did you see the
demonstration?' he asked. 'How did it go?'

'More like a bloody riot than a demonstration.'

'What do you mean?'

Baker sat down and thanked Saidee for the beer. He took
a long drink. He paid no heed to Srinavasan who had sat
down too, licking his lips.

'Did you see Leila?' asked Sandilands.

'Yes, I saw her.'

'How was she? Was she all right?'

'It depends on what you mean by all right.'

'She's not hurt or anything like that?'

'Has she been arrested?' asked Mr Srinavasan.

Baker ignored him. 'Who said Savuans couldn't get
stirred up? The buggers have taken over half the town.'

Sandilands was thunderstruck. 'How could they?'

'There were thousands of them. All smiling. At first
anyway. I noticed one thing. They had left their kids at
home. Two things, really. There weren't any women. Except
Leila, of course. Three things, for Christ's sake. The third
thing was, though they were laughing there was something
else about them I had never seen before. They looked as if
they meant business. After all, fuck it, Sandilands, they had

had the dirty done on them and they were going to do something about it.'

'What about our students?' asked Sandilands.

'I didn't notice them. They must have kept well to the back. Except Dusing, Jerome Dusing. He was up there, at the front, with some other young fellows, Chinese mainly, whose looks I didn't like. Maybe I should say whose looks I did like. They looked as if they were going to get satisfaction or else.'

'Were Chia and Lo among them?'

'Yes, they were. Dangerous young bastards, Lo especially. Mind you, I saw no weapons. If there was an enquiry I'd swear to that. It was the police who had the weapons. Well, when they got to Government House they found it guarded by cops, commanded by your mate, Maitland. I don't know what the hell he thought he was doing. His duty, I expect he'd tell me. His duty my arse. He was just being bloody officious, like cops everywhere. He stood there on the steps, like bloody Horatio, and ordered them to bugger off. Didn't they know they were breaking the law? The cops had their holsters open, ready to draw their guns. I was sure they didn't have bullets in them or maybe blanks, but it turned out I was wrong. Anyway little Abad very politely held up the petition they wanted to be presented to His Highness: a document as big as the Magna Carta, for Christ's sake. Like a bloody fool Maitland refused to take it. You'd have thought it was a poisonous snake the way he drew back. Evidently he'd had his orders. The crowd got angry then. They shouted, they waved their fists. There was hatred on their faces, I was astonished. Were these Savuans? Then something – a durian I heard later – was thrown and hit Maitland on the head and knocked his hat off. It wasn't just his hat he lost, it was his self-control too. He yelled to his minions to arrest Abad. They weren't keen, as you can imagine. So he did it himself or tried to. Bloody idiot. He grabbed hold of the old man. Leila tried to prevent her father from getting hurt. Some of the young fellows I mentioned went for Maitland and roughed him up a bit. His second-in-command, Major Simbin, didn't know what the hell to do, so he did the worst thing he could. He pulled out his pistol and fired it, over the heads of the crowd or at least that's what I think he meant to do, but he was terrified and his hand was shaky, so one of the bullets hit the crowd. It was a real bullet too. Someone was hit. There was a scream.'

'Good God,' cried Sandilands, now very much afraid for Leila. 'Are you sure it wasn't Leila?'

'No, it wasn't her, though it easily could have been. It was a man. They carried him away on one of the banners. His shirt was bloody but he was alive. I think he was hit in the shoulder. Well, while the rest of the cops were trying to make up their minds whether to be live cowards or dead heroes the crowd charged. Guns were grabbed. I saw some automatic rifles. God knows where they came from. I didn't hear any more firing, though. Major Simbin got a bang on the nose. You couldn't see his face for blood.'

'Was Maitland badly hurt?'

'Not his person anyway. His dignity, yes. The crowd shoved open the door and rushed into Government House. I saw Abad and Leila leading them. I have to say, Sandilands, she was doing her share of the shouting. Their intention seemed to be to occupy the Council Chamber. Some of the crowd dashed off, to capture the town. I heard they'd taken over the telephone exchange and – would you believe it? – the hospital. So I thought I'd better come and tell you so that you could go and get Leila out of it; or at least you could try.'

'You think she's still in Government House?'

'I would say so. People are going to be hanged for this, Sandilands. If she was my wife I'd get her out of the country.

She's gone too far. That kid you've got staying with you, her
father's a fisherman, isn't he? She'll know other fishermen.
It should be easy enough to get a boat to take you to the
Philippines. But you'd have to hurry. Troops will be flown
in. British troops.'

Sandilands was on his feet. 'Will you come with me?'

'Sure.'

'Can I be of assistance?' asked Mr Srinavasan.

Again they ignored him.

'I'll leave my bike here,' said Baker. 'Bring money,
Sandilands, as much as you can lay your hands on. This
could be your farewell to Savu. But what about the kid?
Where is she?'

'She's with friends at the beach.'

'Will you want to pick her up too?'

'We'll see.'

22

On their way to the town they met the students trudging
back to the College. Sandilands stopped the car. They gathered round it. Their mood was very different from that earlier
when they had set out. Then they had been joyful and
light-footed, now they were frightened and downcast. Their
banners were rolled up as if they did not want the inscriptions to be seen; they were no longer demanding justice.

Some of the girls had been crying.

Sandilands was dismayed to find that though they were
concerned about Leila they seemed to have lost faith in her.
They did not altogether absolve her from blame for the
violence they had seen.

They had been talking among themselves as to what was likely to happen to the leaders and to themselves. They asked what he thought.

'I don't know,' he said. 'Are all of you here?'

'All of us, except Jerome Dusing. He stayed with Albert Lo. Some said they saw him with a gun.'

'Are you going to bring Leila back, Mr Sandilands?'

'If I can. When you get back to the College report to Miss Leithbridge.'

'Will they do anything to us, Mr Sandilands?'

'I don't think so.'

Sandilands drove on.

'I hope you're right,' said Baker, 'in saying nothing will be done to them. Every damned one could be expelled.'

'The country needs teachers.'

'They could be brought over from Malaya. One thing's certain, anyway, you won't see our students taking to the streets again. Whatever happens from now on they'll sit at their desks, with their heads down. Ironical, isn't it? They set out to help establish democracy and freedom, and what have they helped to do? Turn the place into a bloody police State.'

In the town it was as if an earthquake had just taken place and another, even more destructive, was thought to be inevitable.

Sandilands had to drive slowly because of groups of men on the streets, discussing the morning's events. Few had gone back to work. The bars were full. Women had ventured out to shop. The fruit and fish markets had reopened; as had the banks. Street sweepers were busy. Traffic policemen were at their posts. Surely signs of sanity and normality.

There was, though, that sense of a calamity about to happen. Both Sandilands and Baker felt it, the former more keenly because of Leila. It was incredible that in an hour or so he might be fleeing from the country, with Leila, he hoped. Suddenly their whole future was altered. Luckily most of his money was invested back in Edinburgh. He could find a teaching job, Leila one in a lawyer's office, in that city of lawyers. They could build a new life.

There was the problem of Mary. Would she after all be left with the Andaus?

But first Leila had to be rescued from her own folly.

He felt a spasm of anger. Her ambition had gained nothing and ruined everything.

Moments later a surge of self-contempt swept that anger away. She had said his Malay was inadequate; so too, it seemed, was his love. She was in great danger and all he could do was blame her. He was fit to be a nurse's husband, not a revolutionary's.

Baker was feeling more and more uneasy. He wasn't really a friend of Sandilands', who was too righteous and correct for his taste, but he realised that the big Scotsman was heading straight for tragedy.

He wasn't sure how to convey his somewhat qualified sympathy.

'What'll you do if she refuses to come with you?' he asked, as they approached Government House.

The Savu flag flew over it.

He was pretty sure that she would refuse. She was the kind of woman who would die, and cause other people to die, for principle. A heroine, some would say. A pain in the arse, Baker himself said. Sandilands, stubborn bugger, would stay on in Savu while she was arrested, tried, and maybe hanged. That was to say, if they let him; which they probably wouldn't.

Sandilands was no hero but that was the part he had been given.

They left the car and walked the last hundred yards. There

was little to show that a short time ago hundreds of angry men had been here. No damage had been done to trees and bushes; no litter dropped; no graffiti scribbled on walls; no beer cans thrown among the flowers. In so orderly and well-behaved a country how could there be public hangings?

On the steps of Government House a number of youths stood guard. They had pistols in their belts. Two had automatic rifles. Most of them were nervously smoking. They looked dedicated and ridiculous: an explosive mixture, thought Baker. He was sorry for Sandilands. Now he became sorry for himself as well. An agitated jerk of a forefinger and he was a dead man.

'Bloody young fools,' he muttered. 'Don't they know they're going to be shot to pieces. But for Christ's sake, don't step on their tails.'

Among them were Chia and Lo and also Jerome Dusing.

Lo seemed to be the leader. He wasn't smoking. That was a weakness he spurned. He confronted Sandilands, with his rifle ready. Did he know how to use it, Sandilands wondered.

'You should not be here, Mr Sandilands,' he said, sternly. 'This is not your business.'

'I believe my wife is inside,' said Sandilands. 'I would like to speak to her.'

'She is not here as your wife. She is here as the leader of the People's Revolutionary Party.'

'When did it change its name? Yesterday it was the People's Party.'

'It has not changed its name. For us it has always been the Revolutionary Party. For Madam Azaharri too.'

'Her name is Mrs Sandilands. Does Dr Abad approve?'

'Dr Abad has given up the leadership. He is an old man. Madam Azaharri is now our leader.'

'Will you please let my wife, Mrs Sandilands, know that I am here and wish to speak to her?'

'You cannot speak to her. She is with the other candidates who won the elections. They are in the Council Chamber, forming the new government of Savu.'

'You must know this is madness, Albert. Troops will be sent for.'

'British Troops, Mr Sandilands? Scottish troops?'

It was more than likely. Scottish troops had often been used by the English to build up their empire and then defend it.

'Whoever they are you will stand no chance against them.'

'If they kill us the whole world will hear of it.'

Baker forgot his own advice not to step on their tails.

'The whole world won't give a mosquito's fart,' he said. 'Want some advice, Lo? Throw away those guns and get the hell out of the country. Hijack a boat to take you to the Philippines. If you stay here sure as Christ you'll either be shot or hanged.' Or both, he added, to himself. What was to prevent wounded men from being strung up, just to make sure?

'We are not afraid to die in a noble cause.'

'Jesus, save us from martyrs. *He* knew all about it. What were they doing when He got nailed to the Cross? Dicing in the taverns. Fucking in the brothels. The world doesn't weep, Chia. It yawns.'

'In Australia, Mr Baker, if the people were cheated as we have been what would they do?'

'Laugh into their beer. They'd think it a bloody good joke. What they wouldn't do would be to get killed.'

'You have a grievance, Albert,' said Sandilands, 'but this isn't the way to set it right.'

'What is the way, Mr Sandilands?'

Sandilands had no answer ready. 'Patience,' he said, at last. 'If you had waited you would have got your democracy in the end.'

'How long should we have waited?'

'As long as was necessary. At least it would have been better than killing or being killed.'

'Is cowardly submission to tyranny better than being killed?'

'It would get my vote,' said Baker.

'You had better go now,' said Lo.

Baker thought it a good idea. He didn't want to get mixed up in this any more than he already was.

'I won't go until I've seen my wife,' said Sandilands

'She doesn't want to see you. Do you not understand? She is your wife no longer.'

Baker thought Sandilands was going to grab the insolent young bastard by the throat and strangle him. Instead Sandilands said, quietly: 'She'll have to tell me that herself.'

Lo called one of the youths over to him. After a whispered consultation the youth went inside.

'I heard there was a man shot this morning,' said Sandilands. 'Was he badly hurt?'

Lo shook his head. He would have preferred the victim to be dead. It would have made better propaganda.

Sandilands felt a little relieved. If there were no serious casualties it was possible that these amateurish revolution-aries might be amnestied. Surely the British Government would advise clemency. And His Highness wasn't a blood-thirsty man.

'It's bloody serious, I know,' said Baker, 'but it's laughable too. I remember Lo telling me that his favourite character in history was Chairman Mao. I never knew Mao was a dem-ocrat. Given the chance this lot would set up a worse tyranny than the Sultan's.'

Sandilands shook his head. 'Not Leila,' he said.

Baker wasn't so sure. He had caught a glimpse of fanati-cism on that lovely face.

Chia's messenger came out.

Sandilands could hardly breathe. If she refused to see him now he might never see her again.

Lo scowled as he reluctantly passed on the message.

'Madam Azaharri will see you,' he said, 'for five minutes.'

'Young prick,' muttered Baker. 'I'll wait here. Good luck.'

Sandilands went into the building. The officials and clerks who worked there had been sent away. It was now in the hands of the People's Revolutionary Party. They stood about in the vast entrance hall, about thirty of them, most of them unarmed. They were silent, not knowing what to say to one another. They were not zealots like Lo or visionaries like Leila. They had made their gesture. They wanted to be given permission to go home. They stared at Sandilands with what struck him as envy. He was free to come and go as he pleased. They did not know why he was there. He was part of their confusion.

Leila was waiting for him at the top of the magnificent marble staircase. She looked tired and impatient. She was wearing the same kebaya and sarong in which she had left the house just a few hours ago. He thought he saw blood on it. Was it hers, or Maitland's, or Major Simbin's, or the wounded man's?

'You should not have come,' she said.

She looked at him as if, he thought, she *was* Madam Azaharri and not Mrs Sandilands. He was a stranger to this woman.

There was a guard outside the Council Chamber door. He had a pistol in his belt. A quick dash, a snatch, a blow, and the gun would be in Sandilands' hand. With it he could fight his way down the stairs and into the street. He would shoot anyone who tried to stop them.

There were two flaws in that plan: he was no cinema hero and Leila would not have come with him.

'I've come to take you away, Leila,' he said. Even to himself it sounded feeble.

'Do you know what we are doing here?' she asked. 'We are forming a new government for Savu. Already we have passed a law abolishing the death penalty.'

It was, as Baker had said, laughable. Did she think that such a law would safeguard their lives? On the contrary, it made their executions for treason all the more likely.

'The people will see what we would have done for them.'

'The people won't know anything about it, Leila. They won't want to know.'

'They'll remember us.'

So they would but as what? Martyrs? Heroes? Fools?

'There's still time, Leila. We could find a boat that would take us to the Philippines. Your father could come with us.'

'My father will never desert his people. Neither will I.'

She turned then and walked away.

'What about Mary?' he cried.

She hesitated and then walked on. The man at the door saluted her and opened it for her.

Sandilands watched her disappear behind the big leather-padded silver-studded door, the person he loved most in the world. Yes, but what did that amount to? Whether it was his upbringing to blame, or his nature, or a selfishness that he had all his life jealously cultivated, he had never been able to love with all his heart. In spite of his teasing of the students he had something of Mr Collins in him. To love Leila as she deserved called for qualities he did not have. He would have been happier, safer, and duller, with Jean Hislop. Leila had shown him how limited and timorous he was; Jean had made it her purpose to praise and flatter him. With his hands grasping the onyx balustrade, as if to prevent him from being dragged away, he was not hoping that Leila would come back to him, for he knew she would not, but he was wishing that he still had Jean to give him courage.

Baker had got into the building and was looking up at Sandilands. He wasn't in time to see Leila but he saw Sandilands and ran up the stairs to him.

'Where is she?' he cried. 'Did you see her? What did she say? She's not coming, is she? Then for fuck's sake let's get out of here.'

He caught Sandilands by the arm and pulled him away. They stumbled together down the stairs.

One of the revolutionaries, a grey-haired man with un-happy eyes, came forward and patted Sandilands on the shoulder. 'It is God's will,' he said, in Malay. 'We must all die some time.'

Outside Lo marched up to Sandilands. He wasn't gloating. He was too high-minded for that. 'She has not come with you, Mr Sandilands. Go home. Go home to Scotland. Forget Savu.'

Shall I, thought Sandilands, as he went along the street towards his car, with Baker still holding him by the arm, ever forget Savu? Yes, he might in time forget the cheerful students, the splendid college, the golf matches with the Sultan, the sails to the islands, and the trips into the jungle in search of orchids, but he would surely never forget Leila. No, but when he was an old man, would he boast to his grandchildren that he had known her?

'Don't blame yourself,' said Baker. 'You've done all you could. Let's get back to the College.'

That was what he himself wanted. A shower, a change of clothes, a cold beer, with Mona his amah seated on his lap.

'No, I want to speak to Maitland,' said Sandilands.

23

To Baker's astonishment the gates of the big police compound were wide open. Everything looked normal and peaceful. In the shade of a big flame-of-the-forest tree a motorist was undergoing a test for a driving licence. He was trying to reverse his car into a square formed by four moveable poles. If he touched one he would fail, but he was given three attempts. His last succeeded. The policeman conducting the test was full of goodwill and was delighted.

In another part of the compound several policemen in white shorts and singlets were playing a leisurely game of volley-ball.

'Those stupid bastards in Government House,' said Baker, 'think they've got authority terrified. It doesn't look like it. Why didn't they try to take over this place?'

'Because they didn't want bloodshed,' said Sandilands.

'You could be right. You know what, Sandilands, it would be bloody easy now, at this very minute, to slip out of the country. Christ, you could buy an air ticket to Hong Kong. There's a flight about four, isn't there? If I was you I'd try to get Leila on it.'

Sandilands shook his head. 'She wouldn't come.'

'A pity. It almost looks as if they're being given a chance

to escape. It would certainly save a lot of trouble for every-body.'

Sandilands got out of the car.

'I'll stay here if you don't mind,' said Baker. 'I don't like police stations.'

In the air-conditioned reception hall the sergeant in charge at the desk was in shirt sleeves. Above him was a large portrait of the Sultan in military uniform, with many decorations from various foreign States.

Sandilands approached the desk. 'I'd like to see Mr Mait-land, the Deputy Commissioner,' he said, in Malay. 'My name's Sandilands. I'm Principal of the Teachers' Training College.'

The sergeant smiled. 'I know who you are, Mr Sandilands. My brother Salim was a student at your college.'

Salim, the jolly traitor.

Did the sergeant also know that Sandilands was the husband of the now notorious rebel Dr Abad's daughter?

Other policemen came and went, all smiling, all looking relieved. They were like men from whom a painful and dangerous duty had been taken. They had been given orders to carry on as usual until the soldiers arrived. It would be the soldiers, strangers, who would do the killing or the dying. It could well be that some of the police had relatives or friends among the rebels.

'Mr Maitland's been trying to reach you all morning,' said the sergeant. 'He will be pleased to see you.'

Maitland's office was upstairs. It would have made every Chief Constable in Britain covetous: air-conditioned, spa-cious, luxuriously carpeted, a huge desk of teak, leather armchairs, a portrait of the Sultan in an ornate frame, paintings on the walls of Savu scenes.

Maitland rose from his desk to greet Sandilands. Being Scotsmen they did not shake hands.

'Glad to see you, Andrew. I've been trying to get hold of you.'

'Why? What have you to tell me?'

'Sit down. This is a hell of a business, isn't it?'

There was a faint bruise above Maitland's right eye. The hat that had been knocked off hung on a peg, quite undamaged.

'I believe you've just come from Government House,' he said. 'What's going on there? Did you see your wife?'

'Yes, I saw her.' Sandilands could not keep bitterness out of his voice.

Maitland noticed it. On the desk was a photograph of his own wife, with his two daughters.

'I expect you asked her to give it up and come home.'

'Yes.'

'And she refused?'

'Yes.'

'Too bad. Anyway it would have been too late. They're in too deep, Andrew. Armed rebellion. Treason. Unlawful assembly. There will be executions.'

'Have troops been sent for?'

'They're on their way. They should arrive during the night. From a Scottish regiment, I believe. You know, I thought Leila was an intelligent woman.'

'She *is* an intelligent woman.'

'Then why the hell has she got mixed up in this imbecile caper?'

'She doesn't think it's an imbecile caper. She thinks, they all think, that they're fighting for their rights.'

'Their rights? What's that got to do with anything? I happen to believe they were badly cheated. I wouldn't be surprised if His Mightiness up there would admit it in private. But that doesn't alter the fact that they're taking part in an armed rebellion, and the penalty for that in this country is

death. I warned you about that at the Residency, if you
remember. But leave that aside. What I want to tell you,
Andrew, is that as I sit here I don't know what my orders
are. It looks as if the Sultan and his councillors don't know
either. So in the meantime I've got nobody watching the
airport or the harbour. I wanted you to tell Leila that. Go
back to her now, Andrew, and tell her, while there's still
time. Just her. Not the others. If I get my orders, and they
could come at any time, I'll have to carry them out.'

Sandilands shook his head. 'She wouldn't come.' Especially if the others, including her father, were to be left
behind.

'I didn't think she would. So far nobody's been badly hurt.
I want to keep it that way.'

'What about Major Simbin?'

'That damned fool. He's all right. A badly swollen nose.
Not a hospital case. Just as well. They've taken over the
hospital. Some revolutionaries! They leave this place and the
airport alone and take over the hospital.'

'Is Jean all right?'

'Jean's in her element. She's got them working for her.
Just what she needed, she said: a gang of hard-working
scrubbers. The hospital's never been so clean. She's anxious
about you. We all are. You're absolutely sure Leila won't
leave?'

'Yes.'

'I spoke to Abad on the telephone earlier. Perhaps I
exceeded my authority but I'll be leaving soon and I'd like
to go with a reasonably clear conscience.'

'What did you say to him?'

'I think I promised to do what I could to help if they gave
themselves up.'

'What did he say?'

'Some nonsense about never deserting his people. Are

they his people? I understood he was born in Malaya and he married a Scotswoman, didn't he? Leila's half Scottish, isn't she? It's one hell of a mess. I feel partly responsible. I shouldn't have tried to arrest the old man. I'm afraid I lost my temper.'

'Would it be possible for me to speak to Leila on the telephone?'

'If some bastard hasn't cut the wires.'

Maitland picked up the telephone. 'It's still working.' He waited. Then he spoke, in Malay. 'This is the Deputy Commissioner speaking. Hold on. I've got Mr Sandilands here. He'd like to talk to his wife. All right, Madam Azaharri, if that's what you want to call her. Yes, we'll wait.'

'They've gone to tell her,' he said. 'They insist on calling her Madam Azaharri. She's in council, it seems.'

'They've formed a new government and are passing new laws.'

'Bloody idiots. Like children playing games.'

'They think they had a right to do it, since they won the elections.'

'They certainly did that.'

'Yet British soldiers are on their way to arrest them and maybe kill them. Do the British people know that?'

'I doubt it. But if they did it wouldn't keep them off their sleep. Savu's too far away and full of wogs.'

Then he was listening to the telephone. 'Who's this?' he asked. 'What authority have you to speak for her? Here's her husband. Tell him.'

But when he handed the telephone to Sandilands the person at the other end had hung up.

'He's hung up,' muttered Sandilands. 'Did he say who he was?'

'No. Sounded as if he was young.'

'What did he say?'

'That Madam Azaharri did not want to speak to Mr Sandilands.'

'Do you think he was telling the truth?'

'Do *you* think he was?'

'Yes.'

'Sorry, Andrew. There's still a chance they'll give up when the soldiers arrive. Those soldiers will have experience of this kind of thing.'

'Of crushing democracy?'

'You know what I mean. They'll use minimum force. It could be that nobody will be hurt.'

'But they'll all be arrested.'

'Aye, they will.'

'What will happen to them then?'

Maitland stared at the photograph of his family. 'Some might get off with prison sentences.'

'And some will be hanged?'

Maitland nodded. 'They were warned, Andrew.'

'I could appeal to the Sultan.'

'You could. You know him personally better than I do.'

'I could write to the British press, telling them that a democratic party's been suppressed by British soldiers, on behalf of a dictator.'

'I doubt if it would be printed. Certainly not in those terms and not on the front pages. The Sultan, you know, has it in his power to do a great deal of damage to the British economy, by withdrawing his money.'

Sandilands sighed. It was almost a whimper. 'What do you think I should do, Alec?'

'You want an honest answer?'

'Yes.'

'I don't really know you all that well, Andrew. You're like me, you've kept yourself too private, but if I was in your place I'd go home, as soon as possible. They'll let you have your full pension, considering the circumstances. They'll give you a good testimonial, as you deserve. You'll easily find a good job in Edinburgh. And – you said you wanted an honest answer – I'd ask Jean to go with me. She's still very fond of you. She's been talking about going home herself. She'd help you get over this.'

'I'm still married.'

There was a pause.

'Even if she was in prison for twenty years I'd wait for her.'

'Aye, I'd wait for Kate for twenty years.'

'They wouldn't hang a woman, would they?'

'It's been done before. They wouldn't waste any time either. There'd be no trial, in public anyway. The sentence would be carried out immediately. There would be the briefest of announcements.'

The telephone rang. Both men were startled. Maitland picked it up. His expression hardly changed as he listened.

'Right,' he muttered, and put the telephone down.

'Too bad, Andrew. I've got my orders. Nobody's to be allowed to leave the country. They've lost their chance.'

He got up, put on his hat, picked up his cane, tapped Sandilands on the shoulder with it, and hurried out.

Sandilands wiped tears and sweat from his face with his handkerchief. He waited for a minute or two to try and compose himself. He must show himself worthy of Leila.

Downstairs he found a great difference. The hive had been disturbed. No one as much as looked at him. Out in the compound vehicles were already leaving, crammed with policemen. All were armed.

'What the hell's happening?' said Baker, as Sandilands got into the car.

'He's got his orders. Nobody's to be allowed to leave the country.'

'Does he have to obey his fucking orders? I always thought he was a bit of a fascist. What about the soldiers? Are they coming?'

'They'll arrive during the night.'

'And that will be bloody that. There's nothing more you can do, Sandilands. For Christ's sake let's get back to the College. I'm knackered. Christ knows how you must feel.'

'I have to pick up Mary.'

'Oh.' Like everybody else Baker had been amazed by the quixotic decision to adopt the daughter of the woman charged with murder. He hadn't, like Mr Srinavasan, thought it an affront to God, in that the child as well as the mother deserved to be punished and not 'pampered'. It wasn't, however, the sort of gesture he himself could have made, being too sensible and, to be honest, not possessing the necessary moral courage. If it had been a difficult undertaking for Sandilands with his wife's co-operation it was surely next to impossible for the Scotsman on his own. Baker had a wife in Sydney who, if he'd brought home a Malay kid who spoke little English and whose mother had been hanged for murder, would have wanted to know if he had gone off his fucking head.

'Where is she?' he asked.

'At the beach, I think.'

'What's going to happen to her now, Sandilands?'

'I intend to take her home with me, to Scotland, if they let me.'

The airport was now in sight. The Cathay-Pacific plane for Hong Kong was still on the runway.

At a P.W.D. house near the beach Sandilands got out of the car and called up to three women on the verandah, asking them where Mary was. One replied that she was on the beach. They were white and, in Baker's view, deserving of praise themselves for allowing their own daughters to play with a kid who wasn't just poor and brown-skinned, usually a repellent combination, but was into the bargain the child of a murderess; and, to add to the grisly catalogue, whose foster mother stood a good chance of being hanged too.

'What's happening in the town, Andrew?' asked one of the women. 'We've heard there's been trouble. Is it all over? Why are there so many policemen at the airport?'

'It's not quite over, Mrs Moore.'

'Do you think our husbands will be all right?'

'I'm sure they will.'

'Are they expecting trouble at the airport?'

'Soldiers are arriving tonight.'

'Why? Is there going to be a war?'

'No, not a war.'

'British soldiers?'

'Yes.'

'Is your wife all right, Andrew?' asked another of the women.

'I hope so, Mrs Pettigrew.' His voice at last was a little shaky.

Baker felt ashamed. He had been under the sneaky impression that Sandilands, though upset about his wife, as any man would be, wasn't altogether shattered by it. Now he realised that Sandilands was suffering torture but didn't dare show it lest he break down and weep. What would a hero have done? Not much different.

The little girls, five of them, four white and one brown, were enjoying themselves on the sand. Mary was not shouting with joy like her friends but she didn't look miserable or sorry for herself. Baker felt more moved than he would have given himself credit for as he sat in the car watching Sandilands go down onto the sand and be greeted by the little dark-faced flat-nosed girl as if he was indeed her father.

He chatted amiably to the other girls as she dried her feet
and put on her socks and sandals.

She smiled at Baker as she got into the car and asked a
question that chilled his scalp. 'Where is Leila?' He did not
have much Malay but he understood that. What answer
could poor Sandilands give her?

Whatever it was it was in Malay, so that Baker did not
quite catch it, but it couldn't have been the truth, for it
seemed to reassure her. Baker almost loved Sandilands then
for the lie, whatever it was.

As the car passed the house the women stood up and
waved. Baker found himself waving back. It was his way of
saluting them. In a world full of bastards it was as well to
admit that there were some decent people.

No more was said until the car stopped outside
Sandilands' house.

'Can I do anything?' asked Baker.

'Perhaps you could go and see that the students are all
right.'

'Sure.'

Saidee came hurrying down the steps to help Mary out
of the car. She was in tears. She knew about Leila. The whole
town would know by now.

'Would it be worth it, appealing to His Highness?' asked
Baker, as he sat astride his motor-bicycle. 'You're a pal of
his, in a way. I'd have a go, Sandilands.'

Saidee had a message for Sandilands. Jean Hislop had
telephoned.

He thought about Jean and what Maitland had said. He
had humiliated her and yet she still loved him, in a way that
did not demand too much from him. She wasn't interested
in politics. 'I'd vote Tory, like my parents, but to tell you the
truth I don't trust anybody who says they're in it to help

people. As far as I'm concerned they're all in it to help themselves.' So she had said in the days before he had met Leila. He had agreed with her. Did he do so now? What were Leila's motives? A desire to bring democracy and freedom to her native country? To be fair she had seldom used those shop-soiled words.

The telephone rang. He let it ring. So anguished and confused was he that he did not know whether he wanted it to be Jean or Leila. It kept on ringing.

Saidee could bear it no longer. She ran in and snatched up the telephone. From her scowl of disappointment he knew it must be Jean.

It was Jean. Her voice was sad but affectionate and the accent was blessedly Scottish.

'Hello, Andrew.'

'Hello, Jean.' His own voice was hoarse.

'Poor Andrew. It's awful, isn't it? I can't tell you how sorry I am.'

'Thanks, Jean.'

There was a pause.

But Leila had to be mentioned and she did it, resolutely. 'I've just heard about Leila. From Alec.'

There was another pause.

'I can't believe it. It's happened so suddenly. Such a talented woman. How could she be so foolish?'

Foolish? The word showed surely a lack of imagination. Yes, she would vote Tory, and wear a hat in church, and send her children to a private school. Would those children be his too?

'How are things at the hospital?' he asked.

Her voice brightened. 'You'd scarcely believe it, Andrew. I ordered them to put down their guns and weapons. Do you know what? They did it, very neatly on the floor. They were so polite the whole time they were here. I told them not to disturb the patients and they kept so quiet. I told them to go home but it was too late by then, the police were waiting for them. They were all arrested. I hope nothing terrible happens to them. Alec says they could get ten years in prison. Most of them are so young.'

She could not quite subdue her elation. 'If I can help in any way, Andrew, you know I'll be very glad to. That little girl you were going to adopt, where is she? What's going to happen to her?'

'She's here. I intend to adopt her, if I can.'

'Will they let you?' Evidently she thought, and perhaps hoped, that they wouldn't.

'I don't know. Probably not.'

'What would happen to her in that case? Did you know they've got quite a good well-run orphanage here? I've met the woman in charge. She'd be well looked after there.'

He heard the roar of Baker's motor-bicycle. 'I'll have to go now, Jean. Thanks for telephoning.'

'Would you mind if I came over this evening? I wouldn't stay long.'

'If you like.' He couldn't forgive her for her too ready suggestion that Mary could be put into the orphanage.

'Good. About seven then. Love.'

He went onto the verandah to hear Baker's report.

'They're all safely back, except Dusing of course. I think you should go and talk to them, Sandilands. They're in a state of shock. The girls particularly. Weeping and wailing and tearing their hair. Literally. I've been a crass bastard. I didn't realise how much it mattered to them; how much Leila mattered to them. Be seeing you.'

He shot off then towards the teachers' flats.

24

Sandilands decided to try and telephone the palace before going over to the students' quarters. If he got through and spoke to the Sultan he might have good news to give them.

To his surprise he got through without difficulty. He asked if he could speak to His Highness. He gave his name, and instead of being curtly dismissed was asked to wait. Had His Highness been expecting a call from him?

After five long minutes another voice spoke, this time in urbane English. It was one of the Sultan's secretaries, educated at Oxford. 'His Highness will speak to you now, Mr Sandilands.'

'Thank you.' Sandilands felt the bones of his skull grow tight with foreboding.

The Sultan sounded friendly but also sombre. 'Good afternoon, Andrew. I do not think you are telephoning to arrange a game of golf.'

'No, Your Highness. It's about Leila.'

His Highness sighed. 'Yes. Why did you not stop her? But I think you must have tried. I remember you yourself are not interested in politics.'

'Yes, I tried.' Sandilands' voice trembled. 'What is going to happen to her?'

'That is not for me to say. That is for the courts. She and her misguided friends have broken the law. They knew what the consequences would be. They must pay the penalty.'

'No one's been seriously hurt, Your Highness.'

'Blood has been shed. They are armed, these rebels. Why do they have guns? Is it to kill me?'

'I don't think that was ever their intention. They don't want to kill anyone. They didn't have guns to start with. They took them from the police.'

'That in itself is a very serious crime.'

Sandilands could have said that they had been severely provoked, but instead he pleaded humbly. 'If she was pardoned I would take her to Scotland with me. I promise she would never take part in politics again.'

'How could she be pardoned and the others condemned? We both know her too well to think that she would accept that. You would not ask that they should all be pardoned? The State would be put in peril. I deeply regret this, Andrew. I shall always remember with great pleasure our games of golf. You will be returning to Scotland soon?'

'Yes, Your Highness.'

'That would be best. I have been told you may wish to take a Savu child with you, as your adopted daughter.'

'If it is permitted.'

'It will be permitted. All your rights will be safe-guarded. You will be treated generously. Believe me, my friend, I feel great sadness. But you will marry again and your wife will be the child's mother.'

That surely was ominous.

'So something good will have come out of this terrible business.'

Then he hung up.

Sandilands imagined the telephone, of gold, being put

down by a hand that wasn't steady. Nor had the Sultan's voice at the end been steady.

With the telephone in his hand Sandilands dialled the number of Government House. He would make a last attempt to speak to Leila.

There was a response almost immediately. Were they standing by the telephone, waiting for an offer of amnesty?

'This is Andrew Sandilands. I would like to speak to my wife.'

There was no nonsense this time about Madam Azaharri.

'Please hold the line, Mr Sandilands.'

'Thank you.' Sandilands felt giddy, as if he was having a heart attack.

If she spoke to him would he be able to keep bitterness and self-pity out of his voice?

It was her voice. He felt a great pang of joy but also, seconds later, a greater pang of fear and grief. She chose to speak in Malay.

'Hello, Andrew. I'm glad you telephoned. I didn't say goodbye as I should.'

Why had she not telephoned him? He did not cast it up. He must not sound sorry for himself. 'What's happening, Leila?'

'They have the building surrounded. We are all prepared to die.'

If they surrendered they would be hanged, if they resisted they would be shot.

'What are you going to do about Mary? Where is she?'

'She's here with me.'

Mary was watching him from the door.

'You will be going home to Scotland soon. Take her with you. Marry Miss Hislop. She is a good person. She will help you look after the child.'

'I already have a wife.'

'I was proud to be your wife, Andrew, but I should not have married you. Love is not always enough. I have brought you great unhappiness.'

'You brought me great joy.'

'Did I? For a little while? I hope so. Go home. Soon. Very soon. Don't wait here.'

Don't wait, she meant, until you hear that I am dead.

'Goodbye, Andrew.' She was weeping as she said that.

His telephone was silent.

He hadn't the strength or the will to put it down. Mary came over and did it for him. She saw the tears in his eyes.

'Were you speaking to Leila?' she whispered.

'Yes, I was speaking to Leila.' He made an effort to smile. 'She was asking about you.'

'What was she saying about me?'

'She said I was to take you to Scotland with me.'

She nodded. 'Are we going soon?'

'Very soon.'

But he could not leave Savu while he thought Leila might still be alive; at the same time he could not bear to wait until he knew for certain that she was dead.

There was nowhere for him to go, nothing for him to say, nothing for him to think. All he could do was endure.

Mary held his hand. She would endure with him.

25

While he was waiting for Jean, not looking forward to it but hoping that she would not change her mind, he had a visit from his staff, all twelve of them, including Mr Srinavasan. The Indian could not quite dissemble his delight, not at the

Principal's misfortune, he was over-sorrowful about that, but at the good fortune about to fall on him. He peered about the house with the satisfaction of its next occupant.

Miss Leithbridge was their spokeswoman. She spoke quietly, with restraint. 'We'll not stay long, Andrew. We know you'll want to be alone. But we want to tell you, all of us, that we're very sorry indeed at what has happened.' Then she did what a moment before she had no idea she was going to do: she burst into tears. 'It's dreadful. It doesn't bear thinking about. Such a beautiful woman.' She could not go on and hid her face behind her hands.

Everyone was silent. Even Mr Srinavasan had nothing to say. Everyone knew what everyone else was thinking; that Leila, such a beautiful woman, would soon be dead, shot or hanged. It certainly did not bear thinking about but they couldn't help thinking about it just the same.

Baker saw that Sandilands was in danger of breaking down. 'Let's get out of here,' he muttered, and led the way.

The rest followed but not before the Asians among them had solemnly shaken Sandilands' hand and Miss Leithbridge had embraced him.

Only Mr Srinavasan spoke. 'I shall pray for you, Mr Sandilands.'

What good was prayer?, thought Sandilands, the atheist. But he would have liked to have asked Srinavasan to pray for Leila.

When they were all gone he sat on the verandah, sipping whisky and gazing at one of Savu's magnificent sunsets. The sky was blood red; so were his hands. So were the trees and the ribbon in Mary's hair. She sat beside him, heedless of mosquito bites on her bare legs.

She said she had been looking for Scotland on a map of the world.

'Did you find it?'

'Yes. Is it cold there?'

'Sometimes. A lot colder than Savu.'

'Does everybody speak English?'

'Yes.'

'I will have to learn, won't I?'

'You'll soon pick it up.'

He had heard her practising in her room.

Something was troubling her. God forgive him, he should have guessed what it was.

'Are they going to hang my mother?' she asked.

It was the second time she had mentioned her mother to him. She had spoken matter-of-factly but he wasn't deceived.

'I don't know,' he said.

'Is Leila going with us?'

He shook his head. 'I don't think so.'

'Will we fly in an aeroplane?'

'Yes.'

'Do you have a house in Scotland?'

'Yes.' The arrangement was that the tenants of his flat would move out if given a month's notice.

'Is it a big house like this one?'

'No, it's quite small.'

That seemed to please her. 'Will I go to school?'

'Of course.'

He realised then what a difficult experience it would be for her. That she trusted him to help her through it could be his salvation.

Jean arrived shortly after seven, when the sunset was fading. In a white dress with red collar and cuffs, and with her fair hair tied up with a red ribbon she was handsome enough, and therefore formidable enough to cause Mary to take one look at her and then slip off to her room.

'Hello, Andrew,' said Jean, as she came into the living-room. 'Was that your little guest I saw?'

'Yes, that was Mary.'

'Mary isn't her real name, is it?'

'No. That's what we decided to call her.'

'I see.'

She kissed him, on the cheek, and then sat apart from him. 'Shy, isn't she?'

'Proud too.'

'Proud?' Jean could not keep out of her voice a little incredulity, a little amusement, and a little indignation per-haps, that this child, whose parents were brown-skinned, poor, and illiterate, and whose mother was in jail accused of a horrible crime, could possibly be proud, as Jean understood the word.

'She never complains.'

'Perhaps because she doesn't really understand the hor-rible position she's in. Who could blame the poor wee thing?'

'She understands too well.'

'Quite a little paragon.' Jean then concentrated her sym-pathy on him. 'Poor Andrew. How are you? Silly of me to ask. You must feel shattered. What's going to happen, do you think?'

He shook his head.

'Is there any possibility of a pardon? Alec Maitland doesn't think there is. He's got no say in the matter, of course. You'll have to face up to it, Andrew. Alec thinks all the leaders will be sentenced to death, and she's one of them, isn't she? I hate to say this, Andrew. What would you do in that case?'

'I'd go home.'

'But what if she was sentenced to imprisonment for life?'

'I'd stay here.'

'Perhaps they wouldn't let you.'

For a minute or so she contemplated that situation. Life here would mean life, there would be no remissions. Surely he would seek a divorce. Not immediately, but in a year or two. Jean would wait that long but not any longer.

'If you do go home what about the little girl?' She asked.

'I shall take her with me.'

'Wouldn't it be a bit irregular for a single man to be given custody of a child, especially a little girl, who's not in any way related to him? I don't think they'd permit it, Andrew.'

'They'll permit it.'

'You seem very sure. Have you spoken to anyone about it?'

'Yes. His Highness. He said it would be permitted.'

'Well, you couldn't go any higher than that. By the way, aren't you going to offer me a drink?'

'Sorry.' He got up and went over to the sideboard. 'Whisky and water?'

'Need you ask? Are any of your students involved?'

'One present student, two former students.'

He brought over her drink.

'Thank you, Andrew. Foolish young men.'

'Brave young men. What are they fighting for? Democracy? Freedom? Which, I believe, was what the last war was fought for.'

'I didn't think you'd approve, Andrew, especially when we see how it's turned out. And you can't really call them fighters. Those that turned up at the hospital were a rabble, to tell the truth, a rather cowardly rabble, to be frank.'

'Why do you call them cowardly?'

'Well, for heaven's sake, there were at least twenty of them, some with guns and others with parangs, and they surrendered to me, a woman. I didn't even have a bedpan in my hand.'

'That didn't show they were cowards. It showed they

didn't want anyone to get hurt. If they'd been the terrorists
that the British press will no doubt call them they'd have cut
your throat. Instead they turned you into a heroine.'

She hid her annoyance. 'I don't see myself as a heroine.
Not like Leila. I can understand why you're bitter, Andrew,
but they brought it upon themselves.'

'They were outrageously cheated. They voted for democracy. They won by a large majority. Then they were told it
was all concelled. What do you think they should have
done?'

When Lo had put that question to him how feebly he had
answered it.

Jean's answer was forthright. 'What they shouldn't have
done was start a rebellion and use guns.'

'They didn't start it. It was a peaceful demonstration to
hand in a petition. Their petition was rejected. An attempt
was made to arrest Dr Abad.'

'Alec was simply doing his duty.'

'The guns they have they took from the police, to keep
them from using them. Major Simbin shot a man in the
crowd.'

'It was an accident, Alec said.'

'I haven't heard of a single instance when they've used
their guns. Those at the hospital gave theirs up, didn't they?
At this very minute they're occupying the Council Chamber:
a symbolical act. They think they have a right to be there.
So they have.'

'No point in getting upset about it, Andrew. Maybe they
have a right of some sort but not a legal right, and that's
what matters.'

'So British soldiers, Scottish soldiers, will come all the way
from Cyprus to force them out. If I had any guts I'd go there
now and stand by them.'

'Stand by her, you mean.'

'She's my wife, you know. If you want to call anyone a coward call me one.'

'It would have been madness if you'd taken part. What business is it of yours? What good could you have done?'

'I could have died with her.'

Jean put her drink down. Her hand shook.

'You're not serious?' she cried. Her voice had become shrill.

Well, he thought, was he serious? He imagined himself breaking through the police cordon, entering the building, and seeking out Leila. They would embrace. They would weep together. He would tell her he had come to die with her.

No, he wasn't as serious as that.

As for Jean she was tempted to jeer: 'Go ahead then.' She would have said it with some contempt, for she knew, as he certainly did himself, that he didn't have the audacity.

She managed not to say it. She had known his weaknesses when she had fallen in love with him; perhaps they had been part of the reasons she had fallen in love. She had always thought that he needed a woman like her who would make him face his real self and do the best with it he could. In spite of his years abroad his was a stay-at-home temperament. As a teacher in some fee-paying Edinburgh school, as the husband of a nursing-home matron there, as the father of, say, three children with fair skins and Edinburgh accents, as the owner of a semi-detached villa in Fairmilehead with laburnum in the garden instead of frangipani, and as a member of some exclusive golf club, he might grumble now and then and yearn for the beach at Tanjong Aru and the jungle with the orchids growing wild, but in his heart he would feel content and safe.

So she determinedly said nothing, looked at him with pity

and love and a little reproach, and took another sip of whisky.

'Well, amn't I to be allowed to meet Mary?' she asked.

He was sulky. 'Do you really want to?'

'Of course I want to. She could be as important to me as she seems to be to you.'

'She's very sensitive.'

'Heavens, Andrew, you don't think I would be unkind to a little girl, especially one as unfortunate as her?'

'All right.' He got up and went out.

She breathed deeply. She had kept her temper but it had been a near thing. Even if she found the child off-putting she would treat her with kindness. She might never love her as she would in time her own children but she would try to cherish her for Andrew's sake. His affection for this child was to his credit. He would love his own children even more.

What mattered now was whether he loved Jean herself. She was sure he did, though he had jilted her to marry his Malay adventuress.

Sandilands knocked on Mary's door. She opened it at once. She must have been expecting him.

'May I come in?' he asked.

'Yes.' She made way for him.

He was glad they were speaking in Malay, that pleasant and intimate language.

He had to be fair to Jean. 'The lady would like to speak to you, Mary. When you come to Scotland you will meet lots of ladies like her. She is a nurse at the hospital. She looks after sick people.'

'I'm not sick.'

'No, you aren't.'

'Why does she want to meet me?'

'She's my friend, so she wants to be your friend too.'

She considered that, nodded, and then went and looked at herself in the dressing-table mirror. It wasn't vanity. She was gathering her resources, before facing another ordeal. It took less than a minute.

Back in the living-room, he watched the confrontation between the child who was to be his adopted daughter and the woman who might become his wife and therefore her foster mother. Mary would not openly show dislike and distrust even if she felt them, she was naturally too well-mannered for that, but he knew her well enough now to be able to read her reaction, and in the same way he would be able to judge whether Jean's compassion was genuine or put on to impress him.

Jean did not get up. She did not gush: that was not her way. She smiled but her scrutiny was sharp and professional. Could she see this very ordinary Malay child as hers, in the villa in suburban Edinburgh? As step-sister to her own children? Dressed in school uniform, attending a private academy in Edinburgh? Being introduced to friends and relatives? No, not yet anyway. Later perhaps, when the child had learned English, when she had become accustomed to civilised ways, and when the coarseness of her features had been modified.

That was his interpretation of Jean's various smiles.

She took Mary's hand and, in adequate Malay, asked her name.

Mary gave her Malay name.

'Yes, but we've to call you Mary, haven't we?'

Mary nodded. She did not turn to look at Sandilands for guidance and protection. She kept staring at Jean with a chess-player's intentness.

'My name's Jean. I'm a nurse. You know what a nurse does?'

Another nod.

'Would you like to be a nurse one day?'

This time a shake of the head.

'Oh. What would you like to be then?'

Another shake.

'Of course you don't know that yet. You're too young. I come from Scotland like Mr Sandilands. It's very far away. It's often very cold. They all speak English there.'

Sandilands interrupted. 'Are you trying to discourage her?' he asked, in English.

'Surely, Andrew, it's only fair to let her know what to expect. It's possible that it would be in her best interests to stay here where she belongs. Besides, there's her mother. Should you be taking her away before, well, to be blunt, before her mother's been tried?'

'What good would her staying here do?'

'She's got feelings, Andrew. Goodness knows, I've often been mystified by the way they react to things, so differently from ourselves, but their feelings are as human as ours.'

'They're not orang-utans.'

'Don't be bitter. You know what I mean. Listen, Andrew, I came here to speak frankly and I'm going to. This is an awful time for you. The next two or three days are going to be absolute hell. You can't possibly be in a state of mind to make a sound judgment on such an important matter as whether or not to adopt this child and take her away thousands of miles to a country she's never seen and might not be happy in.'

'When will I be in a state to make a sound judgment?'

'I don't know, Andrew. But I want to help you make it. Remember how we used to talk about our future together in Edinburgh?'

She had talked about it, he had listened.

'It's still there for us, that future. Isn't it?'

He didn't answer. He was thinking of a future without Leila.

'Isn't it? You've got to tell me now, Andrew. I don't want to be let down again. I couldn't bear it. I'm not proud. I'll accept almost any conditions. I'll take this child, even if I have doubts as to whether it's the best thing for her. I'll be as good to her as if she was my own child, or I'll try very hard. But you must tell me now if we do have a future together. I love you, Andrew. That's why I'm asking you now, at this terrible time.'

But if he agreed that his future lay with her he would be acknowledging that he had no future with Leila. He was not ready to face up to that yet. When would he be ready? In five years' time when his memories of her had faded, like the colours of the sunset? Or in the next day or two when he learned that she was dead and his memories of her were still vivid and bloodstained, like the sunset at its grandest?

Jean would not wait five years.

He would need her help. Hadn't Leila advised him to marry her?

She was still waiting for his answer.

There was then a distant roaring in the sky. Aeroplanes, big ones, three at least, were coming down to land. The troops had arrived.

He hurried out to the verandah where the roaring was louder. The sky was dark now, with streaks of red.

Jean was beside him, gripping his arm.

He thought, wildly, that he must drive to the airport and talk to the officer in command. He would explain that they had come all that way to quell not a gang of terrorists but a democratic party that had just won a fairly contested election.

'I'll stay the night,' whispered Jean. 'Just to keep you company. I've got the day off tomorrow.'

The roaring was gone. The planes had landed. The soldiers would be coming out into the warm night, making jokes and eager to stretch their legs after the long flight.

'Scots, most of them, Alec said,' murmured Jean. 'I'll go and get my bag.'

He turned and saw Mary, in the corner, behind plants.

For a few seconds he felt a spasm of hatred. This child represented all his present misfortunes and all the difficulties ahead of him. It was grotesquely unjust, but he needed something or someone to blame, and there she was, dark-faced and secret, a small malign presence.

Contrition and shame followed, but that insane hatred could occur again. He needed help all right but the kind that Jean could not provide. It would have to come from the child herself.

Jean took charge. She got Mary ready for bed and prepared supper for her. She was kind but not sentimentally so, as if she realised that, so soon in their acquaintance, to kiss and hug would have been going too far.

'You're right, Andrew,' she said, when she joined him in the living-room. 'She *is* a proud little girl. She knows how to be grateful without being obsequious. They can be a very obsequious lot, these Savuans. How does she manage to be so special? With such a background too!'

For the rest of the evening they sat well apart, sipping whisky, listening to chichaks, and not talking much. Jean was content for herself, but because she loved him she had to feel some of his suffering. It was real and intolerable but it had in it its own cure. He was not yet looking for consolation but he was realising that it was to be found. Every time he looked at her he realised that. Without being conceited she knew her own value. So, though she now and then shared his agony, like the stab of a recurrent tooth-ache, and was glad that she was sharing it, she felt also a soothing confidence that once these horrible events were past they would find happiness together; indeed their future happiness would be all the more precious and secure because of these present horrors.

It would depend, of course, on what happened to Leila. Should she hope that Leila would be pardoned? Should she pray for that? Those were questions she preferred not to answer.

26

Jean had much experience of telling people that their loved ones were dying or dead, and had acquired the necessary tact and fortitude. She had learned that some had to be given the sad news with a touch of sternness, otherwise they would have broken down. Andrew was one of those. Therefore, that night, when he showed signs of lapsing into maudlin self-pity, only partly induced by the amount of whisky she had let him consume, she rebuked him fondly. When they were in bed, naked, and he showed a rather pathetic desire to make love, she wouldn't have it: not because it would have been adultery, his wife being still alive, but because it would have been on his part an expression of pity for himself and not of love for her. He might even have addressed her as Leila.

Next morning, and all that long anxious day, she kept close to him and dealt with any awkward situation that arose. For instance, that nuisance Mr Srinavasan, whom she detested, called at the house, ostensibly to discuss with the Principal some College business, but really to see for himself if it was true that Sandilands, whose wife at that point was

still alive, so far as was known, was in an adulterous relationship with his former lover, the fair-haired Miss Hislop, with
whom Mr Srinavasam would have dearly loved to have an
adulterous relationship.

'Mr Sandilands has other matters on his mind,' she said,
brusquely.

'But this, dear lady, is a matter of considerable importance. I am Principal Lecturer of Mathematics and prospective
Principal of College, and this concerns arrangements for
forthcoming examinations.'

'I am sure it can wait, Mr Srinavasan.'

And he had to go, thinking not about the examinations
but about her lily-white bosom. He knew it wasn't really
lily-white. He had once seen it almost totally exposed on the
beach and it had been as brown as his sandals; as indeed had
been her buttocks, also immodestly but thrillingly revealed
in part. But he liked to think of them as lily-white and had
so described them in a poem he had written, in Tamil.

A deputation of students came shyly to the house. They
were taken aback to be received by her, especially as she was
so brisk about sending them away again.

'We wish to convey to Mr Sandilands our dreadful
sympathy.'

'Dreadful? You must mean something else. On Mr
Sandilands' behalf I thank you. He intends to call a meeting
of all the students very soon. Till then he wishes not to be
disturbed.'

'We understand. Is it true he will be leaving the College?'

'We must all wait and see.'

They went off, muttering sorrowfully in Malay and
Cantonese.

'What did you tell them?' asked Sandilands, with a sigh.

'That you would be calling a meeting of all the students
very soon. That is what you intend, isn't it?'

'Yes.'

'Before you do, Andrew, we'll have to talk about it. I don't suppose I could be present. We'll see. There could be clypes among them, yes, there could, so you'll have to be careful what you say, not just to them but to everybody. There's a great deal of goodwill for you, Andrew. It wouldn't do to spoil it.'

An hour before she had spoken on the telephone to the Director of Finance, John Halliday, an Englishman, at his house, since his office in Government House was in the hands of the rebels. She had elicited that, on the orders of His Highness himself, Mr Sandilands, his golfing friend, was to be treated with unprecedented generosity. The sum to be paid him for the curtailment of his contract was ten times what it legally should have been: it was therefore considerable. Halliday had not been able to hide his amazement and envy. Also Sandilands' journey home was to be first-class all the way. Jean's own would be economy class but she would pay the difference so that they could travel together. There would be free champagne but any toasts would of course be low-key. The child's expenses were also to be borne by the State: a not negligible sum had been bestowed on her.

'Wish I was a champion golfer,' Halliday had said.

'But, Jack, His Highness can easily afford it.'

'That he can.'

'And really, between ourselves, you could say he's the cause of Andrew having to resign. I mean, speaking in confidence, he has it in his power to pardon them all.'

'He won't do that, Jean. Don't think it.'

'I know, but, again in confidence, it will be a bit thick having them hanged when all they'll have done is stick up for their rights. I simply had to say that, Jack.'

'I understand, Jean, but I wouldn't go about saying it.'

'Of course not. I suppose some bad-minded people are

saying it's done me a good turn, and Andrew too, if we're going to be brutally frank.'

'It's an ill wind, Jean.'

'You could call this a hurricane. Thanks, Jack. Give my regards to Hilda.'

Though she felt very pleased, indeed exultant, about Andrew's sudden affluence, she was cautious when telling him about it. What was money, her tone sorrowfully implied, when life and death were involved. But as she spoke she was reflecting that in Edinburgh they would be not just well-off, they would be almost rich. She could have a nursing-home of her own and the semi-detached villa might after all be wholly detached.

She dealt fairly with Saidee and the other servants. If Saidee felt aggrieved on Leila's account that was fair enough so long as she didn't show it offensively. Each servant was promised three months' pay. Tuan did not know who would take his place but he hoped, and Jean herself hoped too, that whoever he was he would keep them on. Saidee then said peevishly that if it was the Indian Tuan she would rather go back to her village than work for people as black as burnt toast.

When Jean, to amuse him, told Andrew about his dark-skinned ugly little amah's absurd prejudice he disappointed her by missing the point altogether. He muttered something about Saidee's having been a devoted servant to him and Leila.

He kept mumbling that he would have to call Alec Maitland to find out what was happening now that the soldiers had arrived. She offered to make the call for him, but rather huffily he insisted on making it himself.

'All right, Andrew, but for goodness' sake keep calm. Remember it's not Alec's fault. Be careful. You never know who might be listening in.'

She sat with her face close to his so that she could hear what Alec said.

'This is Andrew, Alec.'

'Hello, Andrew. How are you?'

'What's happening? What's going to happen? I know the soldiers have come. I heard the planes last night.'

Jean frowned and drew in her breath in warning.

'So far as I know, Andrew, an ultimatum is going to be delivered to Abad today. He'll be given a few hours to think it over: either surrender or be forced out. By the way, those who were occupying the hospital have given themselves up.'

Jean smiled, demurely.

'What's been done to them?' asked Sandilands.

Jean shook her head: that wasn't at the moment relevant.

'They're in jail.'

'How many?'

'About thirty.'

'Is there room for so many?'

Another shake of Jean's head: no sarcasm, it meant.

'It'll be extended, I have no doubt. Is Jean with you?'

She grabbed the telephone. 'Yes, Alec, I'm here, listening. I know you won't mind. As you can imagine poor Andrew's in a state. It's making him quite ill. Suppose they reject the ultimatum, what then?'

'They'll be forced out. Soon after dawn. Colonel Anstruther who's in command thinks it shouldn't take longer than half an hour. He was surprised at how few of them there are. He said he'd been led to believe there were hundreds.'

'He'll do his best, I hope, to avoid serious casualties?' She was speaking as a nurse.

'Yes, of course.'

Sandilands snatched the telephone back and shouted: 'Has anyone told him what this so-called rebellion is about?'

'That wouldn't interest him, Andrew,' said Maitland, quietly. 'He's a soldier. He just obeys orders.'

Jean was shaking her head vigorously. Sandilands was to keep off that subject.

'Telephone communications with Government House have been cut off,' said Maitland.

It was a hint that it would be useless now for Sandilands to try and speak to Leila again.

'I'm glad you've got Jean with you, Andrew. She'll see you through.'

She smiled and nodded.

'If there are to be executions,' said Sandilands, 'if some are still alive after the colonel has carried out his orders, how soon will they take place?'

'For God's sake, Andrew, don't ask me that.'

'I'm asking it, Alec.'

In spite of Jean's frown.

'There won't be any protracted trials, that's for sure.'

'How soon, Alec?'

'Days, I would think.'

'How many?'

'How would I know that, Andrew? I'm just a policeman. Two? Three?'

'And the British Government will do nothing to stop them?'

'How could it? Savu's not a colony. It's a sovereign State.'

Jean again grabbed the telephone. This time it was easy. Sandilands' grip had gone slack.

'Thanks, Alec. We're grateful. If there are any developments would you let us know?'

'Yes, I certainly will. Do you intend to go home with Andrew?'

'Yes.'

'I'm glad. What about the little girl? Is it settled about her?'

'We're taking her with us.'

'I heard she was to go into the orphanage.'

'That was suggested but we wouldn't have it. We feel we owe it to Leila. Anyway, she's a great little girl and it'll be fun looking after her.'

'Have you considered, Jean, that they might want to make a fuss of you in U.K.? There could be headlines.'

'Don't worry. If there's any publicity of that sort I'll see that Andrew is kept well away from it. Nobody's going to pester him with stupid questions, if I can help it.'

'Good for you, Jean. I hope to see both of you before you leave.'

'Surely, though, there won't be any going-away parties?'

'No. You'll be living in Edinburgh?'

'Yes. We'll be buying a house there. Be sure to look us up when you go home yourself. Perth's not that far. Bring Kate. I'd like to meet her again.'

She put the telephone down, thoughtfully. When it next spoke what would it have to say?

'We just wait now,' she murmured.

27

When it was not quite daylight Maitland telephoned. It was Jean who rushed to answer. She was wearing a dressing-gown. She had been out of bed for over an hour. 'Yes?' She was panting, on the verge of hysteria and tears. The hours of waiting, all through the night, had been almost too much for her.

Sandilands was asleep. She had given him sleeping pills.

'It's you, Jean?'

'Yes. Any news?'

'It's all over. I'll leave it to you to tell Andrew. Where is he?'

'He's asleep. What have I to tell him?'

'They came rushing out but not to give themselves up. Damned fools. Suicidal. Firing guns. They must have been firing them into the air or their aim was rotten, for none of the soldiers was hit. The soldiers didn't know that at the time. *They* didn't fire into the air. That's not their way.'

'Was anybody hurt?'

'Three were killed, eight wounded, how badly I don't know yet. Abad himself wasn't hurt.'

'So he'll be hanged?'

'I'm afraid so.'

Jean found it hard to ask what had to be asked. 'And Leila?'

Maitland found it just as hard to answer. 'She was one of those shot.'

'Shot?'

'She's dead, Jean. She was at the front. She didn't have a gun. She was holding that damned silly petition. If Andrew wants to see her for God's sake tell him he can't, it won't be allowed. Anyway, he wouldn't want to. I saw her. A bloody mess. I don't envy you having to tell him.'

She was sobbing. 'I can tell him because I love him.'

'Yes, that's right.' But the Deputy Commissioner was frowning, as he put the telephone down. He did not quite understand.